Deacon Locke WENT to PROM

ALSO BY BRIAN KATCHER

The Improbable Theory of Ana and Zak

Everyone Dies in the End

Almost Perfect

Playing with Matches

BRIAN KATCHER

KATHERINE TEGEN BOOKS
An Imprint of HarperCollins Publishers

Katherine Tegen Books is an imprint of HarperCollins Publishers.

Deacon Locke Went to Prom
Copyright © 2017 by HarperCollins Publishers
All rights reserved. Printed in the United States of America.

www.epicreads.com

Library of Congress Control Number: 2016957990
ISBN 978-0-06-242252-1

Typography by Michelle Gengaro-Kokmen
17 18 19 20 21   PC/LSCH   10 9 8 7 6 5 4 3 2 1
❖
First Edition

To my wonderful daughter, Sophie,
who's made us so very proud

ONE

THE FANCY COUPLE IN THE STOCK PHOTO ARE GRIN-
ning so wide, their mouths almost look deformed. It's
like something out of a propaganda banner: *Join the Glorious Soviet Army!*

They're not wearing Red Army uniforms, of course.
The boy is wearing a tux, the girl, some sort of dress.

STEPPING OUT IN STYLE
FAYETTEVILLE HIGH SCHOOL SENIOR PROM
TICKETS ON SALE NOW

Stepping out in style. Who the hell comes up
with these themes? There's probably an official,

administration-approved list somewhere. Even I could come up with better names. *Infectious Waste Disposal,* for instance. *96-Hour Psychiatric Hold. The Slums of Bangkok.*

Those would also make good names for college bands, by the way.

Maybe my cynical nature is the reason I've never been to a school dance. And not because the idea of asking out a girl fills me with crippling panic. It's not that. So put that thought out of your mind. Because that's not what it is.

I check the date on the poster. May 6. One month from today. If I'm going to go to this dance, I have to get a date. Like, this week. I'm not going to chicken out this time. Not like homecoming. Or junior prom. Or the spring formal. Or homecoming last year. Or that sock hop thing.

I find Kelli in the back parking lot, directing the loading of boxes of canned goods into the back of a truck. Even in the mild Arkansas spring, she's dressed in heavy black jeans and a tight sweater that shows off her curves. Though she's just over five feet tall, she has a commanding presence. Her minions leap to obey her orders as to how the loot from the food drive is to be stacked and stowed.

Just seeing her there, I'm overcome with an intense feeling of . . .

Uh . . .

Well, not love. Like, maybe. Compatibility. Familiarity.

"Deacon! Come over here!"

There's no other option but obedience.

Kelli blows her nose into a sodden Kleenex, then points to a cart. It's loaded to the gills with pumpkin-pie filling, evaporated milk, Spam, and the other canned-food rejects people give to the poor. "You wanna give us a hand?" Her eyes smile at me through her round John Lennon glasses.

I bend down and grip the cart by both ends, lifting it slightly to get a sense of the weight.

"Deacon?"

Trying not to grunt, I hoist it chest high. I stagger, but don't fall.

"Deacon!"

I nearly topple over backward but manage to stay upright. I shove the cart into the back of the truck.

I turn to see Kelli and her flunkies staring at me.

"Um, thanks. But I just wanted you to pull the ramp out for us."

I quickly grab the toggle and extend the truck's built-in ramp. In retrospect, that makes a lot more sense.

"Thanks. We'll take it from here." She shoots me a tolerant smile, showing off her overbite.

Last year I heard a guy making comments about her teeth, how they would make it difficult for her to perform a certain biological act (I shan't elaborate further). Later, I took him aside and explained how I felt such comments were unworthy of a gentleman. He's avoided us both ever since.

I sit down on the nearby bike rack, which groans slightly, and watch as Kelli's crew makes short work of the remaining cans. For someone so small, she sure takes up a lot of space. I'll never forget the first time I ran into her.

Watch where you're going, you big stupid asshole!

We've talked every day since then. Eaten together. Studied together.

Never did a single thing outside of school together.

She's my closest friend here. I guess, technically, my only friend at Fayetteville High. But I'm the new guy. I only enrolled two years ago.

The other workers wander off. I watch them leave with a sense of foreboding. It's now or never.

Of course, there's always tomorrow. . . .

No! I'm not going to wimp out this time! My great-grandfather was a Scotsman! My grandfather lost his leg in Vietnam! I can ask a friend to go to a dance with me.

Kelli is busy filling out some paperwork on a clipboard. I walk up behind her.

"You're blocking the sun, Deacon."

I force a laugh. It really sounds forced. "The sun is over a million miles in diameter. You honestly think I could block that?"

She sets down her clipboard and looks up. And up. "You? Yeah, I think you could."

I shift uncomfortably. While I'm not the *tallest* guy in school, I . . .

Okay, I am the tallest guy. And not by a little bit.

But then Kelli smiles at me. Her dimples appear. They're so deep they look like a bullet passed through each of her cheeks.

Good one, Deacon. Open with that.

"Kelli . . ."

"Are you okay? You look like you're going to barf or something."

Here goes nothing. "We're about to graduate."

She nods. "Yes, I'm aware of that."

I always feel dumb when I talk to her. Maybe that's why I like her. Since she's impossible to impress, there's no pressure to try.

"And I . . . there's something I'd like to ask you." I've armed the bomb. There's no turning back.

"What's that?"

"Well . . ." *God, why is it so hot out here?* "I wanted to ask . . ."

"No," she cuts in. "What's that?"

She points at something over my shoulder. I turn, grateful for the reprieve.

I can see what's grabbed her attention. Over in the soccer fields, a knight in shining armor has ridden up on a horse. Seriously. A knight.

Okay, he's not so much riding a white stallion as a pony, led by a middle-aged man. And the knight's armor is made out of tinfoil-coated cardboard and a spray-painted bike helmet. But still. The girls' soccer team stops their practicing. One player shrieks and covers her mouth with her hands.

The knight is helped down from the saddle by the horse wrangler. He then falls to one knee. We're sitting too far away to hear what he asks, but the girl's resounding *YES!* echoes off the scoreboards.

As often happens, I don't understand what's going on, and I look to Kelli for an answer. She seems to read my mind.

"A promposal. It's trending."

"Huh?"

She shakes her head and rolls her eyes, which happens at least once during all our conversations. "He's asking her to the prom. Big, fancy spectacle. A lot of people are doing it."

Huh. Now that I think about it, there *have* been quite

a few costumed serenades in the halls this week. That explains a lot.

The girl has now replaced her date on the back of the animal, while the man leads them around the outskirts of the field.

"Hey, Kelli?"

"Yeah?"

I close my eyes, curl my toes, and swallow. "I was wondering."

"What?"

"Would you like to . . . would you like to . . ."

"Spit it out, Deacon."

"Want to go pet the horse?"

She looks up at me and shows me her dimples. "Hell, yes! C'mon!"

She jogs ahead. I follow.

Somewhere, the ghost of my grandfather laughs at me.

"I'm home!" I bellow.

"Deacon Locke, I swear to God if you slam that screen door again I will personally carve out your eyeballs and feed them to the crows!"

"Missed you too, Jean."

It's funny. I've known my grandmother my whole life, but I never once called her grandma, or granny, or nana. She's always been Jean to me.

I find her in the kitchen. While the heavenly smell of tonight's meatloaves wafts from the stove, Jean has taken a break from her cooking. I wince when I see she has her oil paints out and is wearing a smock over her housedress. Her hair and makeup, of course, are perfectly in place.

Not that I have a problem with her crafting obsession. It's just that a guy can only own so many bedazzled sweaters and crocheted toothpaste cozies. I paste on a smile, mentally composing a glowing review of whatever she's painted.

"What do you think?" She cocks her head.

I'm actually kind of floored. It's a portrait, and I instantly recognize the subject.

"Wow, that's amazing. The likeness . . . it's uncanny."

She beams up at me. "You really think so? I thought the mouth came out funny."

"Are you kidding? I'd know that guy anywhere. Ol' Johnny Cash."

Jean's face falls. "That's your grandfather, Deacon."

Whoops. Better laugh it off. "Johnny Cash was my grandfather? Then why aren't we rich?"

"Very funny." She shakes her head and closes her paint box. "Now tell me, how did it go today?"

Trying to ignore the question, I dig in the fridge for a snack. "The usual. School."

Jean removes her smock and folds it. "So did you ask

that girl? What did she say? Do you need money for the tickets?"

I stick my head into the fridge and wince. Living alone with Jean in this old farmhouse . . . I guess I tell her pretty much everything. She's a good listener. But I kind of wish I hadn't shared my plans about asking Kelli to prom. It was a spur-of-the-moment decision, and now that Jean knows, she'll never let me back out.

"I'll ask her tomorrow."

Jean closes the refrigerator door, just barely missing my head. "You've been saying that for days. What's your excuse this time?"

I'm having a hard time meeting her eyes, and not just because of the nearly two-foot height difference. "This horse came onto the soccer field—"

"The truth, Deacon. Even your father could have come up with a better story than that."

I laugh. "I'm serious. It was part of this guy's promposal."

Jean is about to check something on the stove but pauses. "Don't throw your slang at me. I'm too old. Your aunt used to do that. I still have no idea what 'gag me with a spoon' means."

This is hard to explain. I don't even fully understand the concept. "A promposal is like a proposal. To prom. In costume."

She looks perplexed. "Why a costume?"

I pause. "I'm not sure."

Jean rolls her eyes. "Reality TV ruined your generation. Back when I was your age, a boy would simply ask a young lady to the dance. We were honored to be asked and didn't expect more than a sincere smile."

I don't comment on this. Honestly, I can't buy the idea of every boy in the late sixties being a perfect gentleman. I think everyone secretly believes that their generation was the last to have manners and take risks. And the first to have sex. And that *Saturday Night Live* was funniest whenever they first started watching it.

I remember how I could barely even talk to Kelli, despite two years of friendship. Acquaintanceship. Going-to-the-same-schoolship.

"How about you pick up the phone and call her right now?" says Jean.

"Just let me handle it. Is supper ready?"

Jean is having none of my excuses. "We'll eat when we're done talking."

"Jean, you know that song 'Grandma Got Run Over by a Reindeer'? I really like that tune."

She shakes her head. "My favorite grandson—"

"Your only grandson."

"Going to miss what should be a great night, just because he won't get off his duff and ask someone."

This is kind of uncharacteristic of Jean. In her eyes, I can do no wrong. Why is prom such a sticking point with her?

"What's the big deal about some stupid dance? So I can sit around and stare at my date? I'm not exactly a dancer."

"You've no one to blame but yourself. Your father went to his prom, you know. Said he had a wonderful time."

Dad had told me about that night once, when I was still living with him. "Wasn't that when he wrecked Grandpa's pickup?"

She keeps talking as if I hadn't spoken. "You're going to be a college man in a few months. Those girls are going to expect you to be confident. Adult. How are you going to do that if you spend every night here with me?"

"Didn't realize hanging out with me was such a burden for you." That statement sounded a lot less whiny in my head.

Jean stands, wipes her hands on her towel, and walks over to me. She touches my arm.

"Deacon, having you live with me was one of the great joys of my life. But you're no longer a little boy. Well, you were never a *little* boy, but that's beside the point. This isn't about the prom. I just need to know that someday, when I'm not around—"

Why does every old person like to talk about death? Jesus.

"—that you'll be okay on your own. No more excuses. Now, are you going to make an effort to get out more? Start bringing home girls I can disapprove of?"

I think of Kelli. Maybe it's all in my head. Of course it's all in my head. I'll ask her out tomorrow.

"Okay, Jean."

"And you'll make the most out of college, and not lock yourself up in your dorm every night?"

"Yes."

"But not waste your time partying, flunk out twice, and suddenly move to Arizona because that's where the rest of the band is?"

Funny, same thing happened to my father. "No."

"And you'll marry a nice girl and provide me with lots of great-grandchildren to play with?"

"You're really pushing it."

We both laugh. I pick up the plates to take to the dining room. (In Jean's world, eating in the kitchen is reserved for breakfast and informal luncheons.) But then I stop. There's something I need to talk to her about.

"Hey, um, what happened to your taillights?"

She turns and stirs something on top of the stove. "What's that?"

"On your car. I'm pretty sure you had two of them when I left the house this morning."

She doesn't face me. "Someone must have hit me in the parking lot at the Walmart. Drivers today, too busy interneting to pay attention."

I head to the dining room. A distracted driver. That's what she always says when I ask her about the new dents and missing parts on her car.

That driver must have really been distracted. He also managed to gouge a big gash in that pine tree out front.

Jean's driving has gotten a lot worse recently. There's been a couple of close calls at stoplights that scared the hell out of me. But every time I suggest she may not be up for driving anymore, she denies it.

Looks like I'm not the only one in this house who's worried about the future.

TWO

I FIND KELLI IN HER USUAL BEFORE-SCHOOL SPOT, IN that little area next to the vending machines in the cafeteria. The table in front of her is covered with used Kleenexes.

She sneezes hello.

"Allergies again?"

She nods, miserably. "I'll be okay in a couple of days." She blows her nose. "Because I'll be dead."

You ever really, really want to give someone a hug?

She squirts hand sanitizer on her palms, then passes me something from her bag. It's a copy of *Sky and Telescope.*

"There's an article about that WIRO observatory in

Wyoming," she says with a sniff. "I thought you'd like to see it."

I already have a copy of this issue. "Thanks!" I say, maybe just a little too intently and loudly. "Can't wait to read it."

She smiles the miserable smile of the ill.

"Kelli . . ." *C'mon, Deacon.* "Kelli . . ."

"Yes?"

"I . . ."

Her bloodshot eyes bore into me.

Kelli, you and I have been friends for two years. It wasn't easy for me to fit in when I moved here, and I appreciate that you took the time to talk to me, even if it was just to cuss me out at first.

"I . . ."

And, well, school is almost at an end. Prom's coming up, and since neither of us is seeing anyone . . .

"I . . ."

I was just wondering if you'd like to go with me. I think we'd have fun. You don't have to answer today, but just give it some thought, okay?

"I . . ."

"Deacon? Are you all right?"

Why are the voices in my head always so much more suave than me?

"Sorry, my mind was wandering."

I have to ask her. Right now. Before I lose my nerve. Or before she coughs up another wad of mucus and I lose my breakfast.

"Hey!" shouts a shrill, masculine voice from behind us.

It's Elijah Haversham, from my American Literature class. The kid who never shuts up. He reminds me of this novelty parrot toy my dad used to have that would babble gibberish over and over again, long past the point of being amusing.

He pulls up a chair and begins flipping through the magazine Kelli brought me. I'm not sure if I'm more annoyed or relieved at the interruption.

"Whoa, astrology! What's my horoscope? I'm a Gemini."

Kelli winks at me. "Astronomy, Elijah. Real, actual science."

He runs a hand through his thinning blond hair and fixes Kelli with a deranged grin. "I didn't used to buy into the whole star-sign thing either. But get this. My uncle, he was a Cancer. Now guess what he was just diagnosed with?"

She frowns. "Cancer?"

"No, crabs."

Kelli laughs. Maybe a little more than she's ever laughed at anything I've ever said. I'm about to suggest that Elijah find somewhere else to be when a loud trumpet blast cuts through the lunchroom.

When I turn and see a crowd of sequin-suited mariachis march into the room . . . I wish I could say I'm surprised. I truly do.

We stand for a better look. I peer over the spectators' heads.

Yep, should have seen it coming. The grinning guy with the rose in his hand. The teary-eyed girl. The invitation to prom. The applause from the crowd.

"Where the hell do you find mariachis in Arkansas?" says Elijah, hovering at my elbow. He taps his forehead, as if trying to force the thoughts back into his brain. "Seriously, can you believe this? Another promposal. Isn't that a douchey word? What the hell are we coming to?"

He turns and faces Kelli. "You're a girl, right?"

She nods, warily.

"I mean . . . is this what women expect these days? Someone clunking out hundreds of dollars before the dance even happens? Do us poor guys even stand a chance?"

I hold my breath. What if she agrees with Elijah? I'm totally screwed. I can't prompose. Not like that. Please say no.

Kelli rolls her eyes. "Ha! This is nothing but a scam created by the corporate overlords to get us to pour cash into their coffers. Not to mention an attempt by the

patriarchy to reduce women to a subservient and sup-
plicant role."

I don't know what most of that means, but it seems
like she's not impressed by the promposals. I start to
breathe again.

"Although . . ."

Crap.

"I mean, it might be nice if a guy, you know, put a little thought into asking you. Nothing crazy, but it might
make one feel special to know he took a little time to . . ."
She shakes her head, then sneezes. "I have to go. See
you, Deacon."

I watch as she vanishes among the sparkly sombreros.

Wonderful. Even Kelli wouldn't mind some sort of
theatrical promposal. And thanks to Elijah, I can't pretend I don't know this.

"So is she your girlfriend?" asks Elijah, who, it seems,
is still here.

"No, Elijah." I try to do the gravel-voiced "leave me
alone" tone. I apparently fail.

"Why not? Are you gay? 'Cause I'm cool with that."

"No."

"She's kind of cute. You should take her out. Haul
her up the side of the Empire State Building in your
hand." He laughs at his own joke, a braying, donkey-like
sound.

"Elijah, it's not that I want you to go away, but I want you to GO AWAY."

He waves both palms at me. "Hey, you don't have to tell me twice."

He then proceeds not to leave.

"Actually, Deacon, maybe you can help me. You see, I'm kind of having a problem of a romantical nature myself. There's this girl Clara. She's in my math class. She's so funny and smart and . . . wow. She works at C & R Hardware. I was there the other day buying a C-clamp. One of my many vices." He suddenly looks at me with a grin. After a moment, he shrugs and continues. "She was demonstrating a power drill. And normally I find drills so boring." Again, the weird smile. "Hell, did you ever meet a girl and she's all you can think about, and you know you don't have a chance, but you're just going to kick yourself if you don't end up asking her out? Should I go for it?"

Since the semester started, I've maybe said ten words to him. He's said about ten thousand to me. I have no idea why he thinks I, of all people, would have romantic advice for him.

"Sure, man. Whatever."

The warning bell rings.

"Okay. I'll do it. Thanks, Deke." He galumphs off.

Deke?

* * *

That night, I sit on the hill behind our house adjusting my telescope. It's hours after Jean has gone to bed, probably nearly ten o'clock. The sky is a little overcast. I can't really see anything but Jupiter. No matter. Sky gazing near Fayetteville isn't what it used to be, not since the suburban sprawl began edging out here.

When I first started visiting Jean, this place seemed like it was in the middle of the jungle. I must have been five or six. Probably younger than that, right after my mom died. Dad was just beginning to go off on his "business trips." He'd leave me here for days. Sometimes weeks. Jean and I would explore the overgrown meadows behind her old farmhouse. She would have been in her late fifties then, but she always had the energy to chase a five-foot-tall kindergartner around the yard. And when Dad started pursuing financial opportunities around the country, the trips to Jean's were the only stability in my life.

I focus in on the moon but can't see much. It was Jean who gave me my first telescope, actually. A toy thing that once belonged to my aunt. This house was always brimming with cool stuff: my late grandfather's tools, his old army uniform, his prosthetic leg. I would have been the king of show-and-tell, had I ever stayed at a school more than a couple of months.

I have many memories of my father yanking me out of bed in the middle of the night, looking jittery.

"C'mon, Deacon, we have to haul ass. You're going to love Denver. Move it, boy. No, we don't have time to get your books. Now, Deacon!"

I counted once. I think I attended twelve elementary schools. Maybe more. Seven junior highs. It wasn't until my father left for Europe that Jean put her foot down. I was sixteen, and Jean insisted that I move in with her.

Dad . . . he didn't argue. Not even that fake arguing you do for appearance's sake.

"This is just for a little bit, Deacon. I'll send you a ticket, soon as I get things squared away here."

I didn't exactly run out and take Dutch lessons.

I pack up my telescope. The universe is being boring tonight.

I've enjoyed my time here with Jean. Fayetteville's an okay town. It's home to the University of Arkansas, and it rarely snows. But I think even if Jean lived in Detroit, I'd like living with her.

She's my best friend.

But high school is coming to an end soon. And as much as I'd like to, I can't stay here.

I've already been accepted into the U of A, here in town. Don't have a major picked out. They don't offer an astronomy program. Actually, no college offers a worthwhile astronomy program except MIT, and I don't have the grades for that. I don't have the grades for a scholarship, either. I'm going to have some serious student debt when I graduate, and you can't make a living staring at the sky.

But now what? I'm kind of at the point where I have to decide what I want to do with my life.

I can't live with Jean forever. And I don't want to live a selfish life like my father. And that leaves . . . what?

Like the universe, my future is limitless. And like the universe, my future is mostly uncharted and kind of scary.

I guess that's why I want to go to prom. If I go to the dance, even with a friend, I can kind of not be a weirdo. Kind of have a fun high school experience like everyone else. And the clock is ticking. I don't know how long it takes to arrange getting a tux and stuff, but I don't have time to burn.

I swear to the empty heavens, come hell or Elijah, I am going to ask out Kelli tomorrow.

What's the worst that could happen?

See also: ironic foreshadowing.

THREE

REMEMBER THAT MOVIE ABOUT THE MAN WHO makes suits out of human flesh?

When I run into Elijah before school, he looks less sane than that guy.

He's wearing some sort of . . . clothes. It's not wholly a tuxedo, or a dress suit, or office casual. Rather, it's some unholy, Frankensteinish combination.

And he's carrying a bundle of screwdrivers, wrapped in a ribbon.

"I'm taking your advice, Deacon."

This is why I avoid talking to people. I'm quite sure I never advised anything like this.

"I'm going to ask Clara to the prom."

Wow. This cannot end well.

But then I take a second look at the screwdrivers and it suddenly clicks into place.

"It's a bouquet," I guess.

He nods, smiling in a disturbing way.

"Because she works at the hardware store."

He nods again. "She's in the metal shop right now. I'm going to do it. Wish me luck."

"Good luck."

He just stands there. "Um, Deacon, you wanna come with me? Be my wingman?"

Even on a regular day, this offer holds no charm. Today, however, I have a good excuse.

"Um, Elijah, I'm kind of . . . waiting for my friend Kelli."

He looks me over, perhaps noticing that I'm dressed in my finest clothes from Harold's Big and Tall Emporium of Little Rock. He smiles, somewhat madly, and departs.

Kelli will arrive any minute. And while I have no elaborate promposal planned, so what? She's an intelligent, classy girl. And even if she says no, at least I can say I tried.

And what if she says yes? What if she smiles at me with those dimples and I go to the dance with her wearing one of those dresses with the bare shoulders and arms?

She'd be wearing the dress, not me. Just clarifying.

"Hey, Shrek, gimme a hand."

My pleasant daydream is interrupted when someone shoves a massive guitar amp into my chest. I reflexively grab it and look down to see who's being so rude.

Like a lot of people in this school, I've never talked to him. But I still don't like him. He's got that hair. You know the hair. Like he woke up an hour early to brush it so it looks like he just rolled out of bed. And he's got the teeth and the nose and the chin thing going on. And suspenders. Expensive clothes. Creases.

He pulls a guitar out of a case. It's an acoustic, but he's got some sort of adapter for the amplifier. As he reaches to plug it in, he sees the expression on my face.

It is not one of jolly camaraderie.

"Sorry, pal. Could you do me a favor real quick?"

"No, I'm waiting for someone." I try to hand him back the amp.

He smiles in what I guess he thinks is a friendly way. All I can think of is that he must use a special razor to maintain such carefully trimmed beard stubble.

"My name's Jason. Someone hired me to serenade the girl he wants to ask to prom. You can't hear a thing in these halls without amplification, and the guy who was supposed to hold that skipped out on me. Wanna do me a solid?"

The only words I hear are "serenade" and "prom." My mind grinds into action.

"Are you free after school today? Could I hire you?"

He plugs in and starts tuning his instrument. "Sure thing. Fifty dollars, all up front."

I bobble his amp with one hand. "Golly, it would be a real shame if I dropped this."

"Prices subject to negotiation. You ready? Just hold that above your head. Don't smile. All eyes on me. Here she comes."

I resist the urge to drop the thing on his foot, but only because I need his help. Joe Cool here can help me ask Kelli after school today. That'll be a lot easier for me, what with him doing all the work. God, what luck I ran into this guy.

I hoist the amp over my head and am nearly deafened when Jason blasts a chord into my ear. I stand there grinning like a moron as his target girl freezes like a possum on the interstate when she realizes the song is for her. Like a mute Atlas I watch as he finishes his song and promposes on behalf of someone else. The girl, a freckle-faced redhead, breaks into tears when he hands her a rose and requests she accompany some guy named Leo to prom.

Of course she says yes. Lucky Leo.

This is so perfect. Kelli's bound to say yes to a spectacle like this. We'll both have a fun prom memory and I'll be able to claim at least one date before I graduate.

I'll have to ask Elijah about my horoscope today. I bet it's got at least four stars.

As planned, Jason meets me in the commons after school. Kelli will be in the gym, setting up for the student council blood drive. Jason carries his guitar case, I haul his other equipment.

"So what's her favorite song?" he asks.

That's a good question. It's not something we've ever actually discussed. I rack my brain for something Kelli-esque. "'Workers of the World Unite'?"

He shakes his head. "Anything else?"

"'I Am Woman, Hear Me Roar'? 'The Plane Wreck at Los Gatos'?"

"How about I pick something out?"

Well, he's the one with the guitar. "Maybe a good idea."

We stop in front of the gym door. "Do you just want me to sing, or you want me to pop the question too? That's five dollars extra."

I stare at him blankly. I kind of assumed he'd do everything. He misinterprets my confusion for deliberation.

"Let's practice. Pretend I'm Kelli. Charm me, Deacon."

"Uh . . ." I can't do it. Even with Kelli in the other room, I can't manage the words.

"Right. Just let me handle it. Try to look . . . just try not to look ridiculous."

It's a good thing he has a beautiful voice. I have half a mind to fire him, and then just march into the gym and . . .

Who am I kidding? Jason owns my butt.

We slide into the gym. As I expected, Kelli is there, amid the morass of cots, tables, and medical equipment.

But she's sitting down on the job. On one of the cots.

Next to some boy. I recognize him. He's a blocky guy named Hunt. He's on the football team. Not something throwy, something tackley.

It's quiet in the gym. Even though we're not anywhere near them, I can still hear Kelli's voice.

"We'll have fun, Hunt. I mean, even though prom is nothing more than a sexist, capitalist display of . . ."

It's hard to miss the rose in her hand and the grin on her face. We retreat out the door before she notices us.

Six hours. If I had asked her at lunch or before school, I would have been first. But I waited, and I blew it.

I want to throw something. And the nearest something to me is Jason.

He looks up at me with real sympathy.

"Hey, Deacon, that's rough. But listen." He lays a hand on my arm. "I still have to charge you for this."

I stand in the school-bus line, surrounded by people, alone. I'm wearing earbuds, so no one attempts to talk to me. They're not actually hooked up to anything, but it doesn't matter.

I totally blew it. And the sick thing is, it's not losing a chance with Kelli that really bothers me. Well, not just that. It's that she was my one shot at going to the dance. My one shot at normal. My one chance at—I don't know—cool. The sort of guy my dad used to be.

Now I'll start college without ever having a date. I'll end up being that weird guy who never leaves the dorms and eats alone and dies one Friday night but no one notices because it's President's Day weekend and when everyone comes back the smell is terrible and the whole thing gets exaggerated into an urban legend that spawns a bad horror movie.

I blame Jason.

Plus, I have to go home and tell Jean that I won't have a date. And listen to my grandmother rant about how Kelli missed a great opportunity, and I should get right back on that horse.

The thing is, Kelli was the only girl I know well

enough to ask to a dance. And I apparently didn't know her as well as I thought. How the hell does she know this Hunt guy?

Perversely, I wish I could talk to Elijah. His promposal will have tanked by now. Maybe we can get together and commiserate about the fickle natures of women over a soda or two. Manly.

Hey, there he is! He's just coming out of the building, still wearing his obnoxious suit thing. I wave at him.

But he's not alone. There's a girl with him. Short-haired and skinny. She's walking with Elijah. And laughing.

She's carrying a bouquet of screwdrivers.

She must have said yes.

Great.

Good for them.

Buttheads.

FOUR

I COME HOME TO AN EMPTY HOUSE. JEAN IS NOT there to greet me. Good. I'm a grown man, practically. I don't need my grandma to soothe my hurt feelings with a warm cup of cocoa and a lullaby. Hell with that.

In fact, there's no point even in dwelling on what happened today with what's-her-name.

You know. Kelli. The really smart, cute girl who I apparently was crushing on a lot harder than I admitted to myself, and blew my chances with because I waited too long to ask her out. Whatever.

I need a distraction. I consider taking out my telescope, but it's broad daylight. There's only one star up, and you're not supposed to look directly at it.

Instead, I decide to do some of the home repairs that I've been neglecting. I'll start with that sagging gutter. I have no idea how to go about fixing it, but how hard could it be?

As my father used to say, "Just tell the landlord it was like that when we moved in."

By the time Jean putters up an hour later, the drainpipe is in worse shape than before. I've also skinned my knuckles and stuck my hand in a fetid clump of rotten leaves.

Jean stands at the foot of the porch.

"We do have a ladder, you know."

"I'm fine." Peachy. I'd whistle a merry tune if I could whistle. And felt merry.

Jean is silent for a moment. "Everything okay?"

"Dandy. Hand me that roll of duct tape, will you?"

I spend several fruitless minutes trying to reattach a bracket.

Jean doesn't leave. "Why don't you come inside?"

"I'm busy, Jean." Stupid tape, never wants to tear straight.

"I'll fix you a nice snack."

"Leave me alone." Can't she see I'm working? Doesn't she realize I don't want to talk right now?

"Would you like a soda?"

I pound on the dry-rotted roof of the porch. "I said

I'm fine! Leave me alone! LEAVE ME ALONE!"

I press my forehead to the rough shingles.

"Deacon." She touches my leg. "Come inside."

I sit on the living room couch. The haze of self-pity is almost palpable. I don't know what's more pathetic: that Kelli is going to prom with some jock, or that Jean realizes I need cheering up. She's in the kitchen now, probably preparing my favorite snack: mixed fruit, topped with Ding Dongs and Twinkies. And no fruit.

She joins me on the sofa. I'm surprised to see her carrying two bottles of beer. I can't remember the last time I saw Jean drink alcohol; she only keeps the stuff on hand for when she hosts her bridge club. I've had to confiscate the car keys of more than one granny.

I'm a little stunned when Jean hands me one of the bottles. But I'm also kind of cheered up by the adult gesture. We click our drinks and I take a swig.

I think my face gives my reaction away.

"It's an acquired taste," says Jean. "Now do you want to talk?"

I shrug. "You were right. I waited too long. She's going with someone else."

Jean takes a surprisingly long drink of her beer. "I'm sorry, Deacon."

"It's not your fault."

She smiles at me sadly. "It kind of is. I think maybe I pressured you into asking someone. Maybe you didn't even want to go to prom."

I contemplate my drink. "I did. I just didn't realize how much until it was too late. I'm an idiot."

Jean pats my knee. "You're in good company. Your father smashed up Grandpa Howard's old Ford on prom night. And your aunt Karen got into such a raging fight with her boyfriend that the police were called. Heck, the night of my own prom, my friend—"

"Wait, whoa, they had proms when you went to school?" I had always kind of pictured Jean attending a one-room school with a coal-burning stove and an outhouse.

"Yes, smartass. What did you think we had, masked balls and cotillions?"

"Maybe. So what was it like?" Jean doesn't talk a lot about the days before she got married. I'm anxious to hear this story.

She takes a long swig. "Well, it was a Broadway theme. They had the old gym all decorated like New York City. Sinatra was big back then, they played a lot of his songs. Anyway, my friend Peggy had just started dating this guy, Bruce—"

"Hang on. So did you go with Grandpa?" From what

I know about my grandfather, he probably wasn't at all nervous about asking her.

But Jean shakes her head. I'm shocked. Did she go alone? Did she have a boyfriend before my grandfather? If so, do I really want to know about that?

Jean is quiet for a bit. And when she finally speaks, her tone is suddenly grave.

"Your grandfather was a year older than me."

I'm not following. "Yeah?"

"And those days, young men were required to enlist in the armed forces. You know Grandpa Howard served in the Vietnam War."

"Of course."

"We'd always planned on going to the dance together, your grandfather and I. But when he got his draft notice . . ."

It suddenly clicks into place. The Locke family was never rich. Grandpa Howard was probably inducted into the army right after he graduated. Which means . . .

"I never went to my prom. Howard was stationed on the other side of the world at the time. It seemed . . . frivolous to go without him. Disloyal." She stares off into space, her mind a million miles away.

When she finally looks up at me, she's smiling sadly. "I spent my entire senior year terrified of that telegram from the State Department. I did not, as you can imagine, enjoy myself."

"Oh, Jean." I give her a one-armed hug. We finish our beers without talking.

"Deacon, those stupid dances aren't all they're cracked up to be. We're both probably better off not going." She gathers the empty bottles and heads for the kitchen.

Wow, Jean missed her prom. That makes me kind of angry. It makes my problems seem stupid by comparison. I'm going to miss the dance because of my nerves. Jean missed hers because of a freaking war.

Darn you, President Lyndon Johnson!

But what's done is done. I just wish Jean didn't look so sad when she was talking about her prom. I worry that's going to be me in fifty years.

FIVE

WHEN I WALK INTO SCHOOL THE NEXT DAY, I'M relieved that there are no promposals in progress. Just a lot of people milling around. Guys I never hung out with. Girls I never dated. Groups I was never part of.

And Elijah, barreling toward me with his arms outstretched.

I contemplate making a break for it, but that's one of the many disadvantages of being tall: you can't vanish into a crowd.

"Deacon!" he bellows, loud enough that several people turn and look at us. He reaches up and grabs me by the shoulders. "There's the man of the hour. My hero. The guy who single-handedly turned my love life around."

Yeah, people are staring. "Uh, I didn't really do anything. . . ."

"Don't be modest! You were the one who kicked me in the butt! The dude who gave me the confidence to ask out Clara! The guy who led me forward into a land of pure romantic bliss!"

He says that last part really loud and then hugs me. I sheepishly smile at the spectators as I disentangle myself.

"Elijah, all I said to you was 'sure, whatever.'"

"And more inspiring words were never spoken. Such a debt I owe you, my friend."

The scary thing is, I don't think he's being sarcastic. I step away.

"Hang on there, Kong. You never told me what happened with you and your lady love! Did you ask her? Did she say yes?"

Sigh. "No. I mean yes. I mean . . . it didn't work out. I waited too long." Why am I unburdening myself to Elijah?

To my surprise, the goofy expression leaves his face. He looks genuinely concerned. "Sorry, man. Rough break. You going to ask someone else?"

"Nah. Don't know anyone. No biggie, I'll stay home

and hang out with my grandma."

Oh God. How pathetic did that sound? Wow.

Elijah, however, doesn't laugh. He glances around, then moves in closer to me. "I wouldn't give up. I see the way girls look at you."

I nervously glance around, in case anyone is looking at me. But the crowd has moved on.

"I'm serious, Deacon. You've still got a few weeks. If you want to go, go."

I admit it. I'm tempted. But I'm not someone like Elijah who has no sense of fear. Or someone like that guy Jason, with, you know, charm. I can't just run up to some random stranger and ask her to the dance. I've frightened enough babies and animals in my life, and I don't need girls running in fear too.

"Elijah, I just don't know anyone."

He tries to wrap a conspiratorial arm around my shoulder, but can't quite reach. "Don't ask just 'anyone,' my friend. Let's do this logically."

"I have to get to class."

He ignores me. "First of all, does your date absolutely have to be female?"

"Ideally, yes."

"Okay. Now let's get to the important stuff. What're your turn-ons? Turn-offs? You like 'em skinny, blonde, BBW, goth, no tattoos, or what?"

This is going nowhere. "Elijah, I'm not looking to hook up right now. I just want . . . forget it."

"No, c'mon man, tell me."

"It sounds stupid. I just want to go to the dance with . . . someone."

"Wow, that does sound stupid."

How do I put this into words? "I do want to go to prom. But I don't want to spend the whole evening wondering if my date likes me or if she's bored or if we're going to . . . you know."

Elijah laughs.

"I just wanted to go with someone I could have fun with. Like Kelli. Someone I wouldn't have to impress. Someone who could enjoy the dance for the sake of the dance. I guess I just want a friend to go with, and it's too late for that now."

He nods. "Yeah, I already have a date."

"Excuse me?"

"Huh? Nothing. Look. There's got to be someone out there who could tolerate you for an evening. Who do you know who likes you, even in a Jesus kind of way? Someone maybe not that great-looking, someone who probably isn't going to get asked. Someone you can hang out with and have a good time, without putting on an act. Think hard."

I laugh. "Elijah, I don't have a lot of friends. Hell, the

only person you're describing that I know is . . .

"Is . . ."

Holy shit.

My ideal date does exist. She always has. Right under my nose.

Good grief, why didn't I think of this before?

The more I consider this insane idea, the less crazy it seems. I mean . . . it's totally off-the-rails nuts, but . . .

My God . . . we could totally go to prom together. She'd say yes in a heartbeat.

"Deacon! Are you okay? You look funny."

I let out a loud burst of laughter.

"Is something wrong? Should I get you an ice pack? Boil some towels?"

"Elijah, I could kiss you!"

He glances over his shoulder. "Um, okay. Don't tell Clara."

"Be serious. I just thought of someone who'd go with me! Someone wonderful!"

Elijah grins. "Dude! That's great. Who is she? Not a freshman, I hope."

I shake my head. "No, she's out of school."

"Oh, a cougar. How old, nineteen?"

I try to remember. "She's sixty-eight."

His face falls. "Uh, listen. I know I don't know you that well, but—"

I'm too excited to listen. I grab him by the arm. "I'll ask her today. But I need your help. You'll help me, right?"

"Uh . . ."

"Of course you will! This is going to be great!" I slap him on the back.

Then I help him to his feet.

Elijah and Jason sit on my crumbling front porch. It occurs to me that this is the first time I've ever invited anyone over here.

"Thanks for coming out on such short notice, guys."

Jason lays a hand on his guitar case. "Kidnapping, Deacon. The term is kidnapping."

I smile apologetically. Maybe I'd been a little enthusiastic, helping Jason into Elijah's car. He'd calmed down, though, once we explained this was a business venture.

Jason pulls out a comb and begins arranging his hair. "So is she meeting us here or what?"

I look at my watch. "We've got about an hour. She should be back from water aerobics by then."

He snorts. "Water aerobics? What is she, your grandmother?"

"Yes. She is."

He pauses, midcomb. I explain.

"Her name is Jean, she's very special to me, and she

didn't get to go to her own prom." I hope he understands that a joke would be most unwelcome at this time.

He just stares at me. And then, slowly, a smile takes over his face.

"Dude . . . that's awesome."

"Isn't it just?" says Elijah.

I don't *think* they're making fun of me.

Jason claps his hands once. "Okay, let's get rolling. Your grandma, does she have a favorite song?"

That's a good question. All her music sounds the same to me. But I remember something she said the other day.

"Sinatra. I think she likes him."

"I can do that. So where do you want to do this?"

"Um . . . I dunno. Maybe the backyard?"

He rolls his eyes. "Just get her back there. Leave the rest to me."

I'm perversely glad that Jason's here. He seems so on top of things.

"So . . ." It feels so strange to ask this. "You guys want to come inside, grab a soda or something?"

Jason stands. "Sure. You go change."

It hadn't occurred to me I'd need better clothes for this, but I might as well go all out. Hell, Jean deserves the best. Abandoning the guys in the kitchen, I rush upstairs. I then remember that my only nice clothes are the ones I wore for Kelli the other day, and they're in the wash. I start to panic. I don't own what you'd call an extensive wardrobe. When you have my proportions, you get used to limited selection, ugly colors, and half-exposed calves.

Inspiration hits, and I remember that some of my grandfather's old clothes are still hanging in one of the upstairs bedrooms. I never knew Grandpa in life, but Jean always says that's where I got my height. Digging through an old canvas storage case, I finally locate a dress shirt and slacks. There are some neckties as well, but my father never taught me how to operate one.

As I struggle into the tight-fitting clothes, I pause to think. Am I being weird? Asking my own grandmother to prom. How will people react when I show up with Jean as my date?

Maybe I should think this through. Not for my sake, but for Jean's. If people start making fun of her . . .

I catch a glimpse of myself in the wall mirror. The shaggy hair, the caveman brow, the perpetually confused and slightly angry expression. And the fact that I have to bend down to see my reflection.

I'm nearly seven feet tall. No one will have a problem with my choice of date. Not if they know what's good for them.

I return downstairs to find Elijah and Jason drinking

Cokes in the living room. I rush to move their cans onto coasters.

Elijah points to a picture on the end table. "Is that your grandpa?"

"Yep. Jean's husband." He's receiving a medal from a general. It must have been shortly after he was wounded, as he's still in a wheelchair. Despite his uniform and the military pomp, Grandpa Howard still looks like a gawky teenager.

Of course he actually was just a gawky teenager at the time. Funny how different our lives turned out to be.

"Vietnam?" asks Jason.

"Yeah. Lost a leg there. Actually, that's his prosthetic right there."

I gesture to the table lamp that Jean painted and wired up out of Grandpa's old metal leg. With the lampshade, you can't really tell what it used to be. It's the one piece of art Jean created that turned out perfectly.

Jason and Elijah just stare.

"Isn't it neat?" I prompt.

"That's one choice of adjective," says Jason.

I hear Jean's arthritic car stop at the end of the driveway as she gets the mail. We jump to our feet.

"Quick, guys, out the back. We'll meet you there."

Jason grabs his guitar. "You know, we haven't talked cash yet. I charge mileage, you know."

"Out! Out!"

They vanish through the kitchen door.

This is it. In a moment of inspiration, I rifle through Jean's craft supplies and pull out a couple of artificial flowers.

Jean comes through the door. Smile, Deacon. You're on.

She must have stopped at the grocery store, because she's struggling with several plastic bags. I move forward to give her a hand.

She notices me for the first time.

She screams.

Not a startled scream, though. Her hands fly to her cheeks and a horrified shriek escapes her mouth. The groceries tumble across the floor.

"Jean?" I drop the flowers. I almost run toward her, but stop, wondering what's scaring her, and if it's me, and why would I scare her, and would coming near her just make things worse?

And then, just like that, the weird episode stops. Jean falls silent and leans against the doorframe. She laughs weakly and fans herself with her hand.

"Jean?" Tentatively, I approach her.

"I'm sorry, Deacon. Sometimes I forget what a man you've grown into. When I saw you standing there, I didn't recognize you for a moment. I thought you were . . . goodness, I feel foolish."

I take her by the hand. "I'm so sorry. Why don't you sit down and let me get you a glass of water."

She pulls away. "Posh, I'm fine." She bends down to pick up her bags, but then stops. "Did you get new clothes?"

I gather up the rest of the bags and place them on the table. "They're Grandpa's."

Jean is looking at me with a smirk. "And flowers?"

I stoop down to pick up the artificial roses. This is suddenly a lot more awkward than I'd pictured. Things always are.

"Well, I can see you're busy. Do you need to use the car?" Her eyes twinkle.

"Actually, Jean, would you mind coming to the backyard with me?"

She looks quizzical but doesn't say anything. Me, I'm about to hyperventilate.

When we reach the corner of the house, I tell Jean to close her eyes. I then lead her by the hand. Jason is already in position, his guitar on one knee. Elijah holds a phone in one hand, an index finger poised above the screen. He looks like he's about to detonate a bomb. Too late to do anything about that now.

"Okay, Jean, open your eyes."

She gasps when she realizes we are not alone, and for

a moment I fear she's going to freak out again. But she only looks at me questioningly.

Jason strums a chord. Elijah stabs the phone, which comes alive with some sort of backup music.

"Deacon?"

I gently shush her, as Jason starts singing "You Make Me Feel So Young."

Jason has that annoyingly serene look on his face, as if overcome by the beauty of his own talents. Elijah holds the phone rigidly pointed at us, smiling in that deranged way of his. But Jean . . . she doesn't look happy. She keeps looking at me, almost annoyed. Like I've dragged her to an event she is not enjoying. I guess she doesn't understand why this is happening and it's making her uncomfortable.

I think Jason realizes this too. After he finishes the first chorus, he just starts playing gentle chords. Our eyes meet, and he nods at Jean. My cue.

I fall to one knee. Looking Jean in the eye, I hand her the raggedy plastic flowers. "Jean Locke, are you doing anything the first weekend in May?"

I think it takes Jean a moment to process what I've just asked her. Long enough for me to feel awkward kneeling like this and still trying to get her to take the flowers.

Now, when I'd played this scene over in my mind, I'd

pictured Jean getting all flummoxed and giggly. Maybe even teary. Laughter, a hug, and excitement about how she was going to finally get to go to a special dance.

But she's only frowning.

"Deacon, stand up."

I obey, very worried. Maybe she thinks this is some sort of joke. Behind me, Jason's guitar music has faded to nothing, while Elijah's recorded bass line continues to play.

"Jean Locke, will you do me the honor—"

"Stop it." She's really not smiling.

"I just thought maybe you'd like to . . . you know, go to the prom with me." My confidence has left my body. And my voice.

She places her hands on my shoulders. She smiles, but it's not joyful.

"No, Deacon."

And then, without another word, she turns and heads into the house.

I stand alone on my astronomy hill. I have nowhere to go, nothing to make me happy. I'm left lurking up here in the cold, cursing the bleak, empty, godless universe and howling at the yellow moon.

Okay, it's really not that bad. But I'm still pretty annoyed with Jean. I mean, that whole promposal thing was utterly charming. And sincere. A way for both of us to finally go to a high school dance.

Guess she didn't see things that way. Guess she was embarrassed.

I wish she hadn't said no right in front of my friends, or whatever you'd call Elijah and Jason. Fortunately, they were polite enough to quietly leave after Jean turned me down, with Jason only stopping to present me with his bill.

I didn't follow Jean back inside. Instead, I walked to town and back. And when I returned, I didn't go into the house.

I can't even get a date with my own grandmother.

Not that I want to date my grandmother. Not everything you hear about Arkansas is true.

I hear Jean coming up the hill long before I see her. It's a pretty steep climb, and it takes a lot of willpower to stay on my little stool instead of rushing to give her a hand.

"So this is your secret hideout," she says, after catching her breath.

I shrug. I've never given it much thought, but I do kind of have a little camp up here. Just a canvas tarp tied to a couple of trees, some outdoor furniture, a few plastic bins for sodas and my telescope lenses.

"You know, there's an old tent in the basement. And

you could move that picnic table up here if you like."

I don't acknowledge her. I'm too . . . angry is a strong word. But sometimes one needs strong words.

She pulls up a lawn chair. "Deacon, I'm sorry. I didn't mean to be so abrupt. You really caught me by surprise earlier."

"Yeah, well . . . that was kind of the point."

Jean tries to touch my hand but I pull away. Wow. First time I've ever done something like that.

"Listen to me. This was a sweet gesture, but surely you must have a friend you could take."

"Yes! Yes, I do! She's funny and crazy and I've known her a long time. She taught me to shave and to drive, and I tried to teach her how to use the internet. She held my hand when I had that root canal, and I held her hand when we watched *Star Wars*."

"That part with the trash compactor was scary!" she says defensively.

"Remember that time we drove down to Shreveport and you dragged me to that one guy's concert?"

"I'd thank you not to refer to Mr. Neil Diamond as 'that one guy.'" But she's smirking now.

"How about when I tried to remove those wasp nests with the gasoline?"

"That's not a good memory, Deacon! You lit your clothes on fire and got stung!"

"And last Halloween, when we caught those kids egging the house?"

She laughs out loud. "When you came after them, I swear, they screamed like you were the devil himself."

"Well, they probably thought that chain saw still worked." I clear my throat. "Hey . . . remember that time when my father got in bad with some loan sharks and had to leave the country? And how I didn't have to move to the Netherlands because you gave me a place to stay?"

She looks down at her feet. "I was happy to do that."

"Maybe so, but if it wasn't for you, I'd be smoking hash in some Amsterdam tulip bar right now. Look, I know it's crazy. But I guess I'm not going to be able to do things like that with you next year. Not as much." It breaks my heart to say it, but it's true.

"And that's the way things are supposed to be!" interjects Jean.

"Yeah, but prom is the last big high school thing. And I want to share it with my best friend. I know you missed your own dance—"

Jean's head jerks up. "Who told you that?"

"You . . . you did."

A funny look crosses her face. Then she nods. "Yes. Yes, of course."

I pause, a little worried, but I continue.

"I think you and I would have a lot of fun. Let's do

it right. The limo, the tux, the works. Whadya say? Will you go with me? Make the other guys jealous?"

She's smiling. I can see her pearly-white dentures in the dark. "Well . . ."

"C'mon. I didn't rent a hipster guitar player for you to tell me no."

Jean bursts out laughing. "Are you sure your friends won't think this is strange?"

"Of course not." And who cares if they do?

She touches my hand and this time I let her. "Okay, Deacon. Let's do this thing! Prom night! With the most handsome guy I know."

I smile. "That's the spirit!"

"On two conditions."

Damn.

"First, you can back out of this at any time."

"Jean . . ."

"No, listen. I still don't buy this garbage of you not having anyone else you could ask. If you should find a young woman before the dance, I'll happily bow out."

"Fine." Leave it to my grandmother to think I'll overcome eighteen years of awkwardness in under a month.

"And second . . . I'm not much of a dancer. And I don't think you are either. They offer dance classes over at the YMCA. Would you take lessons with me? I'd hate to make a fool of myself in front of all those young people. I'll be uncomfortable enough as it is."

Dance lessons? It somehow hadn't occurred to me that going to a dance meant . . . dancing. "Okay, Jean."

She stands and I follow. "Wow. I'm finally going to prom. And only fifty years too late." She's really smiling now. I take her arm and guide her down the hill.

We're doing this. We're going to the dance together. Yeah, maybe it's weird, but who cares? There's honestly no one in the world I'd rather go with.

Besides, it's not like I'm going to meet the girl of my dreams in the next couple of days.

Stay tuned for the next chapter, where Deacon meets the girl of his dreams.

SIX

I STAND IN FRONT OF MY LOCKER HOLDING MY lunch cooler. A guy in a gorilla suit named Leroy walks by me.

The guy is named Leroy. I don't know what the suit is named.

Another promposal.

Just like the one I arranged yesterday. I'm going to prom. *We're* going to prom.

I'm kind of psyched. The whole experience has given my ego a shot in the arm. Who knows? This time next year, I may be asking out girls who aren't related to me.

I start to head toward the library, where I have lunch with Kelli almost every day. She always reads while I sit near her. Sometimes she talks to me. Lately it's been about her college plans, her biology major, her excitement about higher learning. Sometimes I pretend to be as excited as she is.

But I've avoided her ever since Hunt's proposal, even skipping lunch yesterday. I don't really want to hear about her date. And to tell you the truth, I feel like a change of pace.

Maybe I'll have lunch in the cafeteria. Hey, why not? I'm a senior. It's all about trying new things.

The lunchroom is always crowded, but there are a few seats open here and there. I just have to find a spot and sit down. All casual like. Get to know some of the popular kids.

"Deacon! Deacon, over here!"

Or, I could just eat with Elijah.

As I grab a chair and spread out the food Jean has prepared for me, I realize the girl sitting next to Elijah is there on purpose. I saw her the other day. It's Clara, the girl he stalked into a prom date.

She has short, mousy hair, a knobby frame, and a generous nose.

And is absolutely adorable. Not like supermodel sexy, but definitely out-of-my-league cute. I never thought I'd say this, but I'm kind of jealous of Elijah.

"You must be Deacon," says Clara, with a smile that

puts me at ease. "Elijah has told me so much about you."

Told her what? This is Deacon. He's twelve feet tall and lives in the middle of nowhere.

Elijah reaches for my baggie of carrot sticks. "Hey, Deke, rough go yesterday. But if you're still interested in prom, Clara's cousin—"

"Actually," I interrupt, "Jean said she would go with me."

"How sweet!" says Clara, before Elijah can react. "Does she go here? What's she like?"

I exchange a knowing look with Elijah. "I've known her forever. We're good friends. She's a lot of fun. And beautiful."

"Totally hot," agrees Elijah. "Smoldering sexy."

"Elijah!"

"I call it like I see it. Hey, listen, you wanna go half-sies on the cost of a limo?"

I think about this. "Wouldn't that be like eighty thousand dollars?"

Clara giggles.

"No, smartass," says Elijah. "Seventy bucks each. You in?"

That's kind of a steep price. But I did promise Jean that we'd do prom right, and this might help defray the already mounting expenses (those tickets were costly, and I still owe Jason his fee). Of course, that would mean riding there with Elijah, but no plan is perfect.

"Sure, man."

Clara and Elijah begin discussing reservations and things. They keep asking me to contribute to the plans, and before I know it, the bell rings. I only had a chance to eat two of my sandwiches.

So how about that. I ate lunch with a total stranger and it wasn't nearly as uncomfortable as I'd expected. And it only took me two years.

According to that one song, the YMCA is supposed to be a fun, crazy place. But the real building in Fayette-ville is a bland, unassuming structure. This is where Jean goes several times a week to attend those adult educa-tion classes on arts and crafts. She doesn't admit it, but I think she holds out hope that she'll discover some latent talent and end up being the next Grandma Moses. I encourage her projects: the lopsided pottery, the creepy paintings, and the wonky calligraphy. I even went to her recital when she took that belly-dancing course. Ten postmenopausal women in harem pants. I still cringe when I hear sitar music.

I was hoping all the dance classes would be full, but wouldn't you know it, there's one starting this very Thurs-day. Jean beams as we cross the parking lot. "We were lucky a class was open. The last time your grandfather took me dancing, disco was still big. Is that break-dancing thing still popular?"

I shake my head and smile. Jean's pop-culture references end in the late eighties, when my father left home. And I haven't exactly been a good source of what's trendy these days.

The first letter in YMCA stands for "young," but the building is full of senior citizens. Jean takes me by the arm and leads me to a classroom with a sign on the door:

BEGINNING DANCE
TUESDAY/THURSDAY
4:30–5:30
SORAYA SHADEE, INSTRUCTOR

I'm guessing this Soraya learned to dance when the polka was the latest thing. I'm not encouraged when we enter the room. There's about twenty people here, twice as many women as men. I'm pretty sure they're all on the older side of fifty. Some by quite a bit. One woman even has a portable oxygen tank strapped to her belt.

Jean seems quite at home and says hi to a couple of the women.

"And this is my grandson, Deacon."

There's a simultaneous gasp from her pals.

"Her grandson!"

"That's so sweet!"

"How adorable."

"Shirley, that's her grandson!"

"What's that?"

"I said her grandson brought her here!"

I plaster on a smile. Much as I'm not looking forward to this, I kind of have to take this class. I want to do prom right. Which means I actually need to get out on the dance floor. Jesus, I haven't danced with anyone since square dancing in eighth-grade gym class. My poor partner. She forgave me for stepping on her foot. Even let me sign the cast.

I suffer through countless descriptions of how adorable I am. One woman pats my cheek. I'm about ready to fake a need to use the bathroom when the instructor walks in.

Turns out I was wrong about her being ancient. She's young, probably about my age. And she's . . .

Okay, here's the part where descriptions become difficult. It's easy for me to conjure up her face. It's hard for me to relate it without sounding like I'm filing a missing person report. I mean, how would you describe the Mona Lisa? An Italian girl with a weird smile? Is the Grand Canyon just a big hole in the ground? Is Beethoven's Ninth just a catchy tune?

Well, by now you're probably picturing Soraya as

looking like your own dream date, so allow me to fill in the blanks. For starters, she stands out from the typical pasty-faced Arkansan. She's not black, but has kind of a medium complexion, like she's from Italy or Mexico or Arabia or North Africa or . . . well, you get the picture. Her hair is the darkest I've ever seen, so straight and long, hanging down over her shoulders. Her eyes—and I admit, they are not the first feature I notice—are big and brown. Her nose is narrow, her smile wide, and her legs slender.

She's dressed in sweatpants and a Razorbacks shirt, and she carries a boom box.

I nearly have to take a hit of that one lady's oxygen to stay upright. The room seems to swim. All the other students, even Jean, vanish. All I can see is Soraya. I have no idea what has affected my brain like this . . .

Oh, bullshit. I know exactly what it is, and it doesn't originate with my brain.

Soraya sets down her radio and strides to the front of the room. I think one of Jean's friends is talking to me, but I face the teacher like a good little student. The non-politically-correct part of my mind wonders if she has an exotic accent.

"Welcome! It's great to see y'all here."

Pure Arkansas Ozarks drawl.

"I see a lot of familiar faces, and I'm pleased to see

some new people as well."

She looks right at me when she says that. Like right directly at me. She's pleased that I'm here.

"For those of you who don't know me, my name is Soraya. I teach dance and piano here. . . ."

Jean, I want a piano for my birthday.

"We're going to learn a lot of dances in these next few weeks, but more importantly, we're going to have fun."

Yes. Yes I am.

"Now let's begin with some stretches."

With Soraya in command, I willingly exercise for the first time in years. Though when she leans back and her shirt rides up, revealing an inch of her belly, I almost tumble over on my butt.

"Okay, let's start off with the Texas two-step. If everyone could pair off. It seems we have more ladies than gentlemen here today, so a few of you women will have to either pair up or sit out this first song."

There's a depressing thought. Even at eighty, you still may have to stand on the sidelines watching the more popular kids dance.

Soraya turns on a twangy tune. I move to take Jean's hand and realize, to my shock, that she's paired up with another guy. A lanky old geezer in a Confederate flag hat. I normally don't like that symbol, but this guy is old enough to have actually fought at Bull Run.

Someone is standing close to me. I look down at a pair of thick glasses and a head of silver hair. I smile.

"Shall we?"

I kind of assumed I'd suck at this, but, much to my surprise, we don't do half bad. Soraya gives instructions and we just sort of follow the rhythm. Once you get the pattern down, it's really not that hard. It helps that I don't take my eyes off our instructor the entire time.

"You're such a sweetheart," says my partner.

"Yeah."

Soraya is going around the room, gently touching the dancers, moving them into more correct positions.

"It's so wonderful that you're doing this with your grandmother. People say teenagers today are selfish, but I don't believe that for a moment. My granddaughter Callie, for instance, you've never met a nicer girl."

"Yeah."

Soraya cuts in on a couple and begins dancing with the hopelessly awkward man. He smiles. I know I would.

"Say, Deacon, is it? I should introduce you to Callie. She's such a beauty, I think you'd like her."

"Uh . . . no thanks."

Soraya moves to the next couple over. She's getting closer to us.

"Why not? Don't you like girls? Wait, maybe you don't. There seems to be a lot of that going around these days."

I'm too distracted to correct her. One more couple, and then Soraya will be with us.

"I should introduce you to my great-nephew, Nicholas. Such a nice boy. I think you'd like him."

Soraya stops to help the final couple fall into rhythm, then turns toward me.

And the song ends.

Typical.

Soraya briefly smiles at my partner, then returns to the stereo. "Okay, everyone, same song. Switch partners, give everyone a chance to lead."

I move over to Jean, kind of forcing her partner to retreat. She smiles at me, but just as the music starts, she suddenly stumbles against me.

"Jean?"

"Oh, it's my darn ankle again. I'll have to sit this one out."

Her ankle hasn't given her trouble in months. "Do you need to see the doctor?"

"I'm fine, Deacon. Look, here's someone who wants to dance with you."

I turn and realize that Soraya has approached us without me even noticing. I think she had come over to check on Jean, but my grandmother quickly trots off and sits down.

Soraya looks at me questioningly. Before I can say

anything stupid, she smiles and takes my hand.

We begin to dance. I'm not sure who is controlling my movements, though it's certainly not me. But I'm happy enough to be the puppet for now.

I don't have nearly enough composure to meet her eyes. I just stare straight ahead, while she looks me in the chest. But she has her hands in mine. And they are so soft and warm. So very warm.

And then the song ends. And just like that, she's back at the front of the class, giving more instruction.

Me, I wish I was a smoker so I could go out for a cigarette right about now.

As the class progresses and I proceed to dance with every grandma in the place, I find my blood pressure stabilizing. Yes, Soraya is beautiful, but so what? That probably just spells trouble. Just because she smiled at me doesn't mean she's not stuck-up or snooty. Hell, I doubt she'd even talk to me, let alone . . .

What's the next step with a girl after talking to them?

The class ends. Jean collapses in a chair, gulping bottled water. I gather our things, determined not to do something stupid and reckless like trying to strike up a conversation with our teacher.

I hear a familiar voice at my elbow. "Hey, got a second?"

I manage to turn, just before my central nervous

system shuts down completely.

"Deacon, right? And is that your grandmother over there?"

I nod. *Dat my grammy!* Soraya smiles. "I think that's wonderful. So many of my students . . . well, they don't have a lot to do during the day. They can't get around like they used to and their families ignore them. It's sweet that you're taking the time to do something like this with your grandma."

She then reaches out and squeezes my arm. Just touches me. Like it's no big deal.

"Anyway, I look forward to seeing you next week. You're not a bad dancer."

And then she turns to go.

Me dance pretty.

Jean is standing next to me with a smug grin on her face. "So what did you think of the class, Deacon?"

Soraya has left the room. I permit myself to blink.

"Not bad. Not bad at all."

SEVEN

"SO I WAS THINKING I'D TAKE PHYSICS AND STATIS-tics first semester to get them out of the way. Or do you think that'll be too much of a course load?"

It's the following Monday and I'm back to having lunch with Kelli. She sits at a library table, a catalog from the University of Arkansas, Little Rock, in front of her. I'm crammed at a nearby computer station, grunting in agreement every so often.

"I mean, math isn't my strong suit. What if I can't hack all that? What do you think, Deacon?"

"Absolutely." The internet is fighting me. I don't get online a lot. We don't have a computer at home. Hell, I don't even own a cell phone. And every time I access an online clothing store, I get an error message saying the district technology department has blocked it.

"Are you listening to me? What the hell are you trying to do there? It's you, so I know it's not porn."

I hunch down. "Just trying to order some new pants." And shirts and shoes. Dance class is tomorrow and, well, maybe it would be nice to dress up a little bit. If I could figure out this online-ordering witchcraft.

Kelli leans over. She glances at the library desk, then enters the override password that she learned as a volunteer here. The lockout message vanishes.

"So why are you shopping online?"

"Because Walmart doesn't carry things in circus sizes."

"No . . ." She scoots her chair over until its arms touch mine. "Why are you shopping for clothes at all? I always figured they'd bury you in those brown Dockers."

I pretend not to understand the question. Sometimes a guy just needs new clothes.

As I scroll through the casual department, I can feel Kelli's smirk boring into the back of my neck. I might as well get this over with.

"Kelli? If a guy wanted to make a, uh, good impression, would that shirt work?"

She laughs. "Deacon, it's not clothes that impress a girl."

"Who said anything about a girl?" My dismissive comment comes out as suspiciously paranoid.

She blows her nose, then reaches over and moves the mouse out of my reach. "You want some advice? As your friend and someone who's known you awhile?"

I turn to her in gratitude. "Yes. Please."

Kelli tents her fingers under her chin and stares at me like a doctor about to deliver unpleasant news. "Okay. First of all, you have a bad habit of not looking girls in the eye. You kind of . . . well, you tend to focus on a couple of much lower points, if you get my meaning."

Oh, God . . . oh, God. I don't . . . I mean . . . surely not. Do I? I don't remember . . . am I really one of those chest-staring assholes? I guess I'm only human, but I don't leer . . . do I? Oh, God, there was that time last spring, when Kelli wore this tank top. . . .

She bursts into laughter. "Jesus, you're funny when you freak out. FEET, Deacon! Every time you're around a girl, you stare at the floor. I assume you're not some kind of foot fetishist, so make eye contact."

I'm making eye contact with Kelli. "I kind of hate you right now."

She doesn't react. "Number two: every time you talk

to anyone, you have this whiny voice, like you're apologizing for existing. And you mumble. You're the biggest guy in this school, so stop acting like you're afraid to talk to people. Good lord, I've been wanting to tell you that for a long time."

Had I actually been hoping to connect with Kelli on a more personal level? "Any other glaring personality flaws you'd like to mention?"

She looks at her watch. "Yes, but we're running short on time. Just one more thing." She smiles, and the dimples show.

"Deacon, for some reason I don't think you like yourself very much. And you don't think people like you. But they do. Or they would if you didn't always keep to yourself." She jams her finger against my forehead. "I know there's an interesting guy in that big blockhead of yours, somewhere. Maybe. Try to let him out sometimes. I'd hate for you to . . . blow it with someone you like."

And just for a moment, as her eyes meet mine, the silliness goes away. For a second, I think I kind of understand what she's implying.

"Kelli . . . thanks."

She stands. "You'll do fine." She punches my shoulder. "Just don't overthink things."

Right. Be suave, confident, and above all, don't be Deacon. I can do that.

"And a one and a two and a stop!"

Everyone in class stops dancing within five seconds of each other.

I'd like to say I'd been paying such close attention to Soraya's instructions that I literally didn't miss a beat, but I'd actually been listening to my dance partner. She'd been telling me about when she'd participated in the original Selma to Montgomery march and how her late husband had lost an eye to a police baton.

I'm starting to feel like my generation was cheated, somehow. *Where were you when the* Avengers *movie came out?* It's just not the same.

Soraya wraps up the class, complimenting each and every one of her students individually. When she tells me I have an excellent sense of rhythm, I almost jump for joy. I really would, if the ceiling was a foot higher.

And now class is over. Jean is having a conversation with Johnny Reb. The other students are leaving. Soraya is alone, gathering her stuff.

For the past two days, I've been telling myself that I'll talk to her after this class. Just go right up to her and say . . . words. I've got it all plotted out.

Me: Something

Soraya: Ha, ha, ha!

Me: Something else

Soraya: Oh, Deacon, you're so funny and charming.

Of course, now that we've reached zero hour, it's not so easy.

I'll talk to her next week. Give myself the weekend to plan. Maybe ask Kelli for some more advice.

Maybe wait until I'm as old as the guys here and come to class to hit on women Jean's age. Damn it, Deacon, just do it!

Do I go in brave, like Elijah, or smooth, like Jason?

Soraya hefts her heavy gym bag over her shoulder, then struggles to get a grip on her radio.

Or maybe I should go in like Deacon.

"Here, let me give you a hand."

She rewards me with a smile and passes me her bag. As I follow her out the door, Jean catches my eye.

She winks.

Great. I'm going to hear about this tonight.

The first ten seconds of walking are fine. But then things start to get awkward. Silence descends upon us like a blanket of peanut butter. And it's still a good two minutes until we'll get to the parking lot.

I must say something. "So . . . you don't go to Fayetteville High, do you?"

"No, I go to a private school."

"Saint Pius?"

Soraya gives me an odd look and shakes her head. I worry that I've offended her somehow, but after a minute, she smiles at me.

"So I see that your grandmother signed up for women's self-defense."

This is news to me. "Tell the instructor to be careful. Jean is the sort of person who'd go for a man's . . . eyes."

Soraya smiles. "That was the impression I got. She's quite a handful, I can tell. Does she live with your family?"

Now it's my turn to be a little sullen. "Jean *is* my family."

I'm afraid I've killed the conversation, but Soraya keeps talking. "Everyone around here knows her. Did she really once paint a shirtless portrait of Tony Orlando?"

"Is that who that was supposed to be? I always thought it was Samuel L. Jackson."

She laughs. So do I. I'm doing it. I'm talking to her. Talking to Soraya. Just all casual. Like I do this every day.

I even remember to hold the door open for her when we leave the building. That's how it's done, Jason. Smooth.

Soraya is parked on the street. I place her bag in the backseat. She hops in the front and rolls down the window.

"Thanks, Deacon. I'll see you next week."

"Okay." I smile, look her right in the eye, and turn to go.

That went well. Very well. By the time this class ends in a few weeks, maybe I'll get up the courage to . . .

Click.

Click. Click. Click.

Uh-oh.

I turn to see Soraya, still sitting in her parked car. She turns the ignition, but nothing happens.

She looks up at me. "I told my dad the battery was no good. You got a set of jumper cables?"

I know that Jean's trunk is filled to capacity with decoupage supplies, scrap metal, reclaimed wood, and a drum of clay, but no cables.

"Uh . . . no." Perfect chance to play the hero and I can't. "Want me to call . . . someone?" *And if you say yes, can I borrow your phone?*

She shakes her head. "I can clutch start it. Can you give me a push?"

I understand the last word. "Sure. Um, how far away do you live?"

Her eyes narrow. "I don't mean push me all the way home. If you can just get me over that hill, I can pop the clutch and get it to turn over manually."

She might as well be speaking Swedish. I know what "over that hill" means, though.

And I totally would push her car all the way to her house if she asked me to.

"Ready when you are," Soraya says through the open car window.

I place my hands on the trunk and shove. Soon we've crested the rise. I jog alongside the car. I hear the engine cough, then start. The car starts to pick up speed.

"Thanks, Deacon!" she shouts as she starts to pull away.

I trot up next to the car and lean down to look through the window. "Hey, no problem! Can I help you with anything else?"

She glances nervously from me to the windshield. "No, I'm good."

"You sure?" We're really moving now. "Maybe we should go over to AutoZone and see about that battery."

"No, really, it's okay!"

"I'd hate if you wound up stranded somewhere is all." I'm flat-out running now.

"Deacon! I have to turn here!"

"Okay." I glance to make sure we can merge safely and I sprint out onto Highway 16.

"At any rate, I'll see you at the next class!"

I think she's about to reply, but someone honks at her and merges into her lane. I can no longer keep up, so I come to a stop.

Huh. That went well. Not only did I talk to Soraya, I kind of saved the day. Two for two, Deacon Locke. Yeah.

"Get out of the road, asshole!"

I'm nearly hit by a Volvo. Quickly, I scamper to the curb.

EIGHT

SORAYA SITS NEXT TO ME ON THE PORCH SWING IN front of Jean's house. She wears a billowing white dress and her long black hair blows free in the spring breeze. Neither of us says anything, but it's not an uncomfortable silence. It's like when you're just so at ease with someone, there's no reason to fill the air with pointless talking. I've never been this calm around anyone, not even Jean.

My hand slowly reaches over. Terrified that I'm making a stupid mistake, I gently lay it on top of hers. Her fingers are so warm, so soft. And they intertwine with mine. Just like on the dance floor. Only now, it's so much more.

Soraya turns and looks at me. She smiles with her

white teeth and says, "I've written an erotic book about punctuation."

And suddenly I realize it's not Soraya I'm sitting next to, but Elijah. And we're not on the porch swing, but in his cramped car. Thank God we're not holding hands.

"An erotic book about punctuation," he repeats. "I call it the *Comma Sutra*."

How I long for a comfortable silence. I try to recapture my daydream, but it's gone.

"Get it, Deke?"

"Yes."

"You're not laughing."

I never actually asked Elijah to start driving me home from school, and he never really offered. The arrangement just sort of developed. Kind of like athlete's foot.

I shift uncomfortably in my seat. Elijah's car is tiny. It's like a novelty prototype. Something from Eastern Europe, assembled in a gulag.

Elijah elbows me in the ribs. "Dude, something's on your mind." He's looking at me and not the road.

"No . . . well . . ."

"C'mon, out with it."

"I met a girl the other day. And I really, REALLY want to—"

"Yeah?" Elijah asks with a leer.

"I want to get to know her."

"Oh."

"Any advice?"

Elijah grins. He then rolls down his window and leans his head to the side so the wind whips back his thin hair. "You've come to the right place, my friend. I got this."

I doubt Soraya would be impressed by a screwdriver bouquet, but I listen anyway.

"Now, Deacon, I've found in my many frustrating years of chasing the female species that there are three things that really grab a girl's attention. Any of them will do. Number one: be cool. Or be rich. Same thing, really."

I shake my head. "No luck there."

"Okay, number two: be really good-looking."

"Again, no."

There's a pause. Elijah starts to say something, but doesn't. Eventually, he continues.

"Number three: do something really, really well. And it doesn't have to be like sports or music or needlepoint. Just become an expert at something and do it in front of her. Never fails. Never."

I feel like jamming my feet through the floorboards like Fred Flintstone. I have no skills. No talents. I'm shy, clumsy, and my dance skills are only just developing. There's nothing I'm good at.

Except . . .

"Elijah, do you think she'd like it if I took her stargazing? I have a telescope."

He rubs his chin. "Let's see, you two, alone in the dark, as you explain the romantic mysteries of the universe? Yeah, that could kind of work to your advantage."

"Jesus, she'll see right through that."

He's unfazed. "So invite Clara and me along. We'll all hang out, and if you want to be alone with her, we'll make some excuse."

He pulls up in front of my house. I'm suddenly almost nauseous with fear. Elijah has given me the perfect opening with Soraya. All I have to do is go up and ask her if she'd like to get her hands on my telescope. What could be more innocent than that?

Elijah is watching me as I struggle out of his car. "Hey, Deke, you get your tux rented yet?"

"No."

"I wouldn't wait on that too long. If Bruce Banner needs something that same weekend, they might run out of jackets in your size. I'm getting mine next Saturday, you want to come?"

"Sure."

As he speeds off, I rehearse my little speech with Soraya over and over again. Every time it sounds worse.

Why has this girl rattled me? Aside from the fact that

she's beautiful and well-spoken and danced with me.

Well, if Elijah can ask out a girl, so can I.

Maybe.

I find Jean in the living room looking through a photo album. She's got her record player on, spinning some tune about painting a door.

"Would you turn that noise down?" I say as I drop my bag.

Normally when I make a remark like that, she'll say, "If it's too loud, you're too old," or rip into modern musicians that I don't actually listen to.

But today she just sits there.

"Jean?"

I realize, to my shock, that tears are running down her face. I rush to join her on the couch.

"Jean, what's wrong?"

She grabs a tissue and dabs at her eyes. "Oh, I was going through some old pictures, and got a little verklempt. Just being a foolish old woman."

I flail my arms in that helpless Kermit the Frog way, trying to think how to comfort her. She never cries! And now that she is, I feel like I'm just going to lose it.

But as soon as she takes away the Kleenex, the episode has stopped. She manages a weak smile. I almost say something, but there's a look in her eyes that tells me to drop it. I change the subject.

"So what are these pictures of?"

She hefts the album onto my knee. "These were taken my junior year of high school. I'd almost forgotten about them. Look, here's your grandfather, just before he graduated."

I have to do a double take when I look at the photo. In every picture I've seen of my grandpa, he has a stiff, almost military bearing. Even my father described him as "a real hard-ass." That's why I'm a little shocked to see him at eighteen, leaning against a lamppost with his shirt off, flashing the "V for victory" sign.

My God, his hair goes past his ears.

"Wasn't he handsome?" sighs Jean. "Oh, here's another good one."

I'm shocked to see my grandfather with an eye swollen shut and a bandage around his head.

Jean titters. "That was when he got in a little dustup with the Kznack brothers. Back then boys were not as . . . sensitive as they are now. They all three got into it at the homecoming game. Howard, God bless him, broke two of Aaron's ribs."

This is a strange and dark corner of my family that I wasn't aware of. "Why did . . . wait a minute. Aaron Kznack? *Principal Kznack?*"

"I believe that's where he ended up. Don't worry, this was a long time ago."

My mind has difficulty processing this information. "Hang on. . . ."

"Damn, your grandfather lived hard before the army. Oh, I'd forgotten about this. You know the Ford dealership on Logan Street? Well, there used to be a pond there. We would all go down there on the weekends and light a bonfire."

I examine the ragtag group of teens. There's Grandpa, shirtless again, grinning at the camera. But he's got his arm around some babe in a bikini top. Quite frankly, I'm surprised Jean chose to save this picture of him putting the moves on . . .

I squint at the black-and-white photo.

Oh, Jesus.

"What's wrong, Deacon? Did you think I was always this age?"

"Yeah, kind of." I focus in on teen Jean's face. "You used to smoke cigarettes?"

"That wasn't tobacco." Her face grows solemn. "Maybe you have a hard time believing that young woman was me, but it's even harder for me to believe it, some days. And when you're my age . . . When you go off to college next year, try to make some memories like this. Those times fly by quicker than you think."

"Hey, I think we're going to be making some pretty kick-ass memories at prom next month."

Jean nods, but I can tell that's not what she meant.

I'm done with the pictures. I don't wish to see my grandmother's belly button. When I close the album, a bundle of envelopes, tied with a ribbon, slides out of the back of the book.

"What're these?"

Jean picks them up and stares at them for a moment. They're old and yellow, with unfamiliar stamps.

"The letters Howard sent me when he was in the army. He wrote me every week, even when he was overseas." Her voice cracks and I'm afraid she's going to start crying again. Instead, she passes me the stack. "Here. You should read these. Letter writing is a lost art. You kids today, communicating God knows how on your electric doodads."

"Who am I going to send a letter to?"

"You could write to your . . ." She trails off. I think she was going to suggest writing to my father. She doesn't know I know this, but the birthday card she sent him came back "addressee unknown." We have no idea where he is.

Jean still cares.

I take the letters from her, but to be honest, I really don't plan on looking at them. Jean's memory is spotty, and there's no telling what Grandpa said in those things. The last thing I want to read is a memory of how my grandparents . . . best not to think about it.

Jean stands and turns off the record player. Fifty years from now, will I be rambling on to my grandson about the way Fayetteville used to be? About Elijah and his screwdrivers, or the time Kelli and I cut class so I could help her prepare for the ACTs?

I have to make some better memories, for the sake of my grandson.

I think I'll name him Kevin.

NINE

DANCE CLASS NUMBER THREE. THE GOOD NEWS IS that I'm kind of catching on to the whole rhythm-of-the-dance thing. Prom is in three weeks, and by that time, I may be actually able to not make an ass of myself.

Jean, on the other hand . . . well, she tries. And she's having a good time. I think if I can get her to let me lead, we'll look darn good on the dance floor.

Right now, she's dancing with Johnny Reb, the Confederate veteran. Frankly, I don't like the way he's leaning into her. If he were a lot younger, I'd think he was trying to feel her up.

Suddenly, he lets out a groan of pain and staggers against the wall. For a second, I think he got too handy and Jean kneed him in the balls. She looks just as surprised as everyone else, though.

"I'm fine, I'm fine!" he snaps, clutching the small of his back, a look of abject agony on his face. "Happens all the time."

A half dozen women try to help him, but he shrugs them all off. He looks like he's going to collapse. "I just need to walk it off! It's okay." He stumbles out of the room.

"Deacon," says Soraya, "go with him, please."

A chance to make a good impression. I find the old man leaning against a wall.

He smiles at me weakly. "I have to remind myself that I'm not eighty anymore."

"Are you sure you don't need to . . . sit?"

Deacon Locke, MD.

"It's better standing. Go back to class. In a few minutes I'll be in a better place."

I don't like the sound of that, so I stay.

"I hate it when this happens," he says after a minute. "Doesn't exactly make me look suave in front of the ladyfolk. Especially Barbara."

I guess I kind of chuckle.

"Something funny, sonny? You don't think I go to this class because I like dancing, do you?"

This time I don't hide my laugh.

"I lost my wife, Miranda, couple of years ago. Finally decided I couldn't take any more *Price Is Right*, so I started coming here. God, you think this would be easier the second time around."

So in another sixty years, I'll still be just as awkward around girls. Great.

"I keep trying to ask Barb to dinner, but she never commits. I can't tell if she's shy, or not interested, or just can't hear me. You got any tips, boy?"

Yeah. For the love of God, don't ask me for advice about women. But I have to say something.

"I know this guy at my school. He'll, like, serenade a girl for you, for money. He's good."

He shrugs. "Maybe. Next time you see him, ask if he'd come down a little on the price."

"I never told you his prices."

"Yeah, see if he can knock twenty dollars off. I'm feeling better. Let's go back."

Class has ended and most of the students have left. Johnny follows Barbara out the door. I see Jean and Soraya sitting on a bench, chatting like old friends. So much for my chances of talking to Soraya alone.

"And that wasn't the last time!" chuckles my grandmother. "When Deacon was eight, he spent the summer with me again. And he had developed a real taste for prunes. I tried to tell him to go easy, but he—"

"Jean, I think it's about time to go!" I say, with all the subtlety of a drill instructor. She and Soraya look at me with giggly expressions. Jean smiles at me and leaves.

I'm hit with indecision. Do I stay and talk to Soraya, or do I panic and run after Jean? Fortunately, Soraya makes the decision for me, by patting the seat next to her. Excited and slightly terrified, I join her.

"I wanted to thank you for helping me get the car started the other day."

Brain: *No problem, Soraya. My pleasure.*

Instead, I grin like a moron.

I should say something. I should ask her if she'd like to go stargazing. Or go out for a soda. Or smack me in the stupid face.

"Hey, Deacon, you feel like going for a walk?"

"Sure."

Huh. That wasn't so hard at all.

We stop by Jean's car to tell her I'll make my own way home. And now . . . I'm walking with Soraya Shadee.

It's warming up. Spring is here, and the weather is perfect.

I couldn't care less. Did I mention that I'm walking with Soraya Shadee?

She doesn't tell me where we're going, and I don't ask. I'm afraid if I talk too much, I'll kill the moment.

We soon come to a park where I've never been before.

It's honestly seen better days. Lots of trash lying around, and the playground equipment is in poor shape. Soraya leads me to the other side of the sports field, where there's a large, fenced-in enclosure with a sign that says *Petting Zoo*. In one paddock, there's a pony, and I swear it's the same animal from that one guy's promposal. In another muddy pen I see two goats, a pig, and something furry sleeping in the dirt. A surly-looking man in overalls reads a newspaper. He looks up at us, nods at Soraya, and returns to the paper.

Myself, I don't much care for animals unless they're cooked. But if this is what Soraya wants to do, then I'll wade through any amount of animal filth.

To my surprise, Soraya takes a leash and a large collar from her bag. She then opens the gate a bit and whistles. The pig looks up and trots over to her. She places the collar on its neck.

"Uh, Soraya, I don't think you're supposed to—"

She ignores me, clipping on the leash. The pig follows her out of the gate, which she closes behind it. The man in the overalls doesn't stir.

"C'mon, Deacon."

God, she's pulling some kind of zany prank like on TV! In a few seconds the man's going to notice us and we're going to have to run off with the pig. The police will show up and I'll have to call Jean to bail me out of jail. This is insanity.

I, of course, follow Soraya without voicing my concerns. When we reach the middle of the playing field, Soraya turns to me.

"Deacon, this is Mr. Oinky Pig."

"You two know each other?" I blurt out, before considering what a stupid thing that is to say.

She giggles. "I raised him from a piglet. Unfortunately, he got too big to keep at home, so he lives at the petting zoo now. Don't you, Mr. Oinky?"

I examine the animal more closely. It's huge, bristly, and I swear it's looking at me with an intense, porcine dislike.

"Go ahead and pet him."

I do not wish to pet the pig. I pet the pig anyway. It snaps at me. This amuses Soraya. She gestures at a food stand.

"Want to buy us a snack?"

I'm not sure if she means the both of us, or her and the pig, or all three of us. I end up buying three slices of cheese pizza from the not-very-clean stand. Soraya ties the pig to a fence, and we lean back against a tree.

For a while, the only sound is Mr. Oinky Pig devouring his pizza. Just when I think I need to say something,

Soraya crosses her legs, puts her elbows on her knees, and bends toward me.

"So are you enjoying dance class?"

What would Jason say? "I have a pretty good teacher."

She laughs. "Think you'll take any other courses?"

Not unless you're in charge. "Nah, I'm just getting ready for prom."

Soraya blinks and sits up straighter. "Yes. Of course. Prom. I . . . I'm sure your, um, girlfriend will appreciate the effort."

I toss my crust to the pig. "Actually . . . I'm going to the dance with Jean."

I find it hard to look right at her when I admit this. It doesn't help when she tilts her head nearly forty-five degrees, with a perplexed look on her face.

"Okay, Deacon. I assume there's a story here."

I suddenly feel stupid for mentioning my plans with Jean. It was one thing to tell Elijah, but . . . he's not the one I've been thinking about every day for over a week.

"It's kind of a long story."

She smiles. "Start at the beginning."

"My grandfather was in the Vietnam War."

She looks at me expectantly. "I'm going to need more backstory than that."

"Uh, okay. In 1954, the Viet Cong defeated the French forces at Dien Bien Phu. . . ."

"Deacon!"

"Long story short, Jean didn't get to go to her own prom. And since I didn't have a date, I thought we'd have fun."

Please don't think this is weird, Soraya. Because if you do, I'm not going to think very highly of you. And that would suck.

Slowly, slowly, Soraya's face cracks into a smile. Not a full one, but sincere. "Okay, so you win the grandson-of-the-year award. But you know there are all kinds of dances for seniors. Are you sure you want to miss out on your big night?"

Should I lie? Should I make up some story about how Kelli and I were a thing but we broke up last month? Should I say Jean has some serious health problems and might not be around much longer? Or pretend that I think prom is a stupid waste of time and I'm going with Jean for laughs?

Soraya reaches up and grabs a lock of her hair. She slowly twirls it around her finger, while looking at me with that faint, probing smile. And I'm suddenly ashamed for even considering not telling her the truth.

"Well, for starters, I don't have a girlfriend."

Is it just my imagination, or does her smile widen, just slightly?

"And I figured if I was going to go, I didn't want it

to be with some friend of a friend. I mean, why spend hundreds of dollars to stand around awkwardly with a girl I have nothing in common with? I do that every day for free."

She thinks this is funny and laughs at me. She's not mocking, and I find myself joining her.

"At any rate, Jean's pretty special. I know this is going to sound weird, but she's the only good friend I've ever had."

"I think you're exaggerating."

I shake my head. "Before I moved to Fayetteville a couple of years ago, I'd never gone to one school for more than a semester. Before I stopped being the new kid, we'd move again."

"Military family? Hey, what's so funny?"

"Sorry. The idea of my father in the army. No. My mother died of cancer when I was about four. I barely remember her. My father . . . he liked to call himself an entrepreneur. One month he'd be selling used cars in Charlotte. A few weeks later, we'd be in Denver, trying to get into the legalized pot business. I missed my eighth-grade graduation because I was helping him raid this demolition site for copper wiring. And I was probably the only fifth grader who knew how to call a bondsman. When I was a sophomore, I think he ended up owing the wrong people a lot of money, and he moved to Amsterdam. He was going to take me, but Jean talked him out of it."

Soraya bites her lip, then reaches over, places her hand on my knee, and squeezes. Then she just leaves it there. Her hand on my knee. She's touching me on purpose.

I think it would ruin the afternoon if I suddenly passed out, so I steer the conversation to the least sexy subject I can think of.

"So Jean and I have lived together ever since. She's a lot of fun, when she's not trying to paint. She taught me how to throw a baseball, drive, and cook." I'm very bad at all those things, but I don't mention it. "I'm moving out in a few months, I guess. I just wanted Jean and me to have a fun time before I leave. Next I'll be at the U of A and we won't see each other as much."

"Hey, I'm going there too! Are you going to live in the dorms?"

My mouth finds it difficult to function as I process the idea of going to the same college as Soraya. "Yes."

Soraya, without removing her hand, scoots closer to me. "That'll be fun. And you can visit Jean on the weekends."

"Maybe. But I have a feeling one of us will be out

hitting the bars every Friday night. And I'll be studying." And probably hanging around your dorm like a pathetic puppy.

Soraya closes her eyes and smiles. "You're lucky to have Jean in your life. My only grandmother is still in Lebanon. I was named after her."

I'm glad she told me. I'd been wondering about her heritage, but there's no polite way to ask something like that. "I was named after my father. His name was Deacon."

"You're funny."

Fortunately, she's mistaken my awkward, compulsive talking for humor. But I think we'll both be better off if she takes the conversational helm again. "So how about you? When's your school's prom?"

She takes her hand off my knee. I manage to swallow my whimper.

"My school doesn't have dances. I . . ." She looks away. Then she looks right back at me. "I go to the Islamic school."

She's looking at me intently, as if I'm supposed to say something. "That's over by the university, right? That building with all the moons on it?"

"Right." Still looking at me.

"So what's it like?"

"My school? It's okay, I guess. My parents, they came here years ago. They're as American as you get, but they

96

didn't want me to forget my heritage. The thing is, most of the other kids are the children of graduate students or other people just in town for jobs. But when you live here your whole life, it's . . ." She trails off. "Sorry, Deacon. Didn't mean to get all whiny."

"No. Please, go on." I want her to keep talking. I want her to tell me her problems. It makes me feel special that she'd share things with me. And maybe . . . I dunno, maybe I could help.

She shrugs. "Most everyone around here is nice. But sometimes people can be real jerks. Take Mr. Oinky."

I look at the pig, who's dozing in the grass. "He's a jerk?"

She frowns, and I think I've said the wrong thing. "When he was a piglet, some assholes dumped him in our yard. He had some nasty graffiti on him. My father was furious, wanted to call the sheriff. But all I could see was a piggy. I wanted to keep him. I was nine."

I can't decide if this story is horrible or touching. I guess it's both.

"I like Fayetteville, but I don't love it. I just hope I'm not making a mistake, staying here for school. I'll give it a year, see if it's a good fit." She then blinks. "Wow. I just told you my whole life story."

"Thank you, Soraya." I mean that, too. No one's ever trusted me with their heartache before.

"So how about you? What're you going to major in?"

Ah, the same question Jean keeps asking. "I'm not sure. I don't have to decide right away."

"Do you think you're going to settle down in Arkansas?"

"Probably."

"Any idea what you want to do for a living?"

"Soraya . . ." I nervously crack my knuckles. "Jean keeps asking me that. So does my guidance counselor. And my friend Kelli. And . . . I guess it makes me weird, but I don't know. I don't know what kind of job I want. I don't know where I want to live, or if I want to get married someday, or travel the world or live next door to Jean. And I'm scared as hell about borrowing a godzillian dollars for school when I can't answer those questions yet. Pretty strange, huh?"

Soraya regards me with her dark eyes. "I think you're kind of an oddball, but you're not strange at all. When the right thing comes along, it'll hit you. Take my father. He's an engineer for the highway department. Started college when he was seventeen, and has been building roads for the past twenty years."

"I guess he must love it."

"Ha! He hates it! You've never heard such bitching. Listen, don't let anyone make you into something you're not."

"Easy for you to say."

Though we're still sitting, she puts her hands on her hips. "What's that supposed to mean?"

"Because you're . . ."

"I'm *what*?"

Perfect. Beautiful. Sophisticated. Kind. Wonderful. "Self-confident."

She leans back against the tree. "If only you knew, Deacon. When I was younger I . . . didn't like where I came from. I tried to pretend that I wasn't . . . Muslim. Lebanese. Nonblond. When I was in sixth grade, I tried to tell everyone my name was really Samantha Jasmine Smith. Have you ever heard of a stupider name?"

"'Deacon Locke' springs to mind."

She smiles wryly. "That's why I started dancing. I guess every little girl around here takes a dance class at some point in her life. I just wanted to fit in. I mean, my mother was the only woman in my neighborhood who wore a hijab. Dancing made me feel more like everyone else. And by the time I got to junior high, I realized I kind of liked it. That's why I kept up with it, even when most of the other girls quit."

"You're really good at it."

She rolls her eyes and shoves my shoulder. I wish she'd do it again.

"I'm serious, Soraya. They wouldn't ask you to teach

if you weren't talented."

She shrugs. "Yeah. Plus I work for free." We're silent for a moment. "Sorry, Deacon, I don't know why I told you all that. I guess living with someone like Jean, you don't know what it's like to be embarrassed by where you come from."

I think about it. "When I was twelve, my father had me deliver a package of something to a bunch of strange guys down on the Miami docks. And when I was fourteen, he made me ride in the trunk when we crossed the Mexican border."

"For God's sake, why?"

I shrug. "He never told me. My point is, everyone is ashamed of their family at some point."

Her eyes are wide. "You win."

"It's not a contest. But thanks for letting me talk."

"Thank you, Deacon." She reaches over and takes my hand. When we stand up, she doesn't let go for just a second. Just for one beautiful second.

"My parents are expecting me. Are you okay to get home?"

"Yeah. Fine. Hey . . ."

She looks at me expectantly. I brace myself.

"I've got some friends stopping by this Friday. We're going to do a little astronomy." Good Lord, that sounds nerdish out loud. "You want to come by? Take a look at my telescope?"

She tilts her head. "That's not a euphemism for something, is it?"

"What? No! Oh God, no!"

She grins. "It sounds like fun."

Wow. I mean. Wow. "Okay. Eightish. The big white house next to the golf course."

"I'll be there. My parents might need the car, is it okay if I have a friend bring me?"

I nod, not trusting myself to speak further. She grabs Mr. Oinky's leash and walks away, pausing once to smile at me over her shoulder.

I did it. I did it. I invited Soraya over to my house.

And she said yes.

Imitating a thousand romantic-comedy characters, I fall back against the tree and slowly slide down to a sitting position, a stupid smile on my face.

I sit there for a while, thinking about Soraya and what she said. I'm kind of enraged that she'd ever think she had any reason to be ashamed. I'd like to find out whoever dropped off the pig and break his legs.

Stupid bigotry. The religious people should get together sometime and work out their differences.

I wonder why no one has ever tried that before.

TEN

SO SORAYA IS COMING HERE. TO MY HOUSE. SHE'S going to show up in about an hour. I'm going to teach her about astronomy. We're going to go up the hill and hang out together in the dark.

I must flee. If I start running now, I can make Louisiana by next week.

No. I can do this. I talked to Elijah. He promised he'd come and bring Clara. And Soraya said a friend might be driving her, though I'm not sure if she's staying. And of course Jean will be here. I doubt she'll want to actually join us at the telescope, but she'll help me break the ice. Everyone likes Jean. She'll fill in the conversation gaps. Provided Elijah leaves us any.

I think this as I clean up two years' worth of soda cans and candy wrappers from the hill, move the picnic table up there, take down my tarp, and spread several old quilts in front of my observation point.

Jean, of course, has gone into full hostess mode. She's cleaned the already immaculate house and put out little trays of snacks.

"Jean, you don't have to do this. I'm just having a few friends over."

"Of course." She begins to wind up the vacuum-cleaner cord. "Anyone I know? That boy with the guitar?"

"No."

"That Kelli girl?"

"No."

She pauses and looks directly at me. "Our dance instructor?"

I sputter.

"It's about time. I was afraid you were going to get scared and I'd have to put up with all that staring for another class."

My guts sink. "Was I that obvious?"

"I wasn't talking about you, Deacon."

This does not relax me in the least.

"I'm just showing everyone my telescope," I insist. "It's not a date or anything."

"Does *Soraya* know it's not a date?"

Oh God.

Jean wipes her hands on a rag and examines me up and down. She adjusts my collar.

"Change your socks, they don't match your pants. I'll see you later."

"What?" Where's she going? It's not bridge night. Or dance night. Or pool night.

"Peggy and Barb have been pestering me to join them for cards. I told them I'd play this evening." She picks up her jacket.

"Wait! Don't leave!" I know that Soraya likes Jean, but she may not find Elijah as charming. And the fewer people here, the more I'm going to be expected to talk. And I can't hope that things will go as smoothly as at the park the other day.

"I'll be back. Just after ten. Enjoy yourselves. No drinking."

"But . . ."

She smiles at me with a twinkle in her eye. "Good-bye."

Two minutes later, I hear her car start up and drive off.

I quickly change my socks so I'll have enough time to sit in the front room and hyperventilate. Soraya is coming and I have no idea how to handle myself.

It's okay. Two or three other people will be here,

besides Soraya and me. Maybe more. Maybe Elijah invited people. I mean, he never said he was going to do anything like that, but you never know. Soraya and I probably won't even have a chance to be alone all evening, gosh darn it.

The phone in the kitchen rings. With a growing sense of dread, I answer it.

"Hey, Deke?" It's Elijah. "I hate to do this, but we gotta bail on you tonight. Clara's got the flu or something."

"What? No!"

"Calm down, dude. It's only a twenty-four-hour bug. She's just feeling a little blah."

I nearly yank the phone out of the wall. "Do *you* have the flu?"

He laughs. Laughs like this is funny. "No, man. We're not that close yet."

"They why can't you come?"

There's a pause. "It's just you and Soraya, right?"

"Probably."

"They why would you want me there? I mean, if Clara was coming too, it would be one thing, but you and me and your date? That's just awkward, man."

"It's not a date!"

He laughs again. "You're going to do fine, bro. I believe in you."

"Then get over here!"

"I gotta run. Deep breaths, Deke. Don't slip her the tongue until your third date." He hangs up.

So my little informal scientific gathering has just turned into a night alone with Soraya on a dark hilltop. What if she thinks this was all some setup to get her alone? What if she gets angry?

What if she likes the idea?

Get a grip, Deacon. You can survive. One step at a time. Just concentrate on what you're going to say first.

Dear God, what do I say first?

For an hour, I rehearse dozens of opening lines. Then, just when the clock strikes eight, I hit upon the perfect greeting.

Good evening.

I roll it around in my skull a few times and decide that it fits. Good evening. Good. Evening. Good evening!

Perfect.

The doorbell rings. This is it. Last chance to make a break for it and start all over in Mexico.

I answer the door.

"Good eeeee . . ."

Here she is, backlit by the front-porch light. She's wearing a sleeveless sweater, a light jacket carelessly slung over her shoulder. She stands there smiling at me, like a model in a clothes catalog. Her beauty strikes me like a crowbar to the jaw. Every time I see her, she grows lovelier.

And next to her stands Jason, the guitarist who helped me prompose to Jean.

Soraya smiles at me. "Thanks for having us over, Deacon. Jason says you two have already met."

"Deacon!" Jason claps his hands one time. "Hope you don't mind me tagging along. Soraya lives on my street and she needed a ride."

I stare.

Soraya clears her throat. "I've been looking forward to this. You can't really see the stars in town."

I stare.

"You can actually see the Milky Way out here," adds Jason.

I stare.

Soraya runs a hand through her silky hair. Moths are beginning to fly into the house.

"Is it just us, or are other people coming?"

I can just slam the door in their faces and lock them out of my life forever. Or say I can't do this tonight because my appendix just ruptured. Or punch Jason in the nose.

But I don't. I force my facial muscles to smile.

"Good evening. Thank you both for coming. My friends Elijah and Clara were supposed to join us, but they were forced to cancel."

I grab a flashlight from a table, then join them on the porch, shutting the door behind me. "Shall we? The stars are this way."

If the universe were a kind and friendly place, it would be overcast and I would have an excuse to cancel.

I can't remember the last time the sky was this clear. And the evening is cool, with just the hint of a breeze. A perfect night for stargazing.

A perfect night for stargazing with Soraya. She's walking just behind me, next to Jason. I lead the way, resisting the urge to make a sweeping gesture with the flashlight and accidentally bop him in his acne-free face. First he charges me a wad to play one song for Jean. And now that I'm genuinely starting to like a girl, here he is with his cheekbones and clean nails.

We scramble up the hill. I turn to offer my hand to Soraya and guide her over the tricky step at the top. Jason is already helping her.

The only thing that keeps me from cursing the heavens is the advice from the prophet Elijah: be good at something and do it in front of her. Okay, maybe Jason has the moves and the looks and can buy shoes in regular sizes, but I'm the astronomer here. This is my arena.

I flip on the battery-powered lantern I left on the picnic table and gesture to a couple of lawn chairs. "Please, make yourself comfortable."

Jason assumes I'm including him in that invitation and sits down next to Soraya. I busy myself with the telescope.

Jason claps his hands once. "So what're you going to show us tonight?"

I target the fifth planet. "Jupiter. Soraya?" She joins me at the telescope. "Just bend over and look through the eyepiece."

She's so close to me. So very close. I resist the overwhelming urge to lay my hands on her shoulders.

"Wow! You can really see it," she says, sounding impressed. "What are those little dots next to it?"

"Those are Jupiter's four largest moons. They were discovered by Galileo. Ganymede is the only known moon to have an atmosphere. Europa has a sort of an ocean, and scientists speculate life could develop there. Io is the only moon with active volcanoes."

I'm doing it. I'm showing off and succeeding.

Soraya stares, enthralled, into the telescope. "That's amazing. Why is the moon named Io?"

"I . . ." I don't know. I have no idea. I know there's a big complicated system for naming solar-system objects, but I never studied that aspect.

"Io was a priestess and a lover of Zeus." Soraya looks away from the telescope to listen to Jason. "She was briefly transformed into a cow, and later became the great-grandmother of Hercules. The Ionian Sea is named after her."

Soraya is no longer paying attention to the heavenly vista I've opened for her. "Are all the planets and moons named after gods and goddesses?"

Jason looks at me, apparently offering me the opportunity to answer. I just stand there like a moron who didn't take five minutes to study planet nomenclature. He turns back to our own goddess.

"All of them except the moons of Uranus." He pronounces it "yer-ANN-us," like he's embarrassed by the name. "They're named after Shakespearean characters: Oberon, Ophelia, Miranda."

"Can we look at those, Deacon?"

I so, so want to say yes. But Jason beats me to the punch. "Not with that telescope."

I massage my temple. Unfortunately, he's right. Uranus would be nothing but a gray smudge through my scope.

I show Soraya Saturn, and she's pretty impressed by the rings, but Jason then starts to go on and on about the Titans.

Stupid moons.

Even when I try to subvert his charm by showing a remote nebula known only by a number, Jason launches into an interesting story about some supernova in the Middle Ages that caused an end-of-the-world scare.

Poophead.

Soraya stretches. Maybe, mercifully, she'll end this evening.

But then she spies the blankets I've laid out. She kicks off her shoes (her toes are so long!) and lies down in the middle. She pats the ground next to her. I join her in a flash.

And Jason flops his grotesquely perfect body down on her other side.

I might as well leave and give them some time alone.

"So do all the stars have names?" Soraya asks.

"The major ones do," I answer, before Jason can. "Vega, Deneb, Polaris, Betelgeuse."

"That's a real star? Which one is it?"

"Um, that big red one, by the horizon."

She lifts herself up on her elbows for a better view. "Beetle Juice. I've always wondered about that name. Why do they call it that?"

I know this! I know this! I don't remember where I read it, but I know this. I burst in before Jason can answer.

"It was actually named by an Arab astronomer. You see, during the Middle Ages, the Islamic lands were the cultural hub of the world. A lot of the famous Western astronomers, like Kepler and Copernicus, based their research on the works of Middle Eastern scholars." And didn't sit around telling namby-pamby tales about goddesses, Jason.

I can see Soraya smile in the flickering lamplight.

"What does the name mean?" asks Jason. He sounds genuinely interested, but I'm sure he's just trying to make me look foolish. But I have the answer to this one.

"It's Arabic for 'the armpit of the giant'!"

Crickets. Literally.

Soraya lets out a sudden giggle. Jason laughs.

I pretend to be interested in the sky. *Armpit*. I'm trying to impress a girl and I start talking about armpits. I'm mentally kicking myself so hard, I almost don't notice the shooting star.

"Ooh!" yips Soraya. "Make a wish."

In 1954, a meteor struck and injured an Alabama woman. I wish for a repeat performance starring myself.

No one speaks for a while. Just when I start to relax and take comfort in Soraya's presence, Jason opens his mouth.

"You know, according to a Cherokee legend, the Milky Way was created when a giant dog . . ."

We are treated to the creation myths of the Chinese, Celts, and Polynesians. Soraya listens with rapt enthusiasm. I assume. I don't dare look over at her. But when Jason starts talking about the Inuit, she says she has to get back home. We all stand.

"Let me walk you back to the car," I say.

"Nah, we'll be fine," says Jason. He claps his hands once. "Deacon, thanks so much for the invitation. I had a great time."

Ever eat a 1.25-inch Sirius Plossl eyepiece, Jason?

But as Jason is dusting himself off, Soraya approaches me. And takes my hand. In both of hers. She looks up at me.

"Yes, thank you, Deacon." Her brown eyes glimmer in the lantern light. "I really had fun."

And then she follows Jason down the hill.

I stare after them, long after Jason's Lamborghini Porsche Rolls-Royce Mercedes vanishes down the road. With Soraya.

For some reason, I think back to an incident that happened when I was about fourteen. We were living in Chicago at the time. One night, my dad took me to meet with some guys in an abandoned warehouse. They were not a friendly-looking bunch, and I'd never seen my father look so scared. I was already over six feet tall then, and just before we left, one of the men took me

aside and told me I could come work for him as a body-
guard when I was older.

One more night like this, and I think I might go look
him up.

ELEVEN

court. I can't remember the last time I've been to a mall.

Elijah chows down on a Taco Bell burrito, while I pick at some weird thing with lots of cheese and sour cream. We've just been measured for our prom tuxes. It took about ten minutes for Elijah to finish. With me, the manager had to make several phone calls before the store branch in Springfield, Missouri, confirmed they had a suit in my size.

Elijah has kind of coached me through the whole prom labyrinth: the tickets, the tux, and the limo, which we're going to be sharing. He won't admit it, but I think

115

he's been mentally planning this night long before he met Clara.

He leans back and lets out a long, satisfied sigh. "They need more restaurants here," he observes, the moment his mouth is empty. "A sandwich shop or something. Maybe I'll open one someday. I'll call it 'Billy, Don't Be a Gyro.'"

Like most interactions with Elijah, I'm not really listening. I think back to last night. To Soraya and Jason. Part of me worries I'm just being overly sensitive. I did tell her that other people were coming over. Why wouldn't she bring her obnoxious little friend? Hell, that wasn't the first time Jason had been over to my house. He probably figured he was welcome.

On the other hand, I could see the way he was trying to impress her. Trying to be all cool and knowledgeable around Soraya. Basically doing the things that I couldn't.

So where do I go from here? I'll see her again at dance class this Tuesday. Should I play it smooth, like nothing happened? Should I ask her out again? Should I just bang my head into the floor? And what is that weird noise? That strange and unusual sound?

It's silence. Elijah is not talking. He's sitting there looking at me.

"Huh?"

"I asked you how the thing with Soraya went. Did you aurora her borealis? Unfasten her Kuiper Belt? Cross her event horizon? Fire your retro rockets?"

"How long did it take you to think all those up?"

"Several hours," he says with a grin. "So spill. What happened?"

"Well, she showed up at my house . . ."

"Yeah?"

"With Jason."

Elijah winces. "Damn."

"It's my fault. I acted like it was just a friendly get-together, like you suggested. So I guess it's really your fault."

"So are they dating or something?"

"I dunno. I don't think so. But I think maybe he'd like that."

Elijah has sucked all the guts out of his burrito. He neatly folds the tortilla and dabs his lips with it. "All is not lost. Actually, this might work to your favor."

"She shows up on our date with another guy, and that works to my advantage?"

"The first date is always awkward. You spend half the evening listening to her talk about how she has a headache, and you'd be better off as friends, and that she's moving to Peru next week. Quite frankly, I consider myself lucky that Clara didn't teargas me the first time I talked to her. Now, you had a bad evening, but I'm sure it wasn't the worst date you've ever been on, am I right?"

"Actually . . ." I rub the back of my neck.

Elijah misinterprets this. "Seriously? That was your *worst* date?" He smooshes his tortilla with his fist. "Of course. I guess rejection is something new for you. You've probably never even had a girl say she forgot her purse in the car, and then drive off."

"Elijah . . ."

"And it was my car!"

"Elijah! Look . . ." I like that he thinks I'm more experienced than I am. But Elijah has a girlfriend and I'd like one. If I'm going to get his advice, I need to be honest. "Elijah, I've never actually . . ." God, it's so embarrassing to say I've never been on a date.

"Never what?"

"I've never . . ." How do I put this?

He suddenly laughs. "Oh! Don't worry, man, lots of people haven't." He glances around, then leans toward me. "Believe it or not, I haven't—"

"No! Oh, God, that's not what I'm talking about." Though it's still true.

"What, then?"

"I've never . . ."

"Been in love? Had to compete for a girl? What??"

"I've never been on a date, okay!" I quickly look around. "I've never had a girlfriend, never gone out with anyone."

He just stares at me. "Seriously? Big guy like you?"

"My family moved a lot. So about Soraya—"

"Hang on. What about junior-high dances? Those count."

"No."

"New year's midnight kiss?"

"No."

"Sitting in a tree? K-I-S-S-I-N-G?"

I'm almost tempted to get up and leave. "No. Never. Happy?"

He grins a very smug, very punchable smile. "It's okay, man. Look. The point is, Soraya knows you, and likes you enough to want to do stuff with you. That's half the battle. Now you just need to make sure that next time you get together with her, you're alone. Get her into a situation where there's no one else around, where Jason can't show up." He waggles his eyebrows.

"What? Like the back of a car or something?" I'm really not comfortable with that.

"Uh, no. I mean like a movie. Or just ask her to go for a walk with you. The more time she spends with you, the more she'll get to know you." He stands and begins gathering our trash. I follow.

"But what if she ends up thinking that I'm a giant, nerdy moron who repels and disgusts her?"

"Then you'll know that too."

TWELVE

IT'S DANCE CLASS DAY. JUST LIKE EVERY TUESDAY.
Except it's not. This afternoon, I'm going to ask Soraya
out to the movies.

I dig through Grandpa's clothes for something stylish to wear. I find an outfit in fairly good shape. It's kind
of neat, actually. The pants legs are wide at the bottom,
and the lapels are great-big. The fabric is so white it
almost glows. I like it. It's very retro.

Jean gives me a long look when she sees me but
doesn't say anything. I'm too busy going over the movie
schedules in my head to worry.

Let's see, *Agent Zero* is playing at the Fiesta 16 at 6:00,

121

7:20, and 9:00; at the Razorback Cinema at 8:00 and 10:00; and the Hollywood Twelve on the hour starting at 6:00. *Brown Eyed Girl* is playing at the Fiesta at . . .

We arrive. When we enter the dance room, I'm surprised when most of my elderly classmates compliment me on my new clothes. Johnny tells me he had the same suit back in 1975.

Yeah, I'm a winner.

Soraya is a little late. She smiles at me as she walks through the door, though she does kind of a double take when she sees my new clothes. I guess she never thought of me as stylish.

The lesson passes in a blur. I'm too busy trying to recall movie times to pay attention, and I end up swinging one of my partners backward into a wall.

Finally, we're finished. I take a deep breath. This is it, Deacon. Time to ask her out. I'm psyched. I'm prepared. I'm calm. I don't even care that I can't remember which theater is showing *Summer Love* at eight. I'm going in.

Soraya smiles when she sees me approaching. I think she knows what's coming. I join her on the bench.

"Interesting outfit."

"Thanks. It was my grandfather's."

She laughs into her hand. "I guess gigantism isn't the only thing that runs in your family."

I laugh with her, not quite catching the joke.

"Hey, Deacon? I hope it was okay that I brought Jason the other night. He was my only ride."

I shrug. "Hey, no problem."

"I had a fun time. I hope maybe we can do something again sometime."

I really have to stop myself from doing the touchdown shuffle right now.

"So, Soraya . . ."

My courage is steadfast. My guts are standing firm. A lone bugle rallies me to action.

No, wait, someone really is playing a horn.

He's standing in the doorway of the classroom, playing smooth jazz on a trumpet.

It's Jason. I don't know how, and I don't know why, but he's here. He's wearing a suit. And a fedora.

In case I haven't mentioned it, he's not a 1930s private eye.

Everyone in the class is watching him, including Soraya. And yeah, he's just as talented on the trumpet as he is with his guitar. But so what? Do you really need everyone to focus on you all the time, Mr. Horny? I hope he's mobbed by rats like the piper in that fairy tale.

Suddenly, three other guys follow him into the room. One has a guitar, another carries a set of bongos, and the last drags one of those enormous instruments that look like giant violins. Wordlessly, they begin to jam with Jason.

Everyone is enthralled. Jean clutches her hands in front of her, a dreamy look on her face. Soraya is grinning. One of the men from class begins tapping his cane to the rhythm.

Jason finishes his song and lowers his instrument, though the other three keep playing. I hope this means the song is almost over. But then Jason says something that makes me realize that all is lost and that the universe is a cold and hateful place.

"Soraya?"

No. No, no, no, no, no!

She stands. She walks forward. She looks hypnotized. I want to grab her, pull her out of the room, but I already know it's too late.

Jason smiles. It's a shy, awkward smile. He's totally faking it.

"Soraya, we've known each other since first grade. You and I, we've been through a whole lot together. You're one of my closest friends. And I just wanted to ask you . . ."

He steps forward. He gently takes her hand. She lets him.

"Soraya Shadee, will you go to prom with me?"

The other musicians stop, except for the drummer, who is pounding out a rhythm so faint that I can barely hear it.

And just as I'm slinking toward the door, just as I have my hand on the knob to crawl out of here, defeated and ashamed, Soraya turns. And she looks right at me.

And for one stupid second, I think she's going to tell Jason no. She's going to turn him down, because I was the one she invited to meet Mr. Oinky Pig the other day. Me. Not Jason.

But then she turns back to him.

"Okay, Jason."

The room erupts in cheers. Jason laughs, pretending to look relieved. And everyone in class claps for them. Including me. It's what the loser does. He congratulates the winner, who just effortlessly took away the only thing the loser ever really wanted.

No point in a movie today. Soraya has prom plans to make.

Exit Deacon, stage right.

Jean doesn't say anything on the drive back home and I'm grateful. All I can think about is how excited I'd been over the stupid prospect of asking Soraya to some dumb movie. And now we'll probably never go.

Can't say I blame her. A girl like Soraya deserves someone special. Someone who can play a musical instrument and knows about hair products and Greek mythology.

I just wish she hadn't made saying yes to him look so easy. I wish . . .

Wishes are stupid.

I lie on my bed, staring at the bare ceiling. This used to be my father's room. When I moved in, Jean said I could decorate it however I wanted. As I glance around at the star charts, NASA posters, and clippings from astronomy magazines, I no longer see my comfortable little sanctum. I see the room of a guy who spends his life staring at little white dots in the sky.

Maybe it's not too late to ask out Soraya. I'll see her again on Thursday. Maybe we could go back to the park and talk about . . .

Talk about what she's going to wear to prom.

Do I really want to hang out with a girl who's going to the dance with another guy? Someone she's known a lot longer and who has perfectly straight teeth and good posture?

I need to talk to someone. But Elijah's advice didn't work. Neither did Jean's or Kelli's.

Sometimes I wish I knew more than three people.

I wonder what my father would say. He used to always have women hanging around him, though his dates always had the aura of a business arrangement. And then there was the disastrous time when I was fifteen and he took me to that strip club. The memory almost makes me cringe.

Then again . . .

I can't seek my father out for advice on matters of the heart. But what about *his* father?

Yes, I know he's dead. But he landed Jean. Romanced her. Kept her interested while he was away for over a year. He must have done something right.

And his letters are in my desk drawer. I stuck them there right after Jean showed them to me.

Maybe reading them might help. Give me some inspiration. A little of the ol' Locke charm. Some phrases I can blatantly plagiarize and use to show Soraya that I can be as sensitive and charming as you-know-who.

I spread the letters reverently on my desk. They're crinkly and yellow, with edges worn smooth by time. The postmarks are mostly still visible, and it doesn't take me long to find the earliest one, dated 1968.

C'mon, Grandpa Howard, show me how to be charming.

I open the letter.

Dear Jean,

*It's hot here in South Carolina. Now that basic
training is over, I guess I'm going to be here for a
while. I'll try to come home and visit soon. They've
got me working in the warehouses, but that may just
be temporary. I miss you. Say hi to your parents.*

Howard

Okay. Even I can tell that wasn't exactly Shakespeare. But it sounded like he had just arrived at his . . . base? Fort? Camp? So he was probably just dropping Jean a quick line. I replace the letter and open another. This one is dated a month later, so I guess not all Grandpa's letters are in this stack.

Jean,

*Sorry I haven't written. Thanks for the cookies. The
food here is bad, mostly chipped beef on toast and
stuff. I'm still in the warehouses. I'm getting paid
now, but it's not a lot. Miss you.*

Howard

Seriously, Grandpa? One paragraph? Even I know Jean deserved more. This was back in the days before email and cell phones, so this was probably their only line of communication. I quickly read more letters.

—*My athlete's foot is a lot worse.*

—*Could you send more of those lemony cookies?*

—*There's been an outbreak of food poisoning.*

—*You can't get good soap at the PX.*

Not one letter is over a page long and most are much shorter. All of them talk about the mundane life of a soldier in South Carolina. He never once asks Jean about her life or what's going on back home.

I become disgusted before I'm even halfway through the pile and place them back in my desk. Another dead end.

And it kind of drives home something I've feared for a long time.

Soraya—smart, talented, beautiful Soraya—is out of my league.

Maybe she doesn't realize it yet. But Jason does. I don't have his music. His words. His looks.

And as of about six o'clock today, I don't have Soraya.

I never really did.

The following Tuesday, I sit alone up on astronomy hill. I told Jean I didn't really feel like going to dance class today. Same as last Thursday.

Of course, I can't keep avoiding Soraya. There's only one week left of dance class, and prom comes shortly after. I have to face her. Pretend I'm happy about her prom date.

I hear Jean's car pull up. She's never mentioned the humiliating incident from last week, but I think she wants me to talk about it. In fact, I can hear her walking up the hill. I'm about to get a speech about how things are not nearly as bleak and hopeless as they seem.

There's no use putting this off. I turn to face Jean.

And it's not Jean. It's Soraya.

Great. Now I've gone insane. I'm seeing things.

But she sits at the picnic table, just as graceful and lovely as the day she agreed to go to prom with Jason.

"Your grandmother invited me here. I asked her why you'd missed class, and she said you hadn't been feeling well."

Wonderful. I'm not going crazy. Now I have to pretend to be happy.

I grin. "Just a bit of a bug. Didn't want to spread it to the older folk in class."

She doesn't return my smile. "Deacon, I want to talk

to you about what happened at dance the other day. You ran off before I had a chance to say anything."

"No, it's okay. Please don't worry about it." Please don't. I don't want to hear about what a nice and wonderful guy Jason is.

"No, I have to say this. I really wish Jason hadn't asked me to prom in front of everyone like that."

I perk up. This conversation just took an interesting turn.

"He meant well," she continues. "But sometimes he likes to do things dramatically. He caught me off guard."

I mentally do handsprings. Maybe Jason's promposal wasn't as flawless as I'd thought.

"Well, some guys always have to be the center of attention. So, um, are you still going to go to the dance with him?"

Soraya looks away and I instantly realize it was a false hope. "I've known Jason almost my whole life. We've been friends forever. He's helped me through some really bad times."

"What sort of bad times, Soraya?"

"I'd rather not get into it."

No, that's something you can only share with a real friend. Like Jason.

"The thing is, he wants to go to prom. And I kind of do, too. As friends. I'm just sort of worried that there's weirdness between you and me now. I don't want that."

And now's the time where I have to be the bigger man. I mean, I'm almost always the bigger man, but this time it's hard.

I shrug, like she's silly for even bringing this up. "Soraya, I want you to have a good time. It'd be a shame if you didn't put those dance skills to use."

Her resulting smile is almost worth it. Almost. "I'm so glad to hear that. I was afraid you were upset or something."

It suddenly occurs to me that since Jason goes to my school, Soraya will be going to my dance! My dance! I'm going to have to watch her and Jason all night. Oh, this keeps getting better and better.

"I'll see you there, Soraya."

I think we're done, but she stands and walks over to me. She reaches up and places a hand on my shoulder. Just like when we danced. "Good. I hope Jean won't mind if I steal a dance or two from you that night. And maybe when all this prom craziness is over, you and I will . . . I mean, I hope that just because class ends, we won't stop hanging out."

"I'd like that, Soraya. A lot actually."

She lets go and starts to walk down the hill. Then she turns back.

"I'm glad you're taking Jean to the dance. I can tell she's loving this. But . . . I'm a little jealous." She vanishes down the hill.

I pace around a bit. Open my cooler, then close it again. Adjust my telescope tripod.

Huh.

So maybe I had nothing to worry about after all. Seems she just was going to the dance with Jason for friendship's sake. Probably felt sorry for the poor, insecure guy.

But Soraya still wants to see me. Still wants to do stuff with me when prom is over and done with.

So now I just have to play it cool. Bide my time. And above all, look impressive at prom. Show Jean a good time. And more importantly, show Soraya what she could have had.

You know. If she'd just invented a time machine and met me a month before I asked Jean to prom.

It doesn't matter. That's all in the past. I have to concentrate on what's coming.

Prom is going to be a night none of us are going to forget.

THIRTEEN

MY TUXEDO COMES WITH A LITTLE SHEET OF PRINTED instructions.

That's a good thing. Otherwise I might have worn my cummerbund with the vents facing downward. Can you imagine?

Getting dressed for prom is an involved and somewhat humiliating process, especially when your father cannot help you because he's probably selling guns to Russian gangsters. This shirt was obviously made for a stouter guy. It's tight in the shoulders and billowy around my stomach. The pants are a tad too short, but I'm used to that. And, despite the rental place's assurances, they were unable to locate dress shoes in my size.

I'm forced to wear black sneakers.

Still, as I look in the mirror that I brought in from the bathroom, I don't look that bad. I trimmed my nails. I let one of Jean's friends give me a haircut. I shaved.

Yeah, the bow tie is still crooked and I really feel that I'm wearing the cuff links wrong, but still . . .

I look kind of good.

I mentally go over my checklist for the night. I got the tickets. Elijah rented the limo. I have money. I have everything . . .

Except Soraya.

I shake my head and smile sadly. It is what it is. She won't be with me tonight. I'm going to have to suffer through a night of watching Jason dance with her. A guy who's better-looking, more talented, more . . .

No!

Cut the bullshit, Deacon. Soraya kind of implied that she would rather be your date. She said she wanted to do something with you next week.

I can deal with one night of Soraya and Jason. One night.

I slap on some aftershave (a gift from my father for my ninth birthday) and go downstairs to meet Jean.

"You almost ready?" I holler at her closed bedroom door.

"One second, Deacon."

I lean against the wall and wait. I'm getting pretty psyched about tonight. True, I'm not going to prom with a girl—not really. But Soraya is actually going to be there. And I never would have met her had I not asked Jean to this thing. We are going to have a good time tonight. I'll be able to look back on prom with a smile.

And Soraya and I are going to get together sometime after prom is over. My God, am I actually going to have a date before I get out of high school? If this keeps up, I might have a girlfriend before I'm thirty.

"Here I come!" Jean steps out of her room, and just for a second, I get a glimpse of what 1969 was like.

And it's beautiful.

Her dress, unlike everything else about her, is understated. It's dark blue, not especially revealing, and plain. But somehow, it's fancy and amazing.

Jean is wearing makeup, as usual. Not the caked-on mortician's stuff that a lot of the women from dance class wear. Just some lipstick and cheek stuff. And her hair is all poofy now. And she's wearing nonsensible shoes.

She's glowing. Not like a lightbulb, but like . . . like from inside. But still not like a lightbulb.

"How do I look?" She twirls, giving me a whiff of perfume.

"You look . . . young."

It's not a mindless compliment. It's not at all hard

to picture her as someone my age, a young girl who was supposed to have a special prom night herself.

"Well, thank you. I got this dress for your parents' wedding. I haven't worn it in years, but it still fits."

"You really look great." It's the truth. Tonight, I'm going to have the second-prettiest date at the prom.

Jean smooths out the bottom part of her dress and sits at the kitchen table. "How long until your friends pick us up?"

"About twenty minutes."

"Sit with me."

I obey.

"Would you like a drink? I think there's half a bottle of rum still in the cupboard from mah-jongg night."

I'm touched that she's treating me like such an adult, but I don't think I'd better. I don't want to risk barfing before the big event.

"No thank you."

Jean stares at me for a long moment. "Deacon, how long have you lived with me?"

"About two years." Not counting the various weeks and months when my father had to go out of town and dumped me here.

"I hope you've enjoyed it here. Sometimes I feel like I've really let you down."

Her words are so utterly ludicrous that I wait for the

137

punch line for a few seconds. When I realize she's serious, I let out a sputter. "What the hell are you going on about? If it wasn't for you, I'd be working with Dad, selling fake Rolexes in Prague or something."

She laughs. "Oh, how I wish you were kidding. I just wish . . . I wish that I could do more for you. I wish that I could surprise you at graduation and announce that I'm paying your tuition. Or that I've bought you a car. Or set up a trust fund for you. I wish I had something to give you besides two hundred dollars and a new desk set. Because that's what you're getting."

I swear, I'm almost ready to tear off my shirt like the Hulk, I'm getting so irritated. "Jean, I don't know what's gotten into your brain, but knock it off. Because of you, I learned wood carving, leatherworking, and first aid. If I didn't live with you, I wouldn't have seen you almost get arrested at that political rally. And of course I got to go on that pilgrimage to that quilting museum."

There's a bit of a smile. "I didn't think you enjoyed that."

"Well, not everything was a good memory. But you did all the things my father should have done. And I do not want you to think for a minute it wasn't enough. I can make my own way. I . . . I'm a man now."

"That scares me, sometimes."

I smile. "It scares me too."

The doorbell rings.

"I think that's Elijah."

We stand. "You ready for a night to remember, Jean?"

"Just lead the way."

It's not Elijah at the door, but an older, darker man. He wears a gray suit and one of those brimmed caps like cops wear, though he's not a cop.

"Deacon Locke?" he says, with a slight accent.

I nod.

"I am Rodrigo, I'll be your driver for the evening. Is your date joining us here?"

"I'm coming," calls Jean.

Well, this is it. This guy will be the first to see me out with my grandmother. He can laugh at me if he wants to. But he better not say a word about Jean.

Rodrigo doesn't blink when Jean sashays into view. Seriously. He doesn't blink.

"You are coming with us, ma'am?" he finally asks.

Jean takes my arm. "Yes. My handsome grandson is escorting me to his prom tonight."

Our driver continues to bore into her with his brown eyes.

"How sad." He steps back and gestures to his car with a half bow. "I was hoping perhaps you'd be free later."

Even I catch what he's implying. Is it just the lighting

out here, or is Jean going a little red as Rodrigo holds the limo door open for us?

Elijah and Clara are already in the car, which is so big, they sit facing us. Elijah is busy playing with the passenger controls, gleefully raising and lowering the partition between us and the driver. Clara sits next to him. She wears a loose-fitting dark-green dress that calls attention away from her skinny, angular body and makes you focus on her face. Good call.

She smiles. "You must be Mrs. Locke. I'm Clara."

"Very pleased to meet you, Clara. Please, call me Jean." She turns to Elijah.

"You want some peanuts, Mrs. Locke? They're free, I asked."

Jean clears her throat. "Young man, what's your name?"

"I'm Elijah." Technically, he and Jean have already met, when he picked me up to go clothes shopping. He only got to talk at her for a few minutes, though I find it unbelievable anyone could forget Elijah without a blow to the head.

Rodrigo turns and faces us through the half-raised partition. "Everyone have their seat belts buckled? Then let us be off."

"Ooh, that Spanish accent," Jean whispers to Clara, who giggles.

I had no idea Jean had a thing for guys from Spain.

Clara and Jean make small talk on the ride to the dance. That leaves me facing Elijah and his goofy grin. I can't help but notice that he and Clara are holding hands.

It's a short jaunt to the country club where the dance is being held. Rodrigo rushes to open the door and help Clara and Jean out.

"I'll wait here until you're ready to leave," he says as we stand in the parking lot. He then turns to Jean and hands her a business card. "And if you should need a driver in the future, please don't hesitate to call."

Jean smiles and takes the card. The driver smiles back.

"Remember to ask for me. Rodrigo." He returns to his vehicle.

Clara adjusts Elijah's collar. Jean smiles at me. "Ready, Deacon?"

And suddenly, I am. I'm ready. This evening isn't about Soraya or Kelli or graduation. This is about me and Jean. About a fun night. About making some memories.

I smile at my grandmother. "Damn straight."

She takes my arm and we walk toward the country club.

FOURTEEN

SWARMS OF STUDENTS ARE MAKING THEIR WAY toward the building. Each person is dressed all fancy. Everyone is laughing and talking and touching their dates.

What are they going to say when they realize I'm here with my grandma? I remember watching my father sucker-punch some guy in a bar once. If someone makes fun of Jean, I can't promise I'd be that calm and laid-back.

We line up at the gate. I pull out our more-expensive-than-I-would-have-expected tickets. Up ahead, a teacher is making a student empty his pockets.

I glance at a long list of rules posted on an easel near

the door. No alcohol. No drugs. No overt displays of blah blah blah.

And then I see a rule that makes me freeze.

No one over the age of nineteen admitted.

I get a horrible sinking feeling. They probably instituted that rule to avoid creepy twenty-eight-year-olds hanging around, but still . . . I never thought about this. What if they won't let Jean in? What if this fun evening we've planned ends right now?

The coach who's taking the tickets looks up at Jean. His eyes narrow.

"What're you doin' here?" he asks.

"Excuse me?" responds Jean, in her formal, dismiss-the-telemarketer voice.

"Mrs. Locke! It's me, Mike Harold! I was on the track team with your son, back in the day."

Jean's face breaks into a smile. "Why, Michael, it has been some time."

"You droppin' off some kids?"

Jean pats me on the shoulder. I try to look calm and harmless. "No, my grandson has kindly invited me to the dance."

Mr. Harold finds this hilarious and lets out a bellow of a laugh. "Deacon, your daddy, he was always pulling some kind of crazy stunt. He's living in France, now, ain't he?"

"No, he's in Amsterdam."

"Ah, Germany. You tell him I said hi, okay?" He takes our tickets and we walk in.

Jean leans over to me. "I've known that boy since he was just out of diapers. And maybe they took him out of diapers too soon, if you catch my drift."

We both laugh as we step inside the ballroom.

It's dimly lit, which makes me happy. Hopefully no one will realize I'm wearing tennis shoes. There's crepe paper and fancy decorations everywhere. Up front, a DJ plays a slow tune. Kids are milling about, but no one is dancing yet.

Wow. We did it. We're here at the dance. *I'm* here at the dance. Deacon Locke, the guy who once hid in the bathroom on the day we had to give oral reports in eighth grade. I made it to prom. It's a pretty good feeling.

I look over at Jean, to make some crack about how I hope she didn't sneak any booze into the dance.

But for the first time since I've known her, Jean doesn't look rock steady. She looks kind of scared. Kind of nervous. This is the first time she's been to a teenage social event since Nixon was in the White House. Maybe she hadn't thought this through.

I glance at my two companions. Clara clutches her purse to her chest. Elijah slouches and looks at the floor.

Jeez, is everyone feeling nervous and awkward tonight? I'm glad I'm not the only one for once, but I hope everyone's not expecting me to direct things this evening.

"Deacon!"

It's Kelli. I do a double take. Now that she's lost her glasses, let down her hair, and gotten a makeover, I'm suddenly struck by what a truly beautiful girl she is. Or was she always this lovely and I was too blind to see it?

Just kidding. This isn't a romantic comedy. Kelli's wearing her glasses but not a bit of makeup. Her upper lip is still red and sore from her allergies. She's just as frumpy and curvy and cute as ever. And I'm very glad to see her. She's an island of stability on this unusual night.

She's not alone. "This is Hunt. Hunt, my friend Deacon."

Up close, Hunt looks like a dwarf from an epic fantasy movie. He's not much taller than Kelli, but seems to be built entirely out of muscle and gristle. His head is so square I wonder how he gets his football helmet on.

He nods at me and smiles but says nothing. I turn to my group. "Guys, this is Kelli. And this is Elijah and Clara and, um, my grandmother, Jean."

Kelli smiles at the first two names but stops when she notices Jean. She looks at me, then quickly back at my grandmother.

"Hello. Um, are you chaperoning tonight, ma'am?"

Jean beams. "No, dear. Deacon was kind enough to invite me as his date for the evening."

I don't think Kelli believes Jean is being serious. She glances at me, then at Elijah, who nods.

"Well . . . that's sweet of you to go with Deacon, Mrs. Locke." The look on her face says otherwise. Kelli looks . . . disappointed in me. Like taking Jean was an act of desperation on my part.

I'm about to say something in Jean's defense, but she beats me to the punch. "Sweet of me? It was sweet of Deacon! I tried to get him to ask out a girl from school, but he was determined to show me a fun time. Why don't you ladies join me for a powder and I'll tell you all about it."

Before I know what's happening, our dates are headed for the ladies room. Kelli turns and glances back over her shoulder and winks. I assume at Hunt.

The three of us stand there awkwardly. I'd love to break the silence, but I'm not about to ask a couple of guys to go to the bathroom with me. Girls have it so easy.

Hunt cracks his knuckles. Elijah pulls out a bag of peanuts and starts munching. When he sees me staring, he offers me one. I shake my head.

146

Well. Only three or four more hours to go.

Sometimes I wonder if I'm actually a character in a poorly performing situation comedy.

I look up at the ceiling and beseech the writers for a romantic subplot.

"So, you brought your grandma here?" asks Hunt out of nowhere.

"Yeah. My grandpa was in the army, so she missed her own dance. Thought I'd make it up to her."

I think Hunt has zoned out again, but after a moment he speaks. "My grandma died last year. She was always asking me to visit more." He scratches his chin. "Good for you, man."

I feel just slightly better.

There's a smattering of laughter from the dance floor. The school counselor and one of the English teachers are fast dancing. They're being ridiculous on purpose. Unlike me, they don't mind when people watch them.

Couples begin to pair off. Just a few at first. Most seem less serious than the teachers.

Thankfully, the girls return at this time. All three of them are laughing. I'm glad Jean is fitting in.

Funny, I just thought of my grandmother as one of "the girls."

Kelli directs us all to sit at one of the candlelit tables,

and as none of us have a better idea, we follow her directions. Elijah and I clonk down next to our dates. Hunt gently takes Kelli's wrap, then pulls out the chair for her. I assume he's deliberately trying to make us look bad.

"Mrs. Locke . . . ," begins Kelli.

"Please, dear, call me Jean."

"You never finished that story about your senior prank."

"Oh, it was really nothing. You see, at the time, there was a very antiestablishment attitude. Deacon's grandfather was in the military, and . . ."

I suddenly am rendered deaf to Jean's story. Jason has walked in.

He's wearing a white tuxedo with tails. And a top hat. He's wearing a goddamn top hat. And he has a cane tucked under his arm. I'd like to say he's embarrassing himself and looks to all the world like someone just trying too hard.

But he totally pulls it off. He looks good.

Maybe that's because of his date.

I was prepared for this. I mean, it's not like I expected Soraya to cancel on Jason at the last minute, leaving him humiliated and dateless in front of the entire school. Didn't hope for that at all.

But she's here tonight.

Now in my previous descriptions of Soraya, I may have implied that I find her to be attractive. Perhaps you didn't catch that, it was subtle.

But tonight, she transcends that. Tonight . . . she's regal.

Maybe it's because I've only ever seen her in her casual clothes from dance class. But now, with her hair done, wearing makeup, and with a dress that shows off her bare shoulders and . . . curves . . . she looks like someone from a Hollywood red-carpet event. A woman who should be on the arm of a movie star or a deposed dictator.

It's not just her looks. The way she carries herself. So confident, so strong, so classy.

And she's holding Jason's arm. Not really holding it, just barely touching it. Just touching his arm as he walks next to her and talks to someone he knows.

Soraya Shadee is touching him, but he's not paying attention. He's in the presence of royalty and he blows it off.

It makes me want to just grab him by his perfectly knotted tie and yank.

The very thought is giving me intestinal pains.

No, wait, my guts really do hurt.

I come back to reality and realize Elijah is repeatedly

driving his elbow into my ribs.

"What's your deal, Deke? Calm down."

Right. This night is not about me and Soraya. It's about Jean. I refocus on her story.

". . . and I don't think the principal ever got the cow smell out of his office."

I'll have to ask her to repeat that tale later.

Hmm. I wonder where the fire exit is. I should check.

I look back across the room, where, by an odd coincidence, Jason is standing with Soraya. He's ditched his hat and cane and is leading her to the dance floor by her delicate hand.

She held my hand once.

And now they are dancing. It's a slow dance and he's holding her close. Not obnoxiously close, but near enough.

I feel a gentle hand on my arm. Fortunately it's not Elijah's.

Jean smiles at me. "Shall we dance?"

I stand with a smile. "My pleasure." I offer her my hand and gently help her to her feet. My tablemates follow suit, and soon we're all on the floor.

Jean and I take a moment to find the beat, and soon it's like we're back in class. I deliberately face away from Soraya and her platonic, just-friends, nothing-else-going-on date.

"Are you having a good time, Jean?"

"I am. You know, I was a little nervous at first, but your friends are so charming. We talked quite a bit in the bathroom. That Kelli girl thinks very highly of you."

This is surprising. I kind of assumed she merely tolerated me. "Um, what else did you guys talk about?"

Jean chuckles. "Clara is totally smitten with that Elijah boy. Kelli's not so sure about her date, it could go either way."

"Look at you, gossiping like a teenager."

"Well," says Jean, in a more serious tone, "at least one of us is."

We dance in silence for a minute. In my determination not to watch Soraya and Jason, I realize that Jean and I are being watched ourselves. People quickly look away when they're spotted, but it's easy to see that my older date is causing some heads to turn.

Let 'em stare. I make an effort to stand up straighter. And when the DJ plays a faster number, Jean and I hold our own. Those lessons paid off.

The more we dance, the more people watch us. And the more we're being watched, the more determined I am to dance. This is my prom night, after all. And Jean's prom night, about fifty years in the making. I don't care what anyone else thinks.

After three or four songs, Jean asks to sit down. This

time I remember to pull the chair out for her. She's not expecting this, and my gentlemanly gesture nearly turns tragicomic.

"Would you like something to drink?"

She has out her purse and is reapplying her makeup. "I'm fine. Why don't you see if one of your friends would like to dance?"

"I'm not going to ditch you."

She doesn't look up from her little mirror. "I need a moment to recharge my batteries. Please find someone else to dance with for a minute."

Years of living with Jean make me realize this is an unwinnable argument. "Fine. Where's Elijah?"

I don't see anyone I know, so I wet my whistle at the punch bowl. I briefly worry that someone might have spiked it. Then I decide I've been watching too many situation comedies.

"So spill it!"

I reflexively clutch my drink before I realize it's Kelli who's talking. She's staring at me with an intense grin, as if waiting for me to finish a joke.

"Your grandma!" she clarifies. "What's the story? And don't tell me she was the only person who'd come here with you. There must be two or three girls in Arkansas who would have said yes."

"Well, we're both seniors," I quip.

"C'mon, tell me!"

Her smile is contagious. I'm about to explain about Grandpa and Vietnam and everything, but I stop. Is that really the reason I'm here with Jean tonight? Like Soraya said, I could have brought Jean to a seniors' dance or something, and she would have been just as happy. I take a swig of my punch.

"Kelli, Jean's a lot more than a grandmother to me. Things were pretty rough before I moved to Fayetteville and she kind of adopted me. We've been through a lot together. More than I'd like to talk about. She's my best friend. One of my few friends. And I wanted to share this evening with her."

Kelli's smile widens. "Wow. Just when you think you know a guy."

"What's that supposed to mean?"

"Nothing important." She then stops smiling and moves closer to me. "But I've seen the way you've been acting these past few weeks, with your new clothes and haircut. There's some girl in your life besides Grandma. Fess up."

It's a little embarrassing to talk about this with Kelli, but she'll worm it out of me eventually. "See the girl in the blue dress over there? The one talking to the douche in the white tux?"

"Soraya Shadee?"

"Yeah . . . wait, how do you know her?"

Kelli watches her for a second. "We worked together on a project for famine relief in the Sudan last year." She turns and looks at me. "Wow, Deacon, glad to see you finally went through puberty. Excellent choice."

I think I'm blushing a little bit. "Yeah, well, too bad she's here with Señor Fancypants."

She just laughs. "So make her jealous. Find a pretty girl and ask her to dance."

I set down my cup and hold out my hand. "Shall we?"

"Thought you'd never ask."

A month ago, the thought of dancing this close with Kelli would have filled me with panic. But now that I'm actually doing it, I realize I was worried for nothing. Even with her chest pressing into my lower rib cage, it's like I'm with one of the ladies from class. I enjoy dancing with her, nothing more.

It's a good feeling.

"Hey, Deacon, don't look now."

How am I supposed to not look? I glance over my shoulder, then wince.

Jean is dancing again. Dancing with Mr. Anderson, my American History teacher from last year. The balding, potbellied man who once gave me a D because I had such a hard time working with other people on a group project.

Kelli giggles. "Looks like Jean is making friends."

It looks like Mr. Anderson is going for more than that. He's dancing a bit too close and smiling a bit too much for my taste.

"Go cut in on them, Kelli."

"And dance with Anderson? Ew!"

I distractedly dance as I watch my teacher hit on my grandmother.

"I wouldn't worry about it," Kelli advises.

I force myself to turn away. "You're right. What's the worst that could happen?"

"They get married, and Mr. Anderson moves into your house and makes you start calling him Gramps."

"I'm really going to miss you next year." And you know what? I am.

The song ends and I quickly rescue Jean from my teacher. They both look slightly annoyed, but it's for the greater good. Besides, she's my date.

Unfortunately, the DJ puts on a swingy, jazzy number. Something way out of our league. Something that's probably beyond most of the dancers here. People begin to move to the edge of the floor.

But then someone gasps. A girl cheers. The crowd begins murmuring over the music.

Everyone has moved away from the center of the room. And I know what's coming. I stare over the heads

of the spectators, and my faint hope that it's only a bru-
tal fistfight disappears.

Someone is dancing solo. And not in a pathetic way.
No, he's moving to the music like he's surgically attached
to the rhythm. He's jumping, he's sliding, he weaving.
He bobs and slithers in a way I've only seen on televi-
sion. He's a better dancer than me. Better even than
Soraya. His moves can only be described as beautiful.

It's Jason, of course.

All the students stand and watch, clapping to the
beat, enjoying how Jason is once again making himself
the center of attention. And Soraya stands there, smiling
and clapping.

If she was my date, I wouldn't ignore her. Never. I'd
make damn sure she knew how much I enjoyed being
with her. I'd have made this evening all about Soraya.
Not about me.

In front of us, a couple of girls whisper and giggle as
they watch Jason's performance.

Funny. I go through life hoping no one notices me.
Jason can't stand it when people don't notice him.

I guess my question is, which does Soraya prefer?

As the song climaxes, Jason leaps in the air and lands
in a perfect split, something that should be impossible
for a male in rented pants. Soraya comes over and helps
him to his feet as the crowd cheers.

I feel a hand on my arm.

It's Jean.

She doesn't say anything. Doesn't insult Jason or tell me to ignore him, or say that Soraya would rather be with me. I guess she realizes I don't need empty words right now.

Instead, she just takes my hand and smiles. And much as I wish Soraya was with me tonight, it doesn't matter. I'm here with my friend. I'm having a good time. That's all that's important.

"You ready to show 'em how it's done?" I ask.

"Just try and stop me."

FIFTEEN

NEITHER JEAN NOR I SIT DOWN FOR ANOTHER THREE hours. I'm not entirely sure what happened. One minute, Jean and I are dancing. The next thing I know the song is over and some guy is standing in front of her with his hand out and a grin on his face. Not a teacher this time. A classmate.

She ditches me for the new guy. But I'm only alone for a second before his date has pulled me out on the floor. And so it begins.

Every time a song ends, Jean and I are shunted off to another partner. At first, I worry that guys are asking her to dance because they think they're being funny, or worse, because they're trying to be polite to an old woman. But then people keep coming up to me, complimenting me on my date.

"She is so adorable, Deacon!"

"Dude, your grandma kicks ass."

"Hey, Deacon, do you think she'd buy us some beer?"

Eventually, I just roll with it. Besides, every time Jean dances with someone, I have to entertain his date.

And after practicing with the grandmas at the YMCA for a month, I can actually dance with a girl my own age without sweating.

So how about that. I'm meeting people. Fitting in. Just like a regular guy.

A guy who needed his grandmother to help him make friends, but still.

There's just one final step. One last thing I need to do to make this evening truly great.

I haven't lost sight of Soraya since we got here. I glance at her whenever I get a chance. Sometimes she's dancing with another guy. Sometimes she's sitting with other girls. Most of the time, she's with Jason. Sometimes he even remembers to include her in his dance moves.

And suddenly, he's gone. Probably to the restroom to powder his nose. And prom will be ending soon.

It's now or never.

I regret my long legs as I cross the floor in a matter of seconds. She sees me coming and smiles.

"Soraya?"

This shouldn't be hard. I've danced with her a half dozen times before in class.

Five times. Exactly five times.

But now we're no longer teacher and student. She's a beautiful girl, standing at a dance alone, and I'm . . .

Oh, dear God. I'm Deacon Locke.

Kind of wish I'd remembered that before I came over here.

"Would you like to dance?" I hear myself say.

She doesn't answer. She just places one hand on my shoulder and the other in my palm.

And tonight, I lead.

At first, we don't make eye contact. We both kind of look off to the side. But after a few beats, we start angling our necks. Slowly, like stalking a deer. Afraid a sudden move will startle the other one. And after a minute, I'm looking into Soraya Shadee's endless eyes.

We smile.

"It seems my lessons paid off," she says softly.

"I had an excellent teacher." God, I can smell her perfume. It's not the scent she wore to dance class, though in retrospect, that might have just been her deodorant.

"Deacon, can I tell you something?" She looks nervous. I stiffen, unsure of what's coming.

"When you first told me you were taking your

160

grandmother to prom, I thought . . . I thought that was strange. Not weird strange," she quickly amends. "I just was wondering what your angle was. At first I thought you were some kind of hipster, just trying to be ironic. And then I wondered if maybe you had a social anxiety disorder, or your father had really screwed you up. But when I finally got to know you and Jean, I realized something."

I hope it's not something bad. I'd just as soon she not tell me.

"I realized that you're unique."

I try to smile. "That's one way of putting it."

"I mean it in a good way. You wanted to have fun at prom, and so you brought Jean. That took courage, but it also took a genuinely nice guy. Someone who doesn't try to be normal."

"Sometimes normal isn't an option." I'm trying to be funny, but she smiles like I've said the most profound thing in the world.

There's a burst of laughter. We turn to see Jean, dancing with a basketball player. Everyone around her is cracking up, but in a friendly way. She's having a good time.

I'm shocked when I feel Soraya pull me closer to her. "Don't ever change. I know too many people who live their life trying to be what they're not. With you, what you see is what you get, and that's kind of great."

She thinks I'm great.

"Soraya, I'm glad I brought Jean here tonight. But it's not like . . . well, part of me wishes I was here with . . . someone else."

She ducks her head for a moment. I think she's about to speak, but the music suddenly ends. And then the DJ says something about the last song of the evening. I can see Jason approaching. I suppose I should go. I need to get back to Jean anyway. I step away.

"Soraya?"

She's walking toward Jason, but she turns and looks in my direction.

"Call me," she mouths.

An hour later, I lie back in my seat in the limo. Across from me, Clara leans on Elijah's shoulder. She's lightly dozing. Elijah has a look of pure rapture on his face.

Jean hums quietly to herself, a wistful smile on her lips. Without looking at me, she reaches over and takes my hand.

"Thank you. Thank you for a wonderful evening."

"I should thank you."

Rodrigo puts on some slow, sleepy music as he drives us home. I can see the stars through the sunroof. Tonight couldn't have gone more perfectly. Jean finally got her school dance. I went to prom and danced with a bunch of girls.

And best of all, Soraya told me to call her. Dance class has ended, but maybe not us.

I have a very good feeling about the future.

The end. Seriously. Deacon learned to come out of his shell, and he's going to go out with Soraya. Book's over. The next two hundred pages are acknowledgments.

SIXTEEN

IT'S EARLY SUNDAY MORNING. DESPITE THE LATE night, Jean is off at the sunrise church services, while the rest of us sinners sleep in. I lie on my back, hugging my pillow and staring at the watermarks on my ceiling.

Last night was pretty amazing. I had fun. Jean had fun. Elijah and Clara had fun. But that's not what's important.

The important thing is that Soraya asked me to call her.

I've watched enough movies to know that there's endless debate about how long you're supposed to wait to call a girl so as not to seem desperate. I rack my brain with indecision. Do I call her this morning, or not until the afternoon? Or should I play hard to get and wait until tomorrow?

Then again, is a phone call the right way to handle this? How hard is it to learn to play the guitar? It's just that the telephone is so impersonal. . . .

The phone. The phone is ringing downstairs.

Neither Jean nor I own a cellular. Jean's kind of a technophobe. I think she's still getting used to a phone you don't have to crank. Me, I never had anyone I needed to call, at least not until this month. The only phones in the house are on the wall in the kitchen and in Jean's bedroom.

They're ringing.

Maybe it's Soraya. It might be. She could be calling me.

I leap from the bed, violently untangling myself from the sheets. I tear down the stairs, barely keeping my footing. God, what if she hangs up?

Stumbling into the kitchen, I catch my toe on the corner of Jean's easel and go sprawling, just as I grab the phone. The cord stretches as I go down, but it stays attached. I do a full-body belly flop on the linoleum, causing the entire house to tremble. Choking back sobs of agony, I breathe into the receiver.

"Hello?"

"DUUUUDE!"

It's Elijah.

I clutch my dislocated toe as painful tears run down my nose. Not the best way to start the day.

"Dude?"

I look at the clock on the oven and count to three. "You're aware that it's seven fifty-five in the morning, right?"

"I tried to text you, but it wouldn't go through."

"This is a landline."

"A what? Look, there's something on YouTube you gotta see."

I consider letting go of the receiver and watching it slingshot across the room as the cord snaps back. "Elijah, is someone holding you hostage? Clear your throat if there's a gun pointed at your head."

"I'm serious. You got to see this."

"I don't have internet access."

Silence. I think he's going to hang up, allowing me a dignified death here on the kitchen floor.

"I'll be right over."

"What? No . . ."

The line goes dead.

He makes good on his threat and shows up on my front porch, barely seven hours after we parted company last night, still wearing his prom shoes. He smiles when I open the door and attempts to come in.

I do not move aside.

"Elijah, I am a large man and it's very early. I'm not sure it's advisable for you to be here at the moment."

He just grins and holds up a sack from the doughnut place.

I sigh. "C'mon in."

He's got his phone out before we're even seated in the kitchen.

"You gotta look at this, Deke."

I personally never saw the allure of internet video things. "It's not the monkey drinking its . . ."

"No! Look!"

I squint at the screen. It's a shaky amateur clip. Looks like it was filmed at some kind of dance. Some huge guy is dancing with an older . . .

Shit. I glare at Elijah.

"I didn't film it! But look, over two thousand hits since last night. You've gone viral!"

I jab at the screen in an attempt to shut down the video. Eventually, he takes the phone away from me and does it himself.

"Is there any way I can get these YouTube people to take that down?"

He looks more baffled than usual. "Why would you want to do that? You're famous!"

I glower at him and he scoots away just a bit. "I don't care about me. It's Jean. If she's out there in computer land, people are going to see her."

"So?"

"So? Elijah, correct me if I'm wrong, but are people on the internet always respectful and polite when discussing strangers?" Especially a sweet little old lady at a high school prom.

He looks down at his phone. "I see what you mean. But I wouldn't let this shake you. Tomorrow, you'll be replaced by the latest celebrity nip slip."

"Oh boy."

We're silent for a moment. "Did you really come all the way over here just to show me that?"

"Yes." He answers far too quickly. "Well . . . did you and Jean have fun last night?"

"We did." It's clear he wants me to ask the same question. "Did you and Clara?"

I swear, it's like a cork being popped.

"YES! God, yes! I mean, I couldn't tell if she was really into me or not, but last night everything totally freaking worked! I mean, wow! She told me I was funny! She said I looked good in my tux! She's already talking about things we can do this summer. And last night, after the limo dropped us off, we sat on her porch swing and . . . wow. Okay, I'm done. But wow."

I can't help but smile. "I'm glad it worked out for you."

"But the twenty-seven-dollar question is, how did it go for you, Deke? Was Soraya there? Did you ask her to dance?"

I'd like to brag how she totally asked me to call her (and, by implication, eventually buy a retirement condo together in the Carolinas). But my past catches up with me and I'm suddenly not so confident. I mean, I'm bound to blow this somehow, right?

Elijah is still waiting for an answer. I shrug, then wave my hands helplessly as I try to think of a way to describe my situation.

Surprisingly, he nods solemnly. "Been there myself, man."

Is everyone's love life as screwed up as mine? Doubtful. But Elijah's solidarity calms me down, just a bit.

We both turn as we hear Jean come in through the front door and enter the kitchen. "Deacon? Who parked that little clown car—" She stops when she sees Elijah. "Oh, hello, kiddo."

"Good morning, Mrs. Locke. Did you know you and Deacon are trending on YouTube?"

She turns to me. "Tell your friend he can stay for breakfast if he learns to speak English."

Elijah grins. Soon, we're both sitting in front of a stack of banana pancakes, the doughnuts long forgotten.

No matter what happens to me at college next year, I'm going to miss the home-cooked meals. I'll have to enjoy this while I can.

Jean joins us. We're about to dig in when she turns to Elijah with a smile.

"So, young man, do you go to Deacon's school?"

At lunch that Monday, I sit in the library consumed with worry. Jean spent all of Saturday evening with Elijah. Then on Sunday morning, she doesn't recognize him. He blew it off as a joke. But I can't stop thinking about her memory lapse.

It was just a senior moment, right?

It's got to be. All morning long, classmates stopped me in the hall, asking about Jean and talking about how fun she was. Her behavior at prom, that wasn't the way a doddering old lady would act. She's just a little forgetful, that's all.

Hell, my teachers are always joking about their memory, or their backs, or their eyesight, and they're mostly much younger than Jean. It's just a part of getting older.

Still . . .

A hand swats me in the back of the head, soft enough to be playful, but forceful enough to kind of hurt.

"Hey, Kelli."

"Deacon, could you come with me to the campus

today? I need to set up the stage for the Haitian relief thing, and I think there's going to be heavy lifting."

I don't turn around. "Not today, if you don't mind."

"Whoa, what's wrong? The pressures of fame getting to be too much?"

I wonder if I should talk to her about the incident with Jean. "No, I . . . wait, what?"

"Have you seen this?" She shoves her phone at me.

"That YouTube thing? Yeah, Elijah showed me."

"No! This just went up. Look!"

I squint at the tiny screen.

KZAR Tulsa. REAL ROCK RADIO.

The station's logo shifts to the face of some hip guy, apparently the DJ.

"And for those of you rockers who couldn't get a date for the big dance, check out what this young stud did."

It cuts to a clip of Jean and me dancing. It's not the same one from the other video. How many people were filming us the other night?

The disc jockey continues his smooth voice-over. "This gentle giant apparently brought his grandmother to prom! Not sure of the story here, but look at them go!"

Kelli chuckles as I violently dip Jean.

"Hope this couple had fun!" says the DJ. "And why not? And least he didn't have to worry about getting her back in time for curfew . . . just *Wheel of Fortune.* And forget about trying to sneak beer into the dance, how about a flask of Metamucil?"

On the screen, I twirl Jean.

"Seriously, we wish these two the best. If any of you rockers know who they are, drop me a line. We'd love to have them on. . . ."

A loud, prerecorded message takes over.

"MADCAP MIKE MYRON IN THE MORNING, KZAR NINETY-NINE POINT ONE, TULSA!"

Kelli laughs. "How do you like that? You and Jean are famous."

"No, we're not." Famous people are manufactured in a factory near Hollywood.

"Check out the comments, Deacon."

I read them with a growing sense that Oklahomans are desperate for entertainment.

TOTALLY ADORBS

HE COULD TAKE ME TO A DANCE ANY DAY

KIND OF A SEXY FIGURE FOR A 80 YR OLD

BEND OVER AGAIN BIG GUY

U KNOW WHAT THEY SAY ABOUT CHICKS WITH NO TEETH

"I need to call that radio station and lodge a complaint."

Kelli smacks me in the back of the head again. I'm beginning to find it less endearing. "Don't be an idiot. You should enjoy this."

I'm helplessly trying to search for the station's phone number on her phone. "Why? And what about Jean? Look at the way people are talking about her!"

Kelli shakes her head, removes her glasses, and begins to clean them on my shirt. "Your grandmother is a big girl and won't care. Seriously, Deacon, you should be proud of this. When did you learn to dance, anyway?"

I'm not sure if I should believe her. "Why would anyone care about stuff like this?"

She rolls her eyes. "Maybe you don't see it, but I do. The dominant paradigm in our society places an emphasis on outcome-based models of constructivist nomenclature, overarching the taxonomy of nontraditional matriarchal neoclassism."

"What the hell does that mean?"

"*Girls*, Deacon. Call up Soraya tonight." She takes the phone back from me and stands. "She'll say yes."

I ponder this exciting prediction. "Yes to what?"

"To whatever you ask. So don't be a dick." She turns to go. But there's something I want to ask.

"Hey, Kelli? What's up with you and Hunt? Never pictured you being into jocks."

She grins her evil grin. "I'm just full of surprises, aren't I?"

✷ ✷ ✷

As I go to class, I notice Jason pass me, all perfectly primped.

He sees me about the same time I see him.

He continues to walk toward me, not breaking eye contact.

We just stare at each other. Not angrily, but not friendly, not at all.

He even turns his head and continues to watch me as he walks away. He's not paying attention to where he's going and falls down an open elevator shaft and dies.

No, I have to be honest with you, that didn't really happen.

But he did stare at me. Angry like. As if I wronged him somehow. Like he didn't get to take Soraya to the dance.

What the hell's up with that?

Elijah sits on the roof of his car in the lotus position. Everyone else has gone home for the day. The school parking lot is empty.

I pace in circles around his car, clutching his phone. He watches me like a nonserene monk.

"Just call her!" he repeats.

Easy for him to say. He has a girlfriend. Me, I just went to prom with my grandmother.

"Tell me again how you asked out Clara."

"I went up to her and asked her out."

I stop walking and place my foot on the hood of his car. "But you had screwdrivers and dressed up and stuff."

"That's because I'm a little strange. You're big and strange. Just call her."

"What if I forget what to say?"

"Put her on speaker. I'll feed you lines."

I take a deep breath and close my eyes. Then I open them because I can't see the numbers. I dial.

Soraya picks up after only one ring. "Hello? Who is this?"

Oh, God. I've annoyed her.

"Deacon!" Elijah stage whispers. "Your name is Deacon!"

"Oh, uh, this is Deacon."

"Oh, hi!"

She didn't hang up. That's a good sign.

Elijah frantically motions for me to say something.

"Uh . . . how are you?" I ask. Elijah nods encouragingly.

She giggles. "Fine. Deacon, I have to say, you and Jean did me proud at the dance. Have you seen that You-Tube video?"

Elijah rapidly nods. So do I.

Wait . . .

"Yes, I have."

"Next time you're online, maybe you could get on the comments and recommend the dance class?"

"Okay! I'll do that right now!"

I move to hang up the phone.

Elijah half leaps, half falls from the top of his car. With surprising strength, he grabs my wrist and shoves the phone up to my face. He is not smiling. I try to move my arm, but his hand is like a wiry set of cuffs.

Here goes nothing. "Listen, would you maybe want to see a movie this Saturday?"

There's a five-hour pause while she thinks of the most polite way to turn me down. Then . . .

"Sure! Look, I have a dance class about to start, but call me tomorrow, okay?"

"Yes."

She hangs up.

I did it.

"She said yes."

"Told you, man."

"Wow. It's totally happening."

"Thanks to me."

I look down at him. "Hey, Elijah?"

"Yeah?"

"You can let go of my hand now."

SEVENTEEN

"JEAN, I'M HOME!" IT'S THURSDAY. TWO DAYS BEFORE I see Soraya. Elijah and Clara have taken me to some clothing stores to pick out something to wear. While my size makes shopping complicated, I do manage to find a few nice things.

"Jean?"

No answer. That's odd, her car's out front, so she must be here.

"Hello?"

There's the sound of water running in the kitchen. She probably can't hear me.

"Hey . . ."

No one is the kitchen. But the sink is running full

blast. And it's stoppered. It overflows out of the basin, across the counter, and down on the floor.

"Son of a . . ." Water splashes over the tops of my shoes as I rush to shut things off. The faucet stops running, but I can still hear water flowing somewhere below me. Draining to a place where water should not drain.

Ripping the roll of paper towels off the holder, I begin to sop up the mess. They're less than useless. I go through three rolls and the water is as deep as before.

"Jean!" No answer. Where could she be? Probably taking a nap or in the bathroom or something.

Giving up on the paper towels, I subsequently fail with regular towels, a mop, and trying to force the water into a bucket. Eventually I remember Jean's wet/dry vac, which does the trick. I expect the roar of the vacuum to get Jean's attention, but I'm wrong.

Just as I'm sucking up the last of the standing water, the phone rings. Jean doesn't pick up after three rings. I almost don't answer it, but what if it's Soraya?

"Deacon Locke?" The voice is cool and self-assured. I'm reminded of Jason.

"Yes?"

"Ah, glad to get ahold of you. This is Madcap Mike Myron, from KZAR Tulsa. How the hell are you?"

Geez, the guy from Kelli's phone. The person who made a big fat deal about me and Jean at the dance.

"How did you get this number?"

He chuckles in his self-assured radio voice. "You're not an easy guy to track down, Deacon. If you have a social media account, I sure couldn't find it."

I see a stream of water trickling toward the dining room carpet. "Um, Mr. Madcap, I—"

"Now, you are the Deacon Locke who took his grandmother Jean to his senior prom last weekend, is that correct?"

I almost hang up, but suddenly, I'm wary. "Why do you care?"

Again, that suave laughter. "Why do I care? Because thousands of my listeners want to know what your story is! Why did this handsome fellow take his grandma to the big dance?"

"It's a little involved, and I'm kind of busy."

"Aren't we all? Look, the reason I'm calling is I'd like to do a quick interview with you. Not right now, let's say tomorrow afternoon. Won't take five minutes."

I'm not sure why this guy would want me to be on his show. Sounds like a chance to make a fool of myself, and drag Jean down with me. "No, thank you."

"Hang on there, buddy." His voice drops an octave. "Listen. You know that clip of you and your grandmother is all over the internet, right?"

"Uh, I guess."

"And you know how people get in the comments sections. Some folks have been saying some pretty unkind things about you two."

"What? What have they been saying?" And what are their names and addresses?

"Nothing I'd like to repeat. And I wouldn't worry about what every weirdo online thinks about you. But this would be an excellent chance to tell your story. C'mon, let us know the real Deacon. And the real Jean."

"I dunno."

"Just let me give you a call tomorrow around, say, five? I promise, it'll be fun."

I can hear the front door open. It must be Jean. I have to go.

Well . . . if people are insulting Jean, I need to stand up for her. "Okay. Sure."

"Great. This is a landline, right?"

"Yeah."

"And you are eighteen years old, right? Wink, wink?"

He actually says "wink, wink."

"Yes."

"And you—"

I hear voices in the front hall. I suddenly realize Jean is not alone. She sounds upset.

"I have to go." I hang up and rush to see what the commotion is about.

My grandmother is there, which is kind of a relief. But in the doorway stands a middle-aged man in checked pants and a polo shirt.

"I told you, I'm perfectly fine," Jean snaps at the stranger. "I was just a little overcome by the heat. I would thank you to leave me alone."

"Ma'am, I just wanted to make sure—"

Jean turns and notices me. "Deacon, I am going to go lie down. Please escort this gentleman off our property."

"With pleasure."

I wait until Jean is out of the room, then stomp toward the guy. I expect him to back off. To my surprise, he stands his ground.

"Are you her grandson?" he asks.

"Leave." I make my voice all low and scary. He ignores me.

"I'm Vincent Durmont. I'm the manager over at the Pines golf course."

Why is he telling me this? "Please get off my porch." I need to go look in on Jean. Make sure she's okay.

The guy still doesn't budge. "Young man, your grand-mother was wandering across the eighth fairway earlier."

"It's a public course." But mentally, I start to worry. The golf course is at least a mile away. And what was she doing out there? Jean never goes for walks.

"She was very nearly struck by a golf ball," Durmont

continues. "I don't have to tell you how dangerous that can be, especially to a woman of her age." He smiles the sad little smile people give you when complaining about your behavior. Or your grandmother's.

"I . . . I'll ask her to be more careful, Mr. Durmont."

He nods. "I only bring this up because I'm worried about her safety. I'd hate for her to accidentally be injured."

"Thank you for your concern." I place a hand on his shoulder and gently guide him out of the doorway and down off the porch. "I'll make sure she's more cautious in the future."

I wait until he's gone.

Why the hell was she wandering out at the golf course? That's very strange. And worrying.

Kind of like how Jean sometimes doesn't notice traffic signals or other drivers. Or how she didn't remember who Elijah was. Or left the sink running.

She's just getting old.

Except she's not that old. Not really. Not nearly as old as some of the women from dance class.

Maybe something's wrong.

Should I . . . talk to her doctor? What would I say? And what if he wanted to run tests on her or something?

What if they wanted to keep her?

This is stupid. What do I care what some golf pro thinks?

Distracted and maybe a little afraid, I kick the downspout.

With a loud, rotten, creaking noise, it falls to the ground, followed by half the gutter.

And from inside the house I hear Jean yelling.

"Deacon Locke! Did you make this mess in the kitchen?"

I need to talk to someone.

"No, operator, I'm trying to call Amsterdam. Yes, the Netherlands. I'll hold . . .

"Yes, hello . . . sorry, do you speak English?

"I'll hold.

"Yes, I'm trying to call the Trocadero Hotel in Amsterdam . . .

"Yes.

"Hi, yes, do you speak English? Um . . . *Ik ben op, uh, zoek naar het Trocadero Hotel te bellen* . . .

"*Ja.*

"Yes, hello, do you speak English? I'm trying to reach Mr. Deacon Locke Senior. No, I don't know which room number.

"I'll hold.

"Oh. When did he check out? I see. Did he leave a forwarding . . .

"I see. Thank you anyway."

It's Friday evening, and I'm helping Jean with the dishes (in Jean's world, a dishwasher is something lazy people own).

"I had the car washed today," twitters Jean, as she passes me a stack of dirty plates. "I know you're taking Soraya out tomorrow. Never hurts to make a good impression."

"Mmm." Funny, my date tomorrow is not the biggest worry on my mind. Right now, I have to do something unpleasant, and I'm kind of dreading it.

I have to tell Jean that I'm worried about her.

"So do you have enough money, Deacon? I know you never want to take anything from me, but I know the cost of things has gone up. You want to impress this girl. Take her somewhere nice."

I stand there with my arms elbow-deep in dishwater, wishing there was some way I could fast-forward what I'm about to do.

"Jean, graduation is in a couple of weeks."

She beams at me. "I'm so proud of you. You'll forgive me if I start bawling, right?"

I dry my hands and attempt to smile. "And I guess I'll be moving out in August. So I was wondering . . . are you going to be okay here alone?"

Her smile instantly vanishes. For a long time she just stares.

"It was that golfer, wasn't it? He made you think I can't take care of myself, didn't he?"

Yes, I feel like an ass. "It's not that. . . ."

"Never trust a man who wears plaid."

"It's not about the golfer." Not just about that, any- way. "I'm just wondering if you've ever thought about selling this place. It's not in the greatest shape, I mean, the gutter fell down all by itself yesterday. And maybe things would be easier if you moved into a condo or something." A place where you wouldn't have to drive as much and maybe people could keep an eye on you.

"Deacon Locke, your grandfather built this house with his own two hands."

"You told me he bought it at an auction when some guy defaulted on his mortgage."

She looks at me sternly. "And he signed the papers with his own two hands. Listen, would you? Look, I know I haven't been as swift as in the past. But Deacon, I'm not ready for the body farm just yet. You let me do things at my own pace. You've got bigger things to worry about.

When's your freshman orientation again?"

She's trying to change the subject. And it's tempting to let her. "Jean . . ."

The phone rings. She answers it. I hope she'll finish the call quickly, so we can finish this discussion.

That's a lie. I hope she talks forever so we won't have to.

"Locke residence . . . yes, he is . . . whom may I say is calling? I see."

She holds the phone to her shoulder and looks at me questioningly. "It's some gentleman who says he's supposed to interview you for the radio?"

Shit, not now. "It's about that stupid clip on the internet. I'd forgotten about this."

"Aha! So I'm not the only one who's not as sharp as they should be, hmm?" She hands the phone to me before I can object. "No bad words."

"But . . ."

She's left the room.

EIGHTEEN

SORAYA SITS ACROSS FROM ME IN ONE OF THE nicest seafood restaurants in Fayetteville. The fish is always fresh. Even in Arkansas.

She hasn't said much since we left the theater, and her normally dark face is kind of pale. I think this date is getting off to a very bad start.

"Soraya, I want to apologize again for that movie."

She folds her napkin. "No, really, it's okay."

"The name threw me. *Missing My Lady.* I thought it was a romantic comedy."

She smiles thinly. "Not exactly."

No, not at all. Especially that scene with the straight razor. I'm going to have nightmares.

"Soraya . . ."

"It's okay, Deacon. I haven't seen a horror movie in years. Sometimes it's good to let out a scream."

"Yeah. Sorry about that, too."

We sit there silently. I obsessively take sips of my water.

She's bored. I'm boring her. I actually have a date with Soraya and I'm not being entertaining.

Jason would be a lot better at this. So would Elijah. Hell, so would a lump of pine tar.

The waiter, thankfully, arrives with a plate of bread. He takes out his order pad, then stops. He looks at me, then smiles.

"You're that guy. The guy with the grandma." He grins as if he's just made an amazing deduction.

"Uh . . ."

"Dude, I love that clip."

I have no idea how to respond to that. "May we move to another table?" springs to mind.

"I'm getting you guys some appetizers, on me!" He vanishes before I can ask for another glass of water.

For the first time since the movie, Soraya is smiling. "I forgot I was out with a famous guy."

Across the restaurant, I see our waiter at the kitchen door. A cook has joined him. Our server excitedly points to our table.

"It's weird, Soraya. Why are people so interested in those stupid clips?"

She shrugs. "The world is an ugly and hateful place a lot of times. Maybe the sight of a guy dancing with his grandmother shows that there's some good left in society."

I ponder this. "I don't think that's it."

"Well, maybe it's because you two made such a cute couple."

I'm not sure that's it either, but I do take note that she described me as cute. Sort of.

"Whatever it is, I hope it ends soon. Some radio station actually interviewed me yesterday. How desperate are they?"

"You're kidding! When does it air?"

"Monday, I think." I suddenly realize that Soraya is impressed by this. "I'll, um, find out. Let you know." 'Cause, well, I'm going to be on the radio. Unlike Jason.

Her smile is wider now. "You know, they were talking about you at my school too. My friends were impressed when I told them I knew you."

"And taught me everything I know about dancing."

She laughs. The waiter arrives with some shrimpy snacks and takes our order. He's not very subtle when he snaps a picture of me with his phone. I think it's time to take the focus off Deacon for a bit.

"So I guess we're both graduating in a couple of weeks."

"Yes, and let me tell you, it can't get over soon enough. My parents are driving me nuts, wanting to invite every one of my relatives out. Hell, there was even talk about flying my grandma in from Lebanon. I mean, that's all I need, thirty family members in town so they can watch me cross the stage for ten seconds."

"It might be fun." You know. Having more than one person at your graduation.

"Meh. So how about you? Are you and Jean doing anything crazy for graduation night?"

I'm just starting to kind of not enjoy being thought of as a grandma's boy. "I dunno. I don't have much of an extended family. I did hear from my aunt Karen for the first time in forever. She sent me a card and said she'd take me out for my first tattoo whenever I wanted."

Soraya bursts into laughter, so I pretend I was joking.

But then she stops smiling.

"Hey, Deacon? Can I ask you a question?"

"Sure." Of course, that would be my answer to any request from her.

She glances around, as if to make sure our waiter isn't secretly filming us. "I know you moved a lot. But I haven't. I've lived in Fayetteville my whole life and, and I haven't really enjoyed it, but . . . God, I'm going to sound dumb."

"No you're not." I'm a little surprised at how kind and soothing my voice sounds.

"It's just that . . . my parents have always been kind of strict, with the curfew and the religious school and stuff. But they've always been there for me. And they're really not that bad, they encouraged me with dancing and music and everything. But now, suddenly, I'm going to be living on campus. Five whole miles from home, but it seems like a thousand. I won't know anyone and sometimes I just feel like I'm going to get to college and freak out. And I know that's stupid because I'm an adult, but the idea of moving out really scares the hell out of me."

I'm stunned. "Wow."

She hangs her head. "Lame, huh?"

"What? No! I mean, it's just I thought you were one of those people who could handle anything. Hell, I was about to ask you for advice about starting college."

I totally wasn't, but I had to say something.

"Look, Soraya, I've moved a lot. Most of the time with less than a day's notice. But there's good things about starting over. New people, new stuff to do, clean record with the local cops . . . well, you get the picture. I think when we start school, we're both going to find great things. And not just because Big Eddie needs an enforcer in the warehouse district."

She breaks down giggling. "I'm sorry. I know I shouldn't laugh."

But I'm laughing too. "You should. I never realize how ridiculous my life sounds until I try to tell someone about it."

"Maybe a change will be good for you too. Are you going to summer orientation?"

"Um . . . yes." I'm not sure, actually. I know I have a letter somewhere telling me where to report and when. Kind of like the one my grandfather got at one time. I have a feeling his orientation was a lot harder.

"You know, I guess that means we only have three months until we have to start acting like adults."

"We have to be adults in college? Has Hollywood been lying to me this whole time?"

She starts laughing again. "I never knew you were so funny."

"Neither did I, actually."

"Well, Deacon, looks like we have the summer to try to have some fun. You with me?"

"Yes!" That sounds way too enthusiastic, so I try to play it off as a joke by holding out my hand for a shake.

But she just takes my hand. And holds it, with a half smile on her face.

Then our waiter shows up to refill our drinks and the moment ends.

Still . . .

It's nearly midnight. After eating our fish and posing for a group shot with our server and some guys from the kitchen, Soraya asked if I'd like to go for a walk. My answer was predictable. We ended up wandering all over downtown Fayetteville. We stopped for ice cream, watched a little concert in the park, and talked.

We both did. In fact, I think I talked more than Soraya. Maybe it's because she's a polite listener. But it could be because I'm more at ease with her.

"And then Jean totally clobbered the guy with her purse. Went down like a sack of hammers. For a minute I thought I was going to have to bail a second family member out of jail."

Soraya rolls her eyes, but I can tell she thinks the story is amusing. Regrettably, we come upon a familiar car parked on the street near the movie theater. It's hers.

"I guess this is good night, Deacon. Let me know when your radio interview will be on."

"I will."

We stand there looking at each other for a moment. The light from a nearby streetlight makes her dark eyes sparkle.

And it suddenly occurs to me that maybe she's waiting for me to kiss her.

It's the end of a date, aren't you supposed to? But was this a date? I mean, it was, but was it really? And what if I start to bend down and she backs away? Damn this height!

Soraya solves my problem by reaching up and gently pressing the back of my neck. I lean forward and she pecks my cheek. "I had fun."

"Me too."

As I watch her drive off, I finally admit to myself that just maybe my interest in Soraya may not be totally and completely one-sided.

Maybe. I could be misreading things. But I choose to believe I'm not. And I choose to believe that starting college with Soraya is going to be a wonderful, wonderful thing.

Checking to make sure that girl from the movie isn't following me, I skip back to the lot where I parked Jean's car.

NINETEEN

JEAN AND I SIT AT THE BREAKFAST TABLE BEFORE school on Monday, listening to our satellite radio. It was a gift from Dad shortly before he left for Europe, and we've turned it on for the first time so we can hear the Oklahoma station.

> *Mike: This is Madcap Mike Myron in the morning. Hello, rockers! It's 7:01 in the a.m., and I hope you remember to call in sick next week, because Lady Gaga will be playing at the BOK Center this Saturday! Stay tuned for how you can win tickets.*
> *(Brief musical interlude, presumably one of Ms. Gaga's songs)*

Mike: Now we have a special treat this morning. For those of you following us on Twitter and Facebook, you've probably seen the footage of Mr. Deacon Locke, a high school senior from Fayetteville, Arkansas. Welcome, Deacon.

(Silence)

Mike: Deacon? Are you there?

Me: Yes.

Mike: Well, say hi to the folks, Deacon!

Me: Hello.

Mike: (clears throat) Now, Deacon recently achieved notoriety when—get this—he invited his grandmother, Jean, to his senior prom. Deacon, I have to say, this is a bit of an unusual arrangement. You'd think someone that good-looking could find a date their own age.

Me: Thanks, but—

Mike: I'm talking about your grandma! Yowza! (inappropriate sound effects). I tell you, my granny Myron was never that good-looking. Course, I only got to see her on visiting days, and that orange jumpsuit wasn't flattering. Now Deacon, is it true that Grandma Jean was the one who taught Elvis to move his hips like that?

(Clip of Elvis singing "That's All Right Mama")

Me: I'm hanging up now.

Mike: C'mon, it's all in good fun. By the way, listeners, have you seen a picture of this kid? I swear, this boy's so tall he once made a slam dunk by dropping the ball! I don't want to start any rumors, but the last time this guy went swimming in Scotland, there was a Loch Ness Monster panic.

(Labored bagpipe music)

Mike: So seriously, Deacon, what's the story behind you and your grandma?

Me: Well, my grandmother didn't get to attend her own prom. My grandfather was in Vietnam at the time.

Mike: Get out! You know, my grandpa tried to sign up for military duty, but they turned him down. And he wore his purdiest dress and everything. Go figure. Now, Deacon, it was sweet of you to take your grandmother and all, but let's be honest. Are you sure there wasn't some lucky girl or other hominid female you would have liked to have gone to the dance with? C'mon, just between you and me . . . and all my listeners.

Me: Your listeners? But I heard they were both out of town.

(Pause. Recorded female voice: Oh no he di'n't!)

Me: Just messing with you. Seriously, I know someone who does the same job you do.

Mike: Um . . .

197

Me: My laptop.

Mike: Ain't you the funny guy. But let's be serious. . . .

Me: Sirius? I thought you weren't allowed to say that word.

(Rim shot)

Mike: Well, I can see when I'm outclassed. Deacon, thank you for being on our show. If you'd like to see Deacon and Jean in action on the dance floor, check out our webpage. And if you'd like a date with Deacon's grandma, call 1-800 . . .

Me: Hey!

Mike: Just messing with you. And, Deacon, as a way of saying thanks, we'd like to send Jean a box set of Tony Bennett Sings Tupac's Greatest Hits *on eight-track. We're also sending you a brand-new Cyborg 500 cell phone, courtesy of Sooner Cellular, your hometown wireless dealer. Stop in today and sign up for a plan that's right for you!*

I lean over and turn off the radio. Jean stares at me over her cup of coffee. I smile sheepishly.

Jean picks up the box containing the cell phone that the radio station overnighted to us.

"I guess he was just joking about those Tony Bennett tapes."

"Sorry, Jean. Do you want the phone?"

She passes it to me. "No, Deacon, something tells me you're going to need it."

I sit next to Soraya on the bench in front of the cellular store. She called me after school to congratulate me on the interview. When I told her about my new phone, she offered to take me out here so I could activate it.

That part was fun. But now she's insisting on setting me up with a social media site. I could do without that.

"And when's your birthday?"

"March eleventh. Seriously, what's the point of this?"

She doesn't look up from my phone. "It's a good way to keep in touch with your friends. Especially when you graduate and you won't see them as much."

I'm not convinced. "I prefer to stay in contact the old-fashioned way. Next year I'm going to take a photo of every meal I eat, and when I get them developed I'll drive to my friends' houses and show them off."

Soraya ignores me. "Help me fill this part out. What kind of music do you like?"

"What do you call the stuff Madcap Mike plays?"

"I dunno, Top Forty?"

"Yeah, anything but that."

She keeps entering information. I stretch to see what she's doing, but she hides the screen. "Almost done. Now we just need some pictures. Smile!"

"Huh?" Too late.

She shows me the photo and grins. "What do you think?"

"You can see right up my nose."

"Everyone can see up your nose. Let's try again. Smile big. No, try not to grimace. Oh, good grief."

Suddenly, she wraps her arm around my neck. She stretches up so our faces are on the same level and snaps a selfie of us both.

Now there's a real smile. On both of us, actually.

"Soraya? Can you set this as my . . . what do you call it?"

"Profile pic? Sure." She hands me the phone.

My online persona is kind of sad. I have one photo (though it's with an amazingly pretty girl). I have one friend (Soraya) and one pending (Elijah). One "like" (Madcap Mike of KZAR, Tulsa).

When Jean was my age, her online profile wasn't this pathetic, and they didn't even have electricity back then. I remember that photo of her, hanging out with her big group of friends. I'd like to be able to show off a picture like that one day.

"Soraya? You're not teaching a class today, are you?"

She shakes her head.

"Want to go do something? Maybe see what's happening on campus?"

"That sounds like fun. Actually, I think Jason's band

is playing at Java Jim's. We could stop by."

"Or . . . maybe we could visit the pig again."

We stand. As I move to slip the phone in my pocket, it vibrates. Elijah has approved my friend request. And uploaded a photo, it seems. No, a video.

It's the clip. The one of me and Jean dancing. And another link to my radio interview. Thanks, pal.

As we get into Soraya's car, I feel the phone buzz in my pocket again. And again.

I'm more interested in my real-life companion, but I can't help but worry.

The sun is going down when we pull up in front of my house. Thanks to my fancy new phone, I was able to call Jean and tell her I was going to be late. Who knew?

Soraya slurps the dregs of the milk shake I bought her. I got one for myself too, but I couldn't even finish half of it. How does she stay so skinny? Must be the dancing.

"Hey, Deacon? Send me that picture you took of me by the fountain."

I hate to admit it, but I'm falling into the dark and addictive trap of taking pictures with my phone. Especially when they're of Soraya. Or of the two of us when we have to squeeze together for us to both be in the shot.

I fumble with the device, trying to remember how

to send a picture. Then a message pops up that kind of throws me.

"Something wrong?" asks Soraya.

"It's nothing. Just a few friend requests."

She looks over my shoulder. Well, not over my shoulder. No one can do that. Around it. "Wow. A hundred twenty is more than a few."

She's right. Some of them are people I know: Clara, Kelli, and Hunt. And then there's people from my school who I've had classes with. Also, disturbingly enough, our waiter from the seafood place.

But many of these names I don't know. Some of them from out of state.

There are also a lot of comments on the video Elijah posted.

ALEXIS: UR TOTES ADORBS, DEACON

SARAH: HOTNESS!

MANDY: DO YOU EVER MAKE IT TO LITTLE ROCK? I'D LOVE TO GO CLUBBING WITH YOU SOME NIGHT.

JENNIE: SWOONWORTHY!

MANDY (A DIFFERENT ONE): I WISH MORE GUYS WERE THIS NICE.

SIMON: DEACON, DOES YOUR GRANDMOTHER HAVE A SOCIAL MEDIA ACCOUNT? I CAN'T SEEM TO FIND IT. MY NAME IS SIMON. I'M 70 YEARS OLD AND I ALSO ENJOY DANCING. IF YOU WOULD BE SO KIND AS TO ASK HER TO DROP ME A NOTE . . .

I turn to Soraya to make a joke, but she suddenly looks frowny.

"You're certainly popular with the ladies."

She's right. Almost all the requests are from girls.

And if I'm not mistaken, this makes Soraya uncomfortable.

"Um, I'll just delete those."

"No!" She clears her throat. "I mean, don't. You and Jean are popular. You should enjoy this." She begins toying with her hair. "You're a good dancer. The clip is cute. It's only natural that people would want to get to know you. Of course, I knew you before all this happened, but hey, whatever."

Oh my God, she's a little jealous.

That's kind of awesome.

I turn off the phone. "Losers. You wanna come in? Say hi to Jean?"

"I'd love to, but I'm going to be late as it is. Good night, Deacon."

Again, that smiley pause where I wonder if I should kiss her or shake her hand or what. I just awkwardly climb out of the car.

As she drives away, I make a promise to myself that if we ever go out again, I'll kiss her.

And then she'll slap you and you'll never see her again.

That won't happen.

It could, though.

She likes me. Why not show her I like her?

Because she only tolerates you. Don't make an ass of yourself.

Shut up!

You shut up!

Wanna make me?

THE PRECIOUS!

It doesn't help my confused state when my phone buzzes with another friend request from a stranger. Shaking my head, I go inside.

Jean's still up, sitting on the living room couch. I'm glad. After all the weird happenings this week, I could really use an hour or so of normalcy with my grandmother.

"Deacon! Guess what!" She jumps to her feet. "We're going to be on TV!"

Wow.

TWENTY

THAT WEEKEND, JEAN AND I SIT IN THE BACK ROOM of Fayetteville's only TV station. They call it the green-room, but it's actually painted beige. A young woman has just applied our makeup.

I really do not care for wearing makeup.

"Deacon, isn't this exciting? I've never been on television!"

I'm not really sure why this happened. Jean said she was contacted by some guy named Jeffery Berkowitz, who's the producer of a local show called *Fayetteville Today*. He said they like to interview local celebrities and wanted Jean and me to be on the show.

Jean was super excited. Me, not as much. But maybe it'll impress Soraya.

Stick that in your guitar hole, Jason.

"Just wait until Peggy hears about this! Maybe she'll finally shut up about being in that life insurance commercial."

Apparently high school never actually ends.

"So how do I look?" Jean asks, touching her hair.

The truth is, she looks great. She looks like she's in her forties. She looks young and vibrant.

"You look wonderful."

There's a rap at the door and Berkowitz enters. "Hey, you two, are you about ready?"

"And waiting!" chirps Jean. "Is there anything we need to know?"

"You'll do fine," the producer replies. He has an odd way of talking, always looking right over your shoulder. Every time we have a conversation, I get the impression there's someone sneaking up behind me. "Just talk to Pamela, not the camera. And relax as much as possible. Think of her as your friend."

Yet another "friend" I've made this past week. I should run for office.

A man with headphones ducks his head through the door. "We ready to go?"

Berkowitz leads us to the stage. It's set up like

someone's living room, except for the lack of ceiling, the lights, the cameras, and the thirty or so chairs where the audience sits.

Pamela Benton, the host, is already in her spot. She's an attractive black woman, and she smiles when she sees us.

"Please, have a seat," she says, indicating two comfy chairs.

She talks to the man in headphones for a moment, then turns to me.

"Don't be nervous. You'll be fine."

I actually was feeling surprisingly calm, but her comment makes me wonder if I look nervous, which unsettles me.

The director guy begins counting down like he's about to launch a rocket or something. Music starts to play.

Pamela apparently has permission to look right at the camera. "Welcome back to *Fayetteville Today*. This morning I'm pleased to introduce Jean Locke and her grandson, Deacon. Welcome."

"We're so glad to be here, Pamela," says Jean, beaming.

"Hi," I say, unsure of where I'm supposed to be looking.

"Jean and Deacon recently became an internet

phenomenon when Deacon escorted Jean to his senior prom."

On a large monitor behind us, I hear the familiar soundtrack of the infamous YouTube clip. I try to smile.

"Aren't they adorable?"

The audience seems to agree. Everyone applauds.

"Jean, I understand that you were unable to attend your own prom?"

Jean looks wistful. "Yes, when I was Deacon's age, I was already engaged to his grandfather, Howard."

Behind us, a large photo of Grandpa Howard appears on the screen. He's in his dress uniform, but he still looks more awkward than macho. Just like his grandson.

"Howard was called up to serve his country, and was wounded in Vietnam. I was unable to attend my senior dance, with him stationed in Southeast Asia."

I feel somewhat uncomfortable about her sharing this story with the world. Pamela reaches over and pats Jean's hand. "So tell me, Deacon, what inspired you to take your grandmother to prom? I mean, surely a guy like you could have had his choice of any girl at your school."

Now is not the time to tell the world about Deacon, the gigantic awkward boy who never had a date. But how can I make myself not sound pathetic?

Ah, hell, this is TV. I lie.

"Well, Pamela, I wouldn't say there were a *lot* of girls I could have asked out." Zero is a number, right? "But when I realized that Jean had missed her special day, how could I not ask her? I mean, I wasn't seeing anyone, and here was my chance to take a very beautiful lady to the dance." I break the rule and face the audience. "Am I right?"

The audience bursts out with applause. Pamela does that thing women do, where she places her fingers at the juncture of her neck and chest, to show that she's touched.

"Deacon, that's about the sweetest thing I've heard. Jean, how did you react when he asked you?"

She laughs. "I was surprised, to say the least. I tried to get him to take one of the girls who are always chasing him, but he wouldn't have it."

The audience claps for a little bit.

"So did you two enjoy yourselves? Jean, was this dance what you'd been expecting?"

"It was even better. I'm lucky to have a grandson as thoughtful as Deacon."

The audience says "awww."

"And Deacon, did you have fun? I'd say that you

did." Again, the little clip plays.

"I had a fine time. We went with a couple of my friends." I face the camera again and wink. "Hey, Clara and Eli."

"Is there anyone *else* you'd like to say hi to?" Pamela's grin is so cheesy I think I'm missing something. Then I glance at the display and realize they're projecting my profile pic. The one of me and Soraya, leaning in close together, smiling.

"Oh, um, that's . . ." *What do I say? What do I say?* "That's my friend Soraya."

Jean snorts. *"Friend."*

The audience laughs. Thanks, Jean.

"Now, your graduation is in two weeks, is that right? What are your plans for after school?"

"Staying here in town, U of A. Go, Razorbacks."

Everyone cheers.

Pamela beams. "Well, Deacon, something tells me that you won't be taking your grandmother to your first college dance. And how about you, Jean? Any plans for the future?"

Jean opens her mouth to answer. But then she stops. Freezes. She looks at the audience, then at Pamela, as if she's not sure who she's supposed to be addressing. And then she looks at me, a plea in her eyes.

I quickly turn to our host. "She's got all sorts of things planned. Karate lessons, painting, more dance, maybe turning my room into a studio. Right, Grandma?"

That's the first time I've ever not called her by her first name. I'm not sure why.

Jean nods and smiles weakly.

"Aren't they great?" says Pamela, oblivious to Jean's confusion. "Ladies and gentlemen, Jean and Deacon Locke!"

I'm too concerned about Jean to enjoy the applause. Which is too bad, because I think it's something I could really get used to.

"And cut!" says headphones guy. Pamela turns to us.

"Thank you so much for coming. I hope you enjoyed yourselves. This segment will air Tuesday at eight."

Berkowitz escorts us back to the beige room to collect our things. We're presented with a little gift bag of *Fayetteville Today* trinkets.

Jean smiles as soon as we're alone. "That was a hoot and a half. You handled yourself well out there. I mean, move over, Jack Nicholson!"

"Jean, are you feeling okay?"

"Never better. Would you like to get something to eat? I'm starving."

"Sure."

Again, she just went dizzy for a moment. I'm sure that's all. Those stage lights were so bright.

But I'm going to make an appointment with her doctor this week. Just in case.

TWENTY-ONE

IT'S IMPOSSIBLE TO MAKE A CALL WHEN YOUR PHONE keeps buzzing in your hand. There's a constant stream of alerts: friend requests, chat requests, emails . . . ever since that radio interview aired, it's like I'm carrying around a swarm of angry bees. I'd turn the thing off, except sometimes Soraya texts me and I can't risk missing that.

I glance at the screen. More messages from strangers.

Meghan: Deacon, if ur ever interested in dancing with someone younger, give me a call

Erin: Awesomesauce!

Meredith: Why can't more guys be like you?

Savannah: Hope to see you on campus next year!

Kandis: <3

Brian: I like to dance too, Deacon. I'm just throwing
that out there.

I'm about to give up and use the wall phone, when
my device jolts again.

Soraya. She's calling me.

I adjust my hair, check my teeth in the reflection
from the fridge, and answer.

"Hello." Did that sound desperate? I think I sounded
desperate there.

"Hey, Deacon! You busy right now? There's a little
street fair going on downtown and I wanted to know
if . . ."

"Sure!" Wait, what if she wasn't asking me to go?
What if she was going to ask me something else? Talk
about presumptuous!

"Great! Meet me by the fountain."

"I'll be there in two minutes!"

"Um . . . could you make it half an hour? I just got
home."

"Yes! See you then!"

I stand stock-still, frozen with indecision. Do I have
time for a shower? Shave? Haircut?

Shit, I don't even have a car.

"Jean?" I holler into the next room. "Can I use the
car tonight?"

"Are you meeting Soraya?"

How did she know that? "Um, yeah."

"Have a good time."

Ten minutes later I pull out of the driveway, riddled with joy and fear.

It's only when I'm halfway to town that I remember why I had my phone out in the first place.

I was going to call Jean's doctor about her confusion and memory loss.

I'll call him tomorrow.

I gaze over the crowd of fairgoers, trying to locate Soraya. It's a good three minutes after I said I'd meet her, and I'm starting to panic. I try to calm my nerves, rationalizing that she hasn't given up on me already or been kidnapped by a group of Russian sailors.

There. Though the streets are packed, Soraya stands in her own little bubble, casually leaning against a food stand, idling scanning the crowd.

And when she sees me, her eyes open just a little wider. And she smiles.

I'm standing in front of her in less than two seconds (sorry, buddy).

And just like that, I take her hands. Both her hands. I'm holding both her hands and looking into her eyes, and we're both smiling.

"Hi."

"Hi."

"Hi."

"Hi."

Still smiling and still holding hands. The meteor can come for me now. I'm happy.

"Soraya, would you like to . . ."

"Yeah. Let's."

We walk off, hand in hand.

One month ago, I would have been too afraid to take the initiative like that. I wouldn't have insisted on trying to win a stuffed pony for a girl at a rigged ball-toss game. I wouldn't have let her drag me to the bumper cars, even though I had to ride kind of sidesaddle to fit in the cab. There's no way I would have agreed to go in the haunted house, especially when the woman painted on the door looked just like the girl from that movie.

And one month ago, there was no way I would have asked a girl to ride the Ferris wheel with me. And when the ride stopped, with just the two of us sitting thirty feet in the air, with the noise and laughter and smells of the crowd wafting up to us, there's no way I would have leaned over, touched her chin, and kissed her.

But that was a month ago.

✳ ✳ ✳

The sun has gone down, but I can't see the stars through the glaring electric lights. Soraya and I wind our way through the crowd, eating our little plates of funnel cakes. She has a small smear of powdered sugar on the bridge of her nose.

It takes a great deal of effort and self-control not to whip out my phone and record every detail of this . . . date. It's a date. And it's not our first one.

There's a bandstand nearby and a painfully bad country trio begins to torture "Okie from Muskogee."

"I used to like that song," I say with regret.

Soraya smiles at me. "Want to dance? Show me that you didn't forget everything I taught you?"

I dump the rest of my funnel cake into a barrel and take her hand to lead her onto the dance floor. Dance patch of grass and dirt.

"See!" shouts a girl at my elbow. "I told you Deacon's girlfriend was real."

I recognize the voice, which is odd, since it's not Kelli. I turn to find Clara staring at me with a smug grin.

Elijah is next to her. He's wearing a hat made out of those long balloons. "I never said she wasn't real, Clara. I said she couldn't possibly be as good-looking as Deacon made her out to be." He glances at Soraya, then winks at me. "Guess I was wrong on all counts."

Well, so much for my brief bout of confidence, as well

as my short friendship with Elijah. But Soraya just smiles.

"This is Clara and Elijah," I say before Elijah can speak again.

Elijah tips his balloons at Soraya. *"Ah, shantee, mi zi bo play!"*

"Is that French?" asks Soraya.

"No, just gibberish. Are you guys going to dance? Did you know Deacon's a really good dancer?"

Soraya chuckles. "I'd heard that, yes."

We eventually disentangle ourselves from Elijah and move toward the music.

"Sorry about that."

She shakes her head. "Nothing to apologize for."

The band stops butchering a song with a guitar and starts truly mutilating one on the fiddle. Soraya and I assume the position.

God, those eyes.

"Deacon? I'm enjoying this."

"Me too. I'm glad you called me tonight."

She sucks her lips into her mouth for a moment. "No. I mean, I'm enjoying *this*."

I know exactly what she means. "You know, I'm excited about going to college with you."

I suddenly want to punch myself. That was really fast-forwarding things. But she smiles.

"Me too, Deacon. I feel like such a kindergartner, but

I'm glad I'll already have a friend on campus." She gets a mischievous look on her face. "Provided your fans let me have any time with you."

I shake my head. "That's old news. Seriously. Can we talk about something else?"

"Fine." She pulls my head toward hers and kisses me.

I'm so pleasantly surprised that I forget to close my eyes.

Which is unfortunate, because I notice someone on the edge of the crowd taking our picture. And it's not a kid. It's a grown man with a camera.

It's after midnight when I get home. Jean's long asleep. I can't wipe the stupid grin off my face.

Maybe it's pathetic that I never kissed a girl until I was eighteen, but I don't care. Soraya was worth waiting for. And apparently she feels the same way, with all that talk about getting together when we're at college.

God, Soraya and I alone together in the dorms.

I'm too excited to go to bed. And too wired to look at the stars. Even though I've gorged myself on fair fare, I decide to check for leftovers in the fridge.

Sure enough, Jean has placed all the food from dinner inside: chicken, baked beans, bread, dirty dishes, half a cup of coffee, the plastic centerpiece from the table, used napkins, and the dish soap.

I close the door, suddenly not hungry, and no longer happy. I press my forehead against the refrigerator's warm, impersonal exterior and try to conquer the growing fear in my gut.

"Yes, my name's Deacon, and I'm trying to schedule a checkup for my grandmother. . . .

"I'll hold.

"No, not for me, for my grandmother, Jean.

"No, a woman. J-E-A-N.

"Just a checkup. I know she went last month!

"Sorry, I'm not trying to be rude. I'd just like someone to talk to her. She's getting a little forgetful and I . . .

"No, not an emergency. I know where urgent care is, we don't need that. I'd just like to speak with a doctor. . . .

"That's a month from now! Can't you see her sooner?

"She doesn't need to go to the emergency room!

"Fine, we'll be there. Call me if something opens up sooner."

TWENTY-TWO

ShadeeLady: Miss u
DeaconLocke: Miss you more

YES, I HAVE OFFICIALLY BECOME THAT GUY. I DON'T care. Soraya is texting me and there's no nicer feeling in the world.

Actually, there are a lot of nicer feelings, but only when she's in the room with me.

Unfortunately, I'm standing in the school commons and class is about to start. But I'll see Soraya again tonight.

"Hey, Deacon?" It's Clara. She approaches me in that quiet, supplicating way of hers. I have no idea how she ended up with loud, crazy Elijah. But then again, I have no idea how I ended up with Soraya.

"Hi, Clara."

"Good picture of you in the paper yesterday."

"Thanks." Then I realize I have no idea what she's talking about. "What picture?"

She tilts her head. "You didn't see it? Look!"

She pulls out her phone and brings up an article from the *Arkansas Times*.

There's a photo of the dancers at the fair we'd been to. And right in the front, right in the middle, there's me and Soraya. Kissing.

Apparently the guy with the camera hadn't been a stalker.

Local dance celebrity Deacon Locke and his companion enjoy a quiet moment at the Spring Festival. For more pictures and 4-H contest results, click here. . . .

"She seems very nice."

I stare at the photo. Soraya looks good. I never realized how big my ears look in profile. I wonder if she's seen this. I wonder if she feels as impressive as I do right now. I hope so.

"Hey, Deacon? My boss at the hardware store saw this, and, well, I kind of sort of maybe mentioned that we were friends." The sentence almost ends as a question, like I'd disagree with her on that point. "So anyway, he wanted to know if . . . look, he's trying to unload all the winter stuff and he's having a barbecue at the store this Thursday. Do you think you could come?"

"Yeah, I'll stop by."

She just stares at me. "Actually, I told my boss that . . ." She starts to mumble and look at the floor. I kind of have to do the limbo to face her.

"What was that?"

She keeps her head down, but her eyes shyly look upward. "I told him you'd help out."

I really do not feel like spending an afternoon moving boxes of snow shovels or whatever, but Clara looks so nervous.

"Okay. I wish you'd asked me first, but I can give you a hand cooking hot dogs or something for an hour or so."

"Oh, it's nothing like that. He just wanted you to show up and have your picture taken."

"I dunno. . . ."

"Please? And maybe record a little radio commercial for the store. And, um, help judge the lawn-mower races. And . . ."

I cross my arms. "And what?"

"Participate in the toilet-seat toss."

I'm about to think of an excuse, but she bats her eyes at me. "I think Soraya would be impressed."

"Fine. But only for a little bit. And next time I need a miter saw, I expect you to hook me up."

She winks at me and we walk off to class together.

It's the first truly hot day of the year, and about a hundred people mill around in front of C & R Hardware. There's loud music, free food, and a small petting zoo (I don't see Mr. Oinky there, though).

Dozens of people, mostly teens, have gathered on the parking lot, dancing to the hip-hop beat. Soraya and I are in the middle of the crowd. Though we never danced to this sort of music at the Y, Soraya still manages to instruct me, without making it obvious that I don't know what I'm doing.

I'd told Clara I could only stay for an hour, and we've been here three. I'm kind of enjoying myself. Mostly because of Soraya, but also because the DJ keeps mentioning my name and pointing me out. People ask to take my picture. Mr. Branson, the manager, brings us complimentary sodas.

Across the lot I spot Clara. She's wearing her work uniform, which she has sweat through as she struggles to load some boxes into the back of a customer's truck. I glance at Soraya.

"I should probably . . ."

"You should."

Before I can give Clara a hand, the DJ interrupts the song. "This is Alejandro Cooper with KWWW. I'm here at C & R Hardware of Fayetteville. C'mon down and enjoy their spring clearance sale! There's free popcorn and hot dogs, along with dancing sensation Deacon Locke. Deacon, why don't you come up here?"

Everyone is staring at me. Hey, why not? I take Soraya's hand and join the DJ at his little stage.

". . . and mention KWWW and receive five percent off your purchase of lawn furniture. And here's Deacon Locke! Deacon, why don't you give a shout-out to our listeners?"

I shrug, then shout into the mic.

"That's the spirit. And is this your girlfriend?"

I'm suddenly at a horrific loss. I have no idea. I can't say yes, I don't dare assume that. But what if I say no and she's offended? I can't even look to her for help, because she'll know I'm too chicken to just answer.

The DJ is looking at me nervously. Dead air.

"This is Soraya. She taught me everything I know about dancing."

Soraya smiles and leans toward the microphone. "I teach beginning dance at the YMCA. New classes are—"

"That's great! This is Alejandro Cooper, talking with dancer Deacon Locke and his girlfriend. Now let's warm things up with the latest hit by . . ."

I feel a tap on my shoulder. It's Mr. Branson, Clara's boss. He's a stout, bearded man whose clothes seem a size too small.

"Deacon, you're a natural, the crowd loves you. Do you mind if we snap a couple of publicity photos? Just lean against the John Deere there."

I try to position myself in a way so that I'm not in front of Soraya.

"Uh, no, Deacon, just you."

Soraya looks embarrassed as she steps out of the shot. As I try to smile sincerely, I notice two guys standing near the radio station van.

They're a couple of older men, dressed in short-sleeve business shirts and ties. They stand in the shade, whispering to each other. This wouldn't be odd, except they're staring directly at me. It's a little unsettling.

"Mr. Branson, who are those guys over there?"

He's looking at his camera and doesn't appear to hear me. "Perfect. Hey, are you two going to be around in another hour? I'm taking the department managers out to dinner at Shogun Steaks. Could you join us?"

I'm pretty sure that's one of those fancy Japanese places where they throw the knives. I'd really like to see that.

"Sure!" I say. Soraya nods.

"Great! In the meantime, you've got a lawn-mower race to judge!"

"Your public awaits, Deacon." Soraya kisses my cheek.

Feeling confident, I strut toward the line of pedal-powered tractors, where a group of grade school kids is ready to compete. As I turn back to smile at Soraya, I glance toward the radio van.

Those guys are still there. And they're still watching me.

It's nearly seven by the time I finish my duties. Soraya has gone inside the store to freshen up. Mr. Branson is pulling the car around. This was an enjoyable afternoon. I just wish I hadn't eaten all those hot dogs earlier.

"Hey, Deke."

I'm surprised to see that Elijah is here, and more surprised at how sweaty and exhausted he looks.

"Hi! I didn't know you came."

He rubs his eyes with the heels of his hands. "I've been here for hours."

"Didn't see you out dancing."

"Yeah . . . I was afraid Clara was going to hurt herself moving some of those boxes, so I helped her."

Jesus. Clara. I've been here since school let out and

I never even said hi to her, let alone offered to help her with anything.

Elijah suddenly shakes his head rapidly and smiles. "At any rate, I'm glad I caught you. Clara just got news that she got into this junior STEM program through the college. Real competitive. It's kind of a big deal. I'm going to surprise her and take her out to Denny's tonight. You and Soraya want to come? I want to show her how proud we all are."

"Oh, uh." I see Mr. Branson's car parked in front of the store. Soraya has already climbed inside. "The thing is, Mr. Branson asked Soraya and me to have dinner with him."

Elijah's smile slowly expands, though not in a good way. It creeps across his face till he's sort of grimacing. "Really. You're eating with Clara's boss. That's nice."

"Um . . ."

"Funny, Clara has worked here over a year, and he still calls her Carla. But hey, you dance around for a couple of hours and he's your BBF. That's great." His smile is so wide, I almost expect it to wrap around and meet at the back of his head.

Should I feel ashamed? Because I don't. It's not my fault I already had plans. I was here as a favor to Clara, anyway.

Elijah's painful smile suddenly vanishes. "No biggie. You guys have fun."

He starts to walk away.

"Hey, tell Clara congratulations."

He waves to me without turning around.

I should do something. Get Clara a card or a present. But should I do that for someone else's girlfriend? I'll ask Soraya.

In the meantime, I'm looking forward to dinner. Hey, we're obliged to go. One does not say no to the manager of one of the largest home improvement stores in northern Arkansas.

TWENTY-THREE

JEAN'S BEDROOM MIRROR ISN'T TALL ENOUGH FOR me to see my full reflection, but I like what I do see. The black shirt. Black pants. New shoes. Red tie. My hair's kind of reached a nice length, just touching my collar. I smile. I resist the urge to snap a selfie.

Jean looks at me with pride. "I told you it was worth it to have that shirt altered. Fits you like a glove."

She's right. Though it strikes me as kind of pointless. When I wear it next week, it'll be under my graduation robes. Still . . .

Jean sighs. "You're leaving high school. It seems like just yesterday that I was graduating. I remember what my father told me."

"What's that?"

"'Jean, you're good-looking. You'll find a husband.' Girls didn't really go to college back then."

I wrap my arm around her and hug her.

"Deacon," she says when she disengages, "I'm glad you have the opportunities I didn't. I wish you didn't have to take out those loans. I wish I could help you out more. I wish . . ."

"That Dad was coming," I finish for her. She nods. Maybe he's planning on popping in and surprising us.

Maybe I'll get a job as a jockey.

"It doesn't matter. You're going to do great at college. Just remember that *Animal House* was a movie, not a documentary."

Before I can answer, my phone rings. It's that special chime that lets me know that Soraya is calling. Jean recognizes it, and busies herself tidying.

"Hey there!" I say.

There's a long pause. I can hear Soraya's voice, but she's talking to someone else. Did she dial me by accident?

"Deacon? Hey. Listen. I . . ." She sounds nervous. "Look, there's no easy way to say this."

I quickly sit down on Jean's bed. I guess I always knew this was coming.

"I hate to do this," she continues.

She's dumping me. That's got to be it. I've screwed up somehow. Or more likely, she just realizes that she can do better. A lot better. I close my eyes and wait for the sugarcoated kick to the groin.

"Deacon, can you come over for dinner tonight? My parents want to meet you."

I almost laugh. She's not breaking up with me!

Then I'm suddenly back in hell again.

Meet her parents?

Soraya lives in a white, single-story house with lots of well-maintained shrubs. The car I pushed that one time is parked in the driveway, next to an SUV. I stand across the street, clutching a bouquet of grocery-store flowers. I'm still wearing my graduation clothes. I have to make a good impression.

One good thing about being terrified of girls—you never have to meet their dads.

What if he doesn't like me? What if I do something stupid? I mean, that's kind of inevitable, but what if I do something *really* stupid?

God, their family is religious. I don't know anything about their culture. What if I offend them?

It's only when I remember that Jason lives in this neighborhood that I finally get the courage to approach

Soraya's house. I can't risk him seeing me standing here freaking out.

Her mother answers my knock. She's a pretty woman with Soraya's cheeks and eyes. She's wearing a dark red-and-white headscarf. I don't think it's a coincidence that those are the University of Arkansas's colors.

"Deacon! It's so nice to meet you." She has a very slight accent. "Please, come in."

I thrust the flowers at her. "These are for you!"

"They're lovely. Let me just—"

"Mom!" I'm relieved to see Soraya rush in from another room. "I said I'd get the door."

"I didn't want to leave your friend outside. Now come help me put these in some water. Deacon, Soraya's father is on the back porch. Why don't you go ahead outside. We'll meet you in a moment."

I'm hoping that Soraya will insist on going with me, but she follows her mother to the kitchen.

"Sorry," she mouths.

Well. Now I have to meet her father with no backup and no gift in hand. Maybe I should have brought more flowers. No, that's stupid. I should have brought some food. Why didn't I bring some of Jean's potato salad?

I find Mr. Shadee manning a barbecue grill. He's a short, shabby-looking man with a mustache. He's dressed

233

in jeans and a T-shirt, making me feel somewhat ridiculous in my tie. He smiles when he sees me.

"You must be Deacon."

"Yes, sir. I am Deacon."

"Soraya's told us a lot about you. Grab yourself a drink."

"Yes, sir. I will." I pull a can of something from a cooler.

"So you go to Fayetteville High? You play any sports?"

"No, sir." I barely manage to stop myself from apologizing.

"Junior ROTC?"

"No, sir."

He flips a couple of burgers and then shuts the grill. "The reason I ask is that you're standing at rigid attention. You're a guest in my home. At ease. Relax."

"I will, sir."

He smiles behind his mustache. Glancing at the back door, he moves closer to me.

"I understand you're kind of a celebrity. I saw you on TV the other day. Your grandmother seems very sweet."

"Yes. She is."

"I wish Soraya could get to know her own grandmother better, but she lives overseas."

"Yes, sir. She told me that."

He stares at me for another moment. I can tell I'm

not holding up my end of the conversation, but at least I'm able to answer his direct questions.

"You're on the net a lot too. And the radio, the paper . . . I'd actually heard the name Deacon Locke before Soraya ever mentioned you."

"Thank you."

He takes a swallow from his soda and glances at the door again. His face grows serious.

"I'd like to discuss something with you, before the girls come out."

Oh, God, that picture in the paper. Of me kissing his daughter. It hadn't occurred to me that he might have seen it. He's probably pissed. He's going to demand that I leave, that I stop seeing her. Why did I come here?

"You okay?"

"Fine, sir."

He suddenly seems as uncomfortable as me. "This is going to sound kind of ridiculous. And maybe I'm just being an overprotective father. But since my daughter is seeing you, I feel I have to mention it."

He looks back at the house while I try to suppress a smile at the confirmation that Soraya and I are a thing.

"Deacon, you know how the internet is. Something gets said, a photo comes out, a video clip becomes popular . . . I don't have to tell you how many people have watched that little film of you and your grandmother. I guess the point I'm trying to make is that I'm not excited about the idea of Soraya getting caught up in all that. She's my little girl, and people . . . well, they can be unkind. I'd just as soon you didn't include her in all this hubbub."

Strangely, his little speech makes me feel more comfortable. "Mr. Shadee? I know exactly what you mean. There are a lot of idiots out there with laptops. I've heard people say things about Jean that I didn't appreciate. To be honest, I have no idea why any of this is happening, but I have a feeling it's not going to go on very much longer. And the last thing I want is for Soraya to be embarrassed."

He smiles. At that moment, the ladies join us on the porch. Soraya looks at me questioningly. I wink at her.

"Deacon," says Mrs. Shadee, "I hope you brought your appetite."

I join the family at a picnic table. "I could eat."

Now I may not be the most politically correct guy in the world, but I like to think I'm fairly tolerant and open to new ways of doing things. But the Shadees . . . a lot of their customs are strange and foreign to me. Very different from the way we do things at my house.

For instance, their plates and napkins are made of paper, unlike the china dishes Jean insists we use, even when we eat outside. And when Jean has company, she has an elaborate ritual of asking each guest if they'd like a certain dish, and laboriously doling it out, one entrée at a time. Mrs. Shadee, on the other hand, commands me to help myself, and to grab seconds. Soraya's father even hurls a burned burger over the fence to a neighbor's dog.

Somewhere between the coleslaw and ice cream sandwiches, I finally manage to relax. Soraya's parents badger me about my college plans, and when they find out I'm going to stay in Fayetteville, they seem pleased.

Eventually, I have to get going. Soraya walks me to my car.

"I like your new clothes, Deacon. Though I'm sorry you didn't wear that white leisure suit you wore to dance class that one time."

I smile at the memory. "Jean said she accidentally took it outside, doused it with gasoline, and burned it. She said she should have done that when my grandfather first bought it."

We both laugh, though I'm not certain Jean had been joking.

"Well, you look better in this. Black's your color, I think." She flicks my tie.

I glance back at her house to make sure no one is watching, then turn to kiss her.

She's not puckering up.

"So what were you talking about with my dad?"

"Huh?"

"When you two were out on the porch. What did he tell you?" She has an intense, irritated look on her face, and I can't tell if it's me or her dad that's caused it.

"Um, he was just worried about me dragging you into all that internet crap. I told him I'd do my best."

Soraya runs her hand through her long hair, twisting it between her fingers. "I told him not to say anything."

I'm suddenly on alert. "Say anything about what? Soraya, what's going on?"

She smiles, thinly. "Oh, he's just freaking out over nothing. You know how parents are."

"Not really. Talk to me, is something wrong?"

She places her hands on my shoulders. "Nothing, Deacon. Nothing at all to worry about. And I'm sorry to make you come over here, but they'd been bugging me to meet you."

"I had fun. I like them."

"That's the right answer." She pulls my face toward hers and kisses me.

TWENTY-FOUR

YOU EVER REALLY LOOK FORWARD TO SOMETHING, like a vacation or the Lyrid meteor shower, and then when it finally arrives, it doesn't seem real?

That's what it's like with me and graduation. Here it is, my last day of high school ever. The ceremony is tomorrow. And yet, I can't work up any kind of emotion. Maybe it'll all hit me when I move out of Jean's house in August.

In the meantime, I sit in the auditorium with the rest of the senior class. Principal Kznack and the other administrators hand out awards. It's purely a delaying tactic to keep the graduates from going nuts on the last day.

Elijah sits next to me. "Now I don't have any problem going to NWACC. None at all. But Clara, she's still stuck in high school for another year. Makes a man worry."

"It'll be fine," I mumble. How the hell did we end up in the second row? Now I can't slump down and take a nap. Not that there's anything they could do to me anyway, with only thirty minutes left of my public education.

"Easy for you to say, Deacon. I don't have a million online fans."

"Neither do I."

I should have known better. He pulls out his phone and brings up that stupid clip. But I'm right. The clip doesn't have a million likes.

Just 720,013.

"Quiet, Elijah. Kelli's on."

Actually, Kelli hasn't been off the stage since they started handing out the academic awards. At first, she would return to her seat after she received each certificate and recognition, but that started to prove tiresome. She stands onstage, carrying an armload of plaques and papers.

"And finally, the award for the most volunteer hours logged . . . big surprise, Kelli Henshaw!"

The audience unenthusiastically applauds as Kelli finally sits down on my other side, staggering under the weight of her loot. I look at the clock. There's still lots of time until the final bell, and I think that was the last award. The crowd is getting restless. How are they going to fill up the end of the assembly? I hope not with speeches.

Mr. Kznack takes the microphone. "We have one more very special award to give out."

There's a pause. Then the lights lower. To the sides, I see faculty members closing the doors. Up onstage, mysterious, dark figures emerge from the wings.

Elijah's breathing grows rapid. "It's a trap. They're going to arrest someone."

Kelli shushes him.

"I'm serious. This is how they got Dillinger."

I'm straining to see what's happening on the darkened stage. One of the people up there has a large video camera.

The principal speaks. "It comes as no surprise to us that one of our Bulldog family has become quite famous this year."

No. No.

This is not happening.

But it is. The screen at the back of the stage fades from the school logo into the infamous clip of Jean and me at the prom.

"Deacon!" screams someone in the audience.

I sit there sweating as the audience hoots and cheers our performance.

There's loud clapping and laughter when the video ends. Will people not let this die?

The lights come back up. "Deacon, would you please come up here?"

I don't want to. And they can't make me. Whatever little certificate they've made up isn't worth it.

But then I feel Kelli's hand on my shoulder. "It's okay, Deacon. You can do it."

Right. Confidence. Let's do this. I stumble and trip past everyone in the row. I should have a sense of humor about this. Like the guy who won the "craziest clothes" award. It'll be over in a couple of minutes.

As I take the stage there's another burst of cheering. "I love you, Deacon!" shouts some girl.

I turn to the principal, trying to smile. But it's not Mr. Kznack standing next to me. It's a strange man in a business suit.

Which wouldn't be worrisome, except I've seen him before.

At the hardware store. He was one of the guys watching me.

Elijah was right. I've been set up, somehow. I look to my friends in the audience. Kelli nods, encouragingly. Elijah looks confused.

I'm aware that the man with the camera is now standing at the front of the stage, filming us. And to the side, someone dangles a boom mic over my head.

Dear God, what's happening?

The man in the suit scoots closer to me. He smiles like we're old friends.

"I'm Patrick Delaney, from the United Broadcast Network." He gently pulls me closer to him and faces the cameraman. "We're here in Fayette, Arkansas, with—" He touches the side of his head and listens to an invisible voice in his earpiece. He then smiles and faces the camera again. "I'm Patrick Delaney, from the United Broadcast Network. I'm here in Fayette*ville*, Arkansas. With me is Deacon Locke, the young man whose dance skills have captivated a nation. How're you doing, Deacon?"

"Very, very confused."

The audience laughs.

"Deacon, are you a fan of our show *Celebrity Dance Off*?"

Nope. I'm going to have to wing it.

"It's that dance show, right? With the celebrities?"

More laughter. I force a weak giggle. Behind me, the logo for the show appears on the screen.

"Mr. Locke, I think we've kept you in suspense long enough." He turns to the crowd. "And I know you all are anxious to hear what your principal has to say."

Everyone laughs. Even Mr. Kznack shrugs in an "Aw, you got me" gesture.

"We at UBN have been watching your dance clips with great interest. And we've come here today to invite you, Deacon Locke, to appear on season seven of *Celebrity Dance Off*!"

The crowd screams. A blast of music fills the auditorium. I assume it's the show's theme song. Teachers, students, and the principal are all clapping.

And I have no idea what's going on. I don't watch this show. I don't know what they want me to do. Did the principal know that was going to happen? Did Jean?

I'm scared and confused and everyone is looking at me. There's a microphone hanging over my head. I glance at Kelli, but she looks as flummoxed as I do.

Mr. Delaney is very subtly nodding at me. I'm trapped. I have no other option.

"I . . ." I clear my throat, face the senior class, and smile. "I can't wait. Go, Bulldogs!"

Chaos. Pure chaos. Screaming. Paper wads flying. People yelling my name.

I stand there next to this strange man, grinning and waving, not knowing what I've agreed to or what's expected of me.

But I do know that hundreds of my classmates are

cheering for me. And that's kind of neat. I wish Soraya could see me right now.

Then it occurs to me that she has a TV. She will see me.

Eventually, silence is restored. The principal joins us. But Mr. Delaney is not finished. Not yet.

"This must be pretty exciting for you, Deacon! And as a special thank-you . . ." An assistant appears at his shoulder and hands him an envelope. "We'd like to present your school with this check for two thousand dollars."

I stand there, holding up the envelope, as photographers capture my stunned expression. Surely this will end soon. Someone will explain everything.

Mr. Kznack approaches the podium. For once, I'm glad to see him.

"Thank you, Mr. Delaney. Thank you, Deacon. Now before we leave, I have a few announcements. . . ."

"Just a moment," says Delaney, subverting Mr. Kznack's authority in front of everyone. "Deacon, we need to take a few more pictures. Can you get a few of your friends up here?"

I frantically gesture for Elijah and Kelli. But it's too late.

Dozens of students rush the stage. Kids I've barely talked to, kids I've had classes with, people I've never spoken to in my life. They crowd into me, touch me, force themselves next to me in an effort to be in the photos. I'm knocked around and nearly lose my footing. The camera flashes blind me. Mr. Delaney is giving me instructions, but I can't hear him over the noise in here.

I just face forward, smile, and pray this will end soon.

Eventually I wind up in Mr. Kznack's office with Mr. Delaney. We are alone. I'm supposed to have gone home by now, but I need answers. Explanations.

Delaney is on his phone and I patiently wait for him to finish. Eventually, the call ends.

"Mr. Delaney, I don't want to appear . . ." Enraged? Panicked? "Ungrateful, but you really kind of took me by surprise back there. What was up with the jump scare?"

He gives me a warm, friendly, and completely fake laugh. "That's kind of our thing at *Celebrity Dance Off*. We like to capture our contestants' reactions when they first find out they're going to be a dancing star. I can show you some clips. . . ."

"Uh, that's okay. And *celebrity* dance-off? I'm not famous. I mean, not even close."

He slaps me on the back as if I just made a joke. "But you are, Deacon. You see, we take our contestants from the ranks of everyday Americans who have found their way into the spotlight and into our hearts. For instance, last season we featured Major John Renwick, a marine who lost his arm in Afghanistan. Such a touching story."

I wonder how he enjoyed it when the camera crew snuck up on him.

"Sir, this is really coming out of nowhere. Does my grandmother know about this? I live with her."

"Oh, yes, of course. In fact, she was supposed to be here today, but I guess she couldn't make it."

This sends me into a fresh spiral of worry. Did she forget? Is she sick? Is this man lying to me? I wish I wasn't here alone. I have to be honest with this guy.

"To tell you the truth, I'm not sure how your show works. What is it you need me to do, exactly?"

He looks slightly annoyed, as if I haven't been doing my homework. As if I'm the only one in the world who doesn't watch his program.

"It's very simple. You'll be paired with a professional dancer. Each week, you'll prepare a routine and perform for our viewers, coast to coast. After two weeks, our panel of celebrity judges will start eliminating some of the couples. If you're voted off, you'll fly home, more popular than ever. But if you make the finals—"

"Wait . . . fly home? You won't film this here?"

This strikes Mr. Delaney as humorous and he laughs at me. Not kindly. "No, Deacon. At our studios in Los Angeles. We have a very nice hotel we'll put you up in."

L.A.? This is getting more and more insane. I have to talk to Jean.

"When would we do all this?"

He checks something on his phone. "You'll arrive late in July. Filming starts in August and could last through Christmas, depending on how well you do. And of course there's promotions and commercials and—"

Time out! "I have to start school in the fall."

This doesn't appear to faze him in the least. "So skip a semester. Skip a year. You're young."

Drop out of college . . . college with Soraya! . . . so I can be on some dippy TV show?

"Mr. Delaney . . ."

He stops smiling. "I can tell you have mixed feelings about this. Of course you do. This is all sudden and surprising and thrilling."

Two out of three.

"But I have to tell you, this opportunity won't last. Right now, those internet clips have put you at the height of your popularity. And if you just continue this way, people will start to forget about you. In three months, everyone will be like, 'Deacon who?' But if you appear on our show, who knows where that might lead? Television commercials, personal appearances, maybe even a recording contract. Do you sing?"

"No."

He keeps talking. "The deal I'm offering you pays fifteen thousand dollars, and that's if you don't make the finals. And there's no reason, if you let me point you in the right direction, you can't make ten times that much over the next couple of years. That'd go a long way toward your college expenses, wouldn't it? How are you planning to pay your tuition? Athletic scholarship?"

"Not exactly."

I remember the frightening student loan contracts I've signed . . . the huge debt I'll owe when I graduate. I remember the look on Jean's face when she said she wished more than anything she could help me pay for school. Is this why she helped set this up? Does she actually want me to postpone college?

Delaney smells blood. "My nephew graduated from UCLA last year with a degree in chemical engineering. You know what he does now? He manages a 7-Eleven. Of course, he still owes his student loan payments. He's living in a studio apartment with two other guys."

I'd like to think I'm smart enough to avoid a situation like that. But am I?

"Deacon, you're about to become a man. And I'm asking you to make an adult decision here. Postpone college for a little bit. Come to California. Have the time of your life. Make your brand grow. Then, in a year or so, you can enter school with your tuition almost paid for. I'd call this a no-brainer."

"Did you talk to my grandmother about this?"

He shrugs. "Our people did. I'm not involved in that end of things."

I'm feeling very overwhelmed. "How long do I have to make a decision?"

He is not smiling now. "Not long. Not long at all." He hands me a thick sheaf of papers. "I'll need this signed by you and your guardian by the end of the week. You can have someone look it over if you wish."

"Sure." I scan the contract, but it's incomprehensible.

"I hope you'll make the right decision, young man. Getting you on this show, it's going to put your school in the limelight. Don't you think your friends would enjoy that?"

Is he talking about Elijah and Kelli, or about all those strangers who mobbed me at the photo shoot?

I try to smile. I shake his hand. "I'll . . . I'll let you know. Very soon. Thank you for the opportunity."

He nods, unsmiling. "Good boy."

School is out. Everyone has gone home. The last day in high school and I'm leaving alone. Just like I first started.

As I walk, I use my phone to look at clips of *Celebrity Dance Off.* Even with their very liberal definition of "celebrity," I still feel somewhat outclassed. There's a woman who once dated a movie star. A guy who used to play for the Chargers. A woman who used to be a judge on a different dance-contest show. That one-armed Afghan war vet (thank God his pecs weren't injured, holy shit). The daughter of a disgraced politician.

The format is simple. The contestants are paired off with a professional dancer and work on a new routine each round. After the first couple of episodes, the judges start eliminating teams. The grand-prize winners get $50,000. And that's in addition to the money we get just for appearing.

The show itself is in surprisingly good taste. Everything seems laid-back and fun, with no nasty comments or backstabbing.

Hey, they wouldn't call it reality TV if it wasn't real, right?

There's just one problem.

Actually, there're a lot of problems. But one bigger than the others.

She's slender, black-haired, and a great dancer. And we have plans to go to school together.

Elijah's worried about losing Clara, even though they'll both be living in the same town.

Now, Soraya, she's worth waiting for. Deacon Locke, not so much.

✳ ✳ ✳

When I reach home, I find Jean sitting on the couch, and for a moment I think she's asleep. But she's not. She's staring blankly at the television, which is playing an infomercial. She's still wearing her robe but no makeup, and her hair hangs down limply over her forehead and shoulders.

"Jean?"

She jumps up with a start. "Deacon! I wasn't expecting you. Is it that late already?"

It's actually quite a bit later than I normally get home.

She stands. "Is something wrong? You look upset." She reaches for her brush and begins fixing her hair.

"Jean, there was a camera crew at my school. They barged in on the awards announcements. People want me to be on some dancing show on TV."

Jean pauses midbrush. "Was that today? Oh, I'm so sorry. I was supposed to be there. How was it?"

I take the remote and shut off the television. "So you did know about this?"

"They contacted me a couple of weeks ago. Said they needed it to be a big surprise or they wouldn't ask you to be a contestant. I hope it didn't upset you."

I fake smile as I sit down across from her. "No, it just really threw me. Um . . . so what do you think about all this?"

She shakes her head. "It doesn't matter what I think."

I lose it. The confusion and frustration that've been building up since I was first ambushed by the dance show spew forth.

"Doesn't matter? Jean, how could you keep this from me? And you've been badgering me about college for years. Now you're saying maybe I shouldn't go? Answer me!"

She stares off into the distance, and for a moment I think she's about to cry. I stand there, waffling between apologizing for my outburst and waiting for Jean to apologize for my weird situation.

She looks back at me, and I'm suddenly struck by how old she looks. Worn-out. Tired.

"I say my opinion doesn't matter because it's not my decision. I'm not the one they offered that contract to, and I'm not the one with college to pay for."

"You're avoiding my question."

She doesn't deny it. "When that show contacted me, I thought it was nothing but stupid Hollywood fluff. But . . . they made some good points. All you'd have to do is work for a few months at something you're good at, something you enjoy, and you'd have an excellent down payment at least for your schooling. It's something to think about."

"Think about? I didn't know about this until today! I was getting kind of excited about college and now I'm supposed to move to California instead? I'm only eighteen, I can't handle this!"

Jean doesn't answer. She just looks past me at a photo on the wall. Grandpa Howard in his army uniform. He was a teenager too.

Okay, maybe I am old enough to decide for myself. But that doesn't make things any easier.

"You think I should do this, don't you?"

"It doesn't matter—"

"Damn it, just answer me!"

Wow. First time I ever swore in front of her. But she takes no notice.

"All I can say is a chance like this doesn't come along often. I'd hate for you to regret not going for it someday."

I press my knuckles to my forehead. "So basically, the risky, regrettable choice is go to college, while the sensible, financially prudent course of action is to drop out of school and move to L.A. and try to be a TV star."

This gets a laugh from Jean. "That sounds like something your father would say. Of course, your father would never be in this situation."

I sit there with my hands between my knees. "I wish someone would just tell me what to do."

"Deacon . . ."

"I know, I know." I stare at my grandfather's portrait. He never had an opportunity like this. "I'm not saying I'd mind, you know, being a TV star. Making some money. Seeing California for the first time."

"You've lived there before. When you were six, I think."

This is news to me. "It all runs together. You know, I'd do this in a heartbeat, except . . ."

She nods, knowingly. "Soraya. Have you told her?"

I shake my head. "Any guy would be lucky to be with her. And for some reason she wants to be with me. I'm not really in a position to move out of state for three or four months."

Jean leans over and takes my face in her hands, something she hasn't done since I was in elementary school. "Just talk to her. You might be surprised."

TWENTY-FIVE

I MAKE IT THROUGH THE GRADUATION CEREMONY without incident. I arrive at the school at the last possible minute, walk across the stage when they say my name, and leave with Jean the moment it's over. She understands. It's not like we have to wait around for my father.

She also understands why I choose not to go to the school-sponsored grad night celebration. I really don't want to discuss my show-business opportunity, not until I've made a decision. I won't miss anyone at the party, except maybe Elijah and Kelli.

But now I'm with someone I want to be with very much. We sit alone on astronomy hill, leaning backward on our elbows, staring at the sky. It's completely overcast, but neither of us cares.

Jean took us out to dinner as a graduation celebration, though Soraya's school doesn't end until next week. Afterward, I asked her if she'd go for a walk with me, by the light of my electric lantern.

She turns and smiles at me. That beautiful, somewhat shy smile that I like to think she shows only me. Good God, am I seriously thinking about moving away?

But I have to at least talk to her about this.

"There's something I need to show you."

She scoots closer to me, her smile widening. It kills me. I almost chicken out. Instead, I take out my phone.

"This happened yesterday."

I show her the clip of my ambush by the *Celebrity Dance Off* producer. Her smile gradually fades as she realizes what's going on.

The video ends and she doesn't move. She doesn't say anything. Just tucks her knees up to her chin and stares down at my house.

"Soraya? I didn't know this was coming. And I haven't agreed to anything. They just took me by surprise."

An eternity passes. Then . . .

"I don't want you to go."

There! At last! Someone giving me some direction. What a load off. I can just call up Delaney and tell him I won't do the show.

Funny, I'm less relieved than I would have expected.

"I won't leave."

She holds up a hand, but still stares off into the night. "You have to do this. We both know that."

"I don't know that at all. Why shouldn't I just stay here and go to school with you?"

She faces me. "Because you're not that great of a dancer. You're good, but not great. The reason you've been invited to this thing is because people like you. You're sweet and nice and funny when you let yourself be. I know it. Jean knows it. Those TV people know it. And they want to pay you and make you famous, at least for a while. I'm not going to be the girl who sits here and tells you to give all that up."

That trembling lower lip. I'm hurting her. How can I hurt her?

"Maybe I don't want to go."

She rolls her eyes. "Of course you want to. You'd be stupid not to want to."

"Then just call me stupid!" Though she's right. If it wasn't for her, I wouldn't be nearly as conflicted.

She frowns at me. "Fine. You're stupid. You're stupid for even thinking about skipping this. You're stupid for not being excited and you're stupid for asking my opinion, because I don't matter!"

She gets up and stomps to the very top of the hill,

standing there with her back to me.

I dig my fingers into the earth. I grind my teeth.

What does she want from me? I told her I'd stay. I told her I didn't want to go. So why is she angry?

"Deacon?" Her voice is thick with emotion.

"Yeah?"

"Now's the part where you walk up silently behind me, wrap your arms around my waist, and we stand there sadly and quietly, but still together."

"Oh. Sorry." This is all still new to me.

I join her at the top of the hill. I wrap my arms around her from behind and kiss the top of her head.

"You're the best thing that's ever happened to me," I say. I feel her body unstiffen slightly. "This TV thing is exciting, but knowing you, it can't compare. And I worry that if I go off to California, when I come back, you'll . . ."

She turns around in my arms. "I'll what?"

"You'll be gone."

She has her back to the lantern and I have trouble reading her face. But I feel it when she shoves me with both hands.

"You're an idiot."

"You said that earlier." Geez, it's like I'm talking to Kelli.

"I'm serious. Where the hell would I go?"

Is this, like, a rhetorical question? "I dunno! Maybe you'll meet some guy who isn't six states away and gone for half a year." Like, perhaps, a certain guitarist who'd probably like to take my place.

Soraya throws up her hands like she cannot believe what I'm saying. "You know what? Forget it! Forget I said anything. I'm done talking about this."

Two-second pause.

"Seriously, Deacon? You're moving off to L.A., you're going to be surrounded by beautiful blond women with fake boobs and tans, you're going to be on TV while the producers try to make you into every American girl's fantasy, and you think *you're* the one who should be worried?" She throws back her head and yells in frustration.

"Yes! I should be worried! Because this . . ." I point to myself. "This is all fake. You really are talented and beautiful and fun, and I feel like such a jerk for leaving, you whiner!"

"Well, we'll just have to wait for each other, you big moron!"

"Fine!"

"Fine!"

I'm not sure how we go from shouted insults to kissing, but you know what? I'm good with it.

* * *

Sometime later, Soraya and I walk, hand in hand, back to her car. We stop in the driveway. I don't think either of us is ready for her to leave.

I reach up and brush a leaf out of her hair. God, she's wonderful.

Her eyes suddenly light up. "I got you a little something. I can't believe I forgot."

She ducks into the car and pulls something out of her purse.

"It's just a little graduation present."

It's a U of A stocking cap, with the Razorback pig on it.

"I thought you'd need it this fall, but I guess you can wear it during those subzero Los Angeles winter nights. Hey, what's wrong?"

I shift my face back into neutral. "Nothing. It's beautiful. Thank you."

It's just that this is the first time someone besides Jean has ever bought me a present. The McDonald's gift certificates and truck-stop toys from Dad don't count.

"I, uh, got you a little something too. Very little." I fish it out of my jacket pocket.

"Oh, a mix CD!"

"Sorry it's nothing better. All my assets are tied up in the Cayman Islands."

She's eagerly looking through the list of songs. My

one contribution. Elijah downloaded them all for me, burned the CD on his computer, and embarrassingly provided the blank CD and paid for the downloads. But I chose the music.

"'Dancing with Myself,'" she reads. "'Save the Last Dance for Me.' 'Music Box Dancer.'"

"It's because we met at dance class," I explain.

"Thanks, that was kind of subtle. Oh, 'Dancing in the Dark,' good one."

"Number ten is my theme song."

She looks down the list. "'Dancing Fool.' Very appropriate." She gently but firmly grabs my collar. "C'mere, fool."

I'm distracted as she kisses me. I am a fool. I'm really going to give this up for months?

"Soraya," I say when we come up for air. "I've been thinking—"

She reaches up and places her fingers on my lips. "Don't say it."

"You don't know what I'm going to say."

"Were you going to second-guess being on TV?"

I toy with the hat. "Maybe."

She looks down at her CD, then up at me. "Deacon, I hate that you're leaving. I didn't expect this. But you're going to have fun. And you're going to come back with a lot of money. And I think I might enjoy bragging about my famous boyfriend."

She shuts me up with a final kiss.

As I watch her drive off, all I can hear is one word.

Boyfriend.

I tiptoe back into the house so as not to wake Jean. But she's still up. She's sitting on the couch, listening to music, and staring at that photo of my grandfather.

I sneak behind her and up the stairs.

I guess I'll be leaving two girls behind. Jean will be fine. I'll make sure her doctor says it's okay for me to leave. And why shouldn't it be? Things have been so crazy lately, half the time I'm as confused as she is.

Still . . .

Los Angeles. That's far.

Big opportunity or big mistake?

If you think Deacon should go to Los Angeles, turn to page 402.

If you think he should stay in Fayetteville, turn to page 501.

TWENTY-SIX

NOW THAT COLLEGE HAS BEEN DELAYED, I'M KIND
of at a loss as to what to do with myself all summer. Last
year, Jean and I took a series of road trips, visiting state
parks and historical sites. She hasn't mentioned doing
anything this vacation, and Soraya is busy volunteering
at the YMCA most weekdays. I research additional dance
classes, but everything is geared toward the high school/
college crowd and is not offered during the summer. I
find myself alone a lot.

Not that I don't have anything to do. Mr. Delaney
has given me plenty of homework. He's big into social
media.

"You really have to get yourself out there," he wrote

me. "Have an online presence as much as possible."

I don't mind constantly posting pictures of myself and writing blog posts, more or less following a script I was given:

COUNTING DOWN THE DAYS TILL SEASON SEVEN! LOOK FOR ME ON THE UBN THIS FALL! #CELEBRITYDANCEOFF

CAN'T WAIT TO SEE THE EXCITING FINAL SEASON OF ZOMPACA-LYPSE, ONLY ON UBN!

JUST TALKED TO MY NEW DANCING PARTNER. TALENT AND LOOKS!

I asked Mr. Delaney who my partner was going to be. He said they hadn't decided yet.

I am a little uncomfortable with the blatant advertising they ask me to do.

HOT AS HECK HERE IN ARKANSAS. WHO'S UP FOR A NICE FRESA ICE TEA BLASTER?

JEAN JUST DEPOSITED HER SOCIAL SECURITY CHECK IN THE FIRST BANK OF MOARK. I'M GLAD THEY'LL BE THERE TO LOOK OUT FOR HER WHILE I'M IN CALIFORNIA.

CAN'T WAIT TO TRY THE NEW PASTA BURGER FROM PIZZA PRESTO. #PIZZALICIOUS

I had to draw the line when Mr. Delaney asked me to adopt a puppy so I could tweet about some dog-food brand.

I sit on the front porch, staring at the broken drain-pipe and trying to figure out how to post about this new brand of selfie stick without sounding like a douche. I decide it's impossible.

My phone buzzes. One of these days I'm going to have to ask Elijah how to change the alerts. Seems all I do these days is accept friend requests. . . .

See? I totally sounded like a douche there. It's spreading.

I try to silence the chat request when I notice the picture is of astronomer Neil deGrasse Tyson. Unfortunately, the name is just Adam.

I'm a little disappointed that it's not actually Dr. Tyson trying to contact me, but I like this guy's style. I respond.

> DeaconLocke: Nice avatar.
>
> AdamF: Holy geez, is this really Deacon Locke?
>
> DeaconLocke: The same.
>
> AdamF: Awesome. I'm Adam, I'm a junior at the U of A.
> I don't know if u remember me. I met you at an Ozarks
> Astronomy meeting. I was the 1 with the Celestron
> NexStar.

I don't remember him, but I remember his telescope.

> DeaconLocke: Right. How's it going?
>
> AdamF: Not as good as you're doing! I saw that u r
> going to b on Celebrity Dance Off.
>
> DeaconLocke: The rumors are true.
>
> AdamF: Guess that means u won't be coming here 4
> college.

DeaconLocke: Not until spring semester.

AdamF: 2 bad. We've got kind of a skywatcher club here. Every Thursday night we take the telescopes out and have a midnight picnic.

That does sound like a lot of fun, and again I'm second-guessing my decision to postpone college.

DeaconLocke: Sorry to miss that. But my girlfriend is starting there this year. Maybe I'll stop by and say hi when I visit her.

Because I totally have a girlfriend.

AdamF: Sweet! Hey, if u r not doing anything tonight, we're having a little party at my apartment. U guys should come by.

Tonight I'd planned to blog about those great new summer fashions from Newstrom and Green.

DeaconLocke: Sounds like fun. Can we bring anything?

AdamF: You'd seriously come? Dude, that's great! I'll send u an evite!

Well. My first college party. Adam sounds like a together guy, so it shouldn't be too insane. This might be fun.

I text Soraya, who's on board. Now all I have to do is borrow the car. That will be easy enough, since it's Friday and Jean usually stays in. Most classes and clubs don't meet on the weekends and Jean doesn't care for traffic and crowds. I find her in her bedroom, primping in front of a mirror. Even on stay-at-home nights, she always makes sure she looks sharp.

Though I'm wondering about that dress she's wearing. It looks new. And somewhat fancy for an evening of old movies on AMC.

"Looking good, Jean."

"Thanks. Hope you don't mind if I slip out tonight. I left you a cold supper in the fridge."

Damn. This is going to be a problem. Maybe I can convince her to get a ride from someone else. "Where are you headed?"

"Oh, out to dinner."

"Do you think you could get Shirley or Peg to drive you?"

She dabs on a bit of perfume. "They won't be there."

"The thing is, I was hoping to use . . ."

Wait a minute. The clothes. The perfume. The unexpected Friday-night plans.

"Um, who exactly are you meeting?"

She continues to stare at her mirror. She mumbles something.

"Jean?"

She stands and picks up her purse. "Otis Harold, from the grocery store."

"That guy who works in the meat department? The one with the beard?" I feel like I've been slugged in the gut. Not that I'm upset about this, just really, really surprised.

"The same. He's been asking me to dinner for quite some time now. I finally decided that if you could find a girlfriend, I can have an evening out with a gentleman."

I'm reeling. I really am. "But . . ."

"I have to go." She kisses my cheek. "Be safe, love you."

"I . . . I'll have my cell!" I yell after her. "Call me if you need anything!"

Okay. Jean has a date. With a guy.

Why shouldn't she? I mean, she's an attractive, mature . . .

She's my grandma! Grandmas don't date!

At least not the hairy-eared butcher from the Safeway.

I suddenly really need to get out of the house. See Soraya. Go to Adam's thing.

I don't have a car. But I have a phone.

"Hey, um, Elijah? You feel like going to a party?"

Adam's place is on the second floor of a small complex of cheap student apartments. As we pull into the lot, I can already see several people hanging out on the stairwell.

It's a relief to get out of Elijah's car. Because of my

long legs, I was forced to ride shotgun with Elijah, while Soraya and Clara sat in the backseat.

I help Soraya out of the car. She's wearing a pair of old jeans and a T-shirt, but she still looks incredible. I'm dressed in a set of preppy clothes that Mr. Delaney sent me. It feels like the new suit you get when they release you from prison.

Elijah thumps me on the back. He holds up half a bottle of Scotch that he filched from his parents. "So who's ready to party?" He hands his keys to Clara, then turns to me. "Lead on, MacDeacon."

I point to the crowded stairs, where a couple of people are already staring down at us. I'm feeling less and less confident. I don't really do small talk, and I have a feeling that if Soraya doesn't take the conversational lead, I'm going to end up standing in a corner, ignored. As Elijah and Clara head to the party, I lean over to my date.

"If you'd like to leave early, just let us know."

She shakes her head. "I had to spin some pretty improbable lies to get out of the house tonight. Let's have some fun. Hey." She takes my chin in her hand. "Maybe there'll be *dancing*."

I can't help but smile. "C'mon."

As we climb the stairs, I notice a few people pointing and whispering.

So you've never seen a tall person before. Get a life.

270

The apartment is pretty large, and there are about a dozen people inside. I'm relieved to notice two manga posters, a guy in a "Bob" Dobbs T-shirt, and an oscilloscope that flashes in time to the music. My kind of crowd.

"Deacon! You made it!" It's Adam. I remember him from the astronomy meeting. He's a skinny Hispanic guy with glasses. "Let me get you guys some drinks. Hey, everybody, Deacon Locke is here!"

The partygoers all turn at once. People smile at me. Someone snaps a photo.

Soraya laughs. Adam hands me a bottle of beer. When I attempt to pop the top, it sticks. Determined not to look like a newbie, I grip it and twist with all my might. I lose some skin from my palm, but it opens.

I then notice Adam still standing there, holding a bottle opener toward me. Oops.

To cover my gaffe, I ask him about his classes. Soon, he has introduced Soraya and me to a half dozen science majors, including several amateur astronomers. I worry that I'm going to be outclassed like I was with Jason, but they keep the discussion purely on the material plane, avoiding the fruity mythological aspects. I think the dry nature of our conversation bores Soraya a little bit, and she joins Clara in the living room.

More people arrive. Is it my imagination, or do they go out of their way to introduce themselves to me? Nearly all of them snap a picture. To hide my awkwardness, I grab another beer. And another.

The music turns up. I haven't had a chance to leave the kitchen area since I got here, because people keep surrounding me. At first, they're all friends of Adam's and his roommates', wanting to discuss astronomy. But as more people arrive, they keep bringing up *Celebrity Dance Off* and that clip of me and Jean. Adam has left to talk to his other guests. I don't see Elijah or Clara, though I spot Soraya, sitting on a couch, talking to some guy.

I best join them.

I try to barge through the increasing crowd, but I'm blocked by a wall of men, big guys who just arrived. They're shouting and friendly, and I don't think this is their first stop of the evening. They badger me with questions about the show, about the hosts, about the dancers. At first I try to avoid the questions by drinking more beer—wait, this isn't beer, what is this?—but I'm surrounded. I pretend to take out my phone and check my messages. That's a mistake. I have over thirty notifications. All pictures of me at this party. Is this why things are getting so crowded? Because I'm here? Nah.

I elbow my way into the living room, where people are trying to dance. I notice Adam and his friends dashing around the apartment, trying to keep order. I think this get-together was a lot bigger than they had planned. I finally find Soraya, leaning against the wall. The chaos of the party doesn't seem to affect her at all. She just stands there looking amused and slightly bored.

"You want to go outside?" I half scream.

She nods. "I could use some fresh air. Let's go." She takes my hand and starts leading me through the crowd.

"Hey, Deacon!" shouts a stranger. "Show off some of your moves! C'mon!"

There is a general scream. Hands push me from behind. People are laughing and yelling.

I'm confused and dizzy and I'd like to leave. I turn to Soraya, who only shrugs.

A new song comes on. It's one from dance class, one we both know. I glance over at one of Adam's roommates, who's clapping to the beat. I look over to a group of girls, who are gesturing me out onto the tiny dance floor.

I'm going to be doing this professionally in a few months. Might as well get used to it.

Soraya and I take a bit to find each other's rhythm. No one seems to care. The second we start moving, everyone goes wild. The phones are out, capturing our moves. Soraya is grinning. For the first time tonight, I'm really having fun.

For about two minutes. Then some girl with way too much spray-on tan kind of barges between Soraya and me. She is not nearly as good a dancer, but that's not the point. I'd much rather dance with Soraya. I wrangle around until I'm facing her again.

Only now someone else barges between us. A guy this time. And pretty soon I'm being knocked around the room by people trying to show off their own moves.

A girl elbows Soraya in the ribs. Someone else spills half their drink down her front. And then . . .

Some big guy is flailing all over the place, mistaking being a public spectacle for dancing. He knocks Soraya against the couch. She loses her balance and starts to fall over backward.

I'm there in a second. Shoving the guy out of the way, I grab her hand and steady her before she goes over. Our eyes meet and we smile.

Only now someone is poking me in the back. Kind of hard. Repeatedly jabbing me, trying to get my attention.

Maybe it's the alcohol, but it takes me a moment to realize he's not poking me, but hitting me. With his fist.

I turn around. While I've never had to look up to face someone, this person comes close. It's the guy who almost knocked over Soraya, and he's not here to apologize. He's yelling something at me, but he's talking so fast and the music is so loud that I can't understand him. I try to move past him, but that only makes him madder.

Elijah appears at my elbow, talking to the stranger.

For some reason I can make out his words perfectly.

"Hey, let's just calm down, pal. Deacon didn't mean anything. Why don't we just all back up and let it go, eh?"

Without breaking eye contact, he shoves Elijah, who almost goes sprawling. And I suddenly realize that this isn't just some loud asshole. I realize that he wants to fight.

Should I grant his wish? I take a step forward.

There's no telling what might have happened in this crowded room if the punches started flying. But at that moment, the music suddenly stops.

Adam is standing on a chair. He does not look happy.

"All right, it's over! Thank you for coming, but I don't know any of you people. I'm shutting things down here. Everybody out."

No one moves toward the door. After a second of silence, everyone starts talking again.

I should do something.

"He said . . ." My voice escapes me like a cannon report. "EVERYBODY OUT!"

The confused partygoers start to make their way to the door. Soon the apartment is nearly empty. The belligerent asshole is one of the last to go.

Once the crowd is gone, I realize why Adam put an end to things. There are spilled drinks and broken glasses everywhere. A framed picture lies shattered on the ground and someone has kicked a hole in the dry-wall.

"Um, want us to help you pick up?" I ask lamely.

Adam shakes his head. "We've got this."

"Thanks for having us," says Soraya.

"Thanks for coming," he replies, but with little enthu-siasm.

We find Clara and go downstairs. The other guests are already making their way to other places, other par-ties. They seem less friendly now.

"Hey, faggot!"

Great, it's the jerk. He's sitting on the bumper of a car next to a couple of his friends. They're all staring at us. Unfortunately, he's parked two spaces from Elijah's car.

I don't want to deal with him. And I don't want to make my friends deal with him. But we have no choice. I take Soraya's hand, and Clara takes Elijah's. We walk forward, ignoring the asshole's taunts.

"You think you're hot shit, being on that candy-ass show? You ain't nothing! Look at me, you ain't nothing!"

Clara beeps the keys and our car doors unlock.

"Yeah, just keep walking, wimp! Goddamn queer dancer. Just walk away."

I have my hand on the door handle, ready to pull it open for Soraya.

276

"Get the hell out of here! You and your raghead girl-friend!"

My hand freezes, the door halfway open.

"Deke . . . ," hisses Elijah.

I turn. I face the other guy.

He should not have said that about Soraya.

And from the look on his face, he realizes that as well.

But now it's far too late.

Five minutes later, we're speeding away from campus, with Clara at the wheel. We'd piled into the car so fast that I wound up in the cramped backseat, next to Elijah.

There's a grim silence in the car. Elijah, of course, is the one who breaks it.

"Ten points on distance, Deke, but I'm going to have to ding you on your form. He flew way out of bounds."

Okay, maybe I kind of sort of hurled that guy across the parking lot like a bowling ball. Maybe he ended up going a lot farther than I expected.

But that thing he said about Soraya . . . I couldn't let that go.

I wish she would say something. It's so hard to read a girl's emotions by the back of her neck.

When we reach Soraya's house, I follow her out of

the car and instruct Clara to drive on. As soon as the taillights vanish, I turn to Soraya. She's standing there, arms folded, obviously angry.

"So are you going to tell me what I did wrong?" I ask, a tad bitchier than I mean to.

She slowly shakes her head. "I don't know, Deacon. Maybe it's that you went completely apeshit on some drunk asshole who wasn't even worth looking at?"

I was afraid of this. Soraya's right, I should have ignored him. But I did it because he insulted her. Doesn't that count for anything?

"Did you hear what he called you?"

"Yes. Yes, I did. And I chose to let it pass. Because he's no better than any of the dozens of other jerks who've called me that or worse. Why did you have to go and pick a fight?"

"Pick a fight?" I begin angry pacing a short distance up and down her street. "You think I started that?"

"You certainly ended it. You're lucky you didn't get hauled in."

Okay, maybe I did kind of lose it there. Maybe I'm a little bit worried that I put that guy in the hospital. But still . . . I wish my own girlfriend would take my side.

"Soraya, it hurts me when people insult you."

"This may come as a shock, but it hurts me too. But I'm a big girl, and I've learned it's better to not respond to morons like that. Don't give them the satisfaction. I don't need you to fight my battles for me."

Great. I wasn't exactly expecting Soraya to melt in my arms and say, "Deacon Locke, you're my hero." But it would be nice not to get a lecture.

"Sorry. Sorry I did anything. Sorry I tried to stand up for you."

"And now you're angry."

I wasn't, really, but the exasperated, condescending way she says this does kind of make me mad.

"What the hell am I supposed to do?" I snap. "Shit-head calls you a name and I'm the one you're pissed at. I'm going home."

We just stand there.

"Don't let me stop you, Deacon." But there's less anger in her voice.

"I want to make sure you get inside okay, first."

It's warm and balmy out. I can clearly see Ursa Major. It would be a wonderful time to kiss someone under the stars. Instead, I'm standing here staring at my girlfriend, wondering which of us is supposed to be offended.

Soraya ends the standoff. "I know you meant well. But I like the Deacon who took his grandmother to prom and pushed my car and made me that CD. When you attacked that guy—and I'll admit, part of me enjoyed seeing that—you kind of scared me. I'd like it if you didn't go around punching people."

"I never punched him."

"I'd like it if you didn't use people as a human shot put. If those dance-show sponsors got word of this, it could mean trouble for you. Okay?"

"Okay." She's right. Of course she's right.

It doesn't feel right, though. Not totally.

"Good night, Soraya."

"Night, Deacon."

I wait until she's safely inside before I begin the long walk back home.

We didn't kiss good-bye. I hope that's not the start of a trend.

I hope I haven't ruined things.

Before I walk a mile, I get a text from Mr. Delaney. It's a link to a video clip.

DANCE STAR LOSES HIS SHIT

It was me, in case you were wondering.

> PDELANEY: Call me first thing in the morning. We need to talk.

TWENTY-SEVEN

SATURDAY MORNING, I SIT IN THE KITCHEN AS JEAN prepares breakfast. I'm still a little angry with Soraya, and angry with the jerk from the party, and angry with myself. It was supposed to be a fun evening, hanging out with smart college students. And now there's a video clip of me acting like a professional wrestler. Over ten thousand hits since last night. Most of the comments are in support of me, even though they have no idea what was going on.

Thank God Jean never goes online.

"You never told me how your date went," I tell her. The words seem so alien . . . Jean. On a date.

She stands there at the stove, pouring out pancake batter and dropping sausages into the skillet. "It was okay. Otis is a nice man, but he does go on. Bit of an ego, really. He barely let me say a word all night. It's too bad more men aren't quiet and polite like you, Deacon."

I'm watching myself kick college boy's ass on my phone. "Yeah. That's me."

The clip is blocked by an incoming call. Delaney. I can't put this off any longer.

"Hello?"

"Deacon! What the hell were you thinking?"

And a pleasant good morning to you, too, sir.

I glance over to make sure Jean is occupied with breakfast, then walk into the dining room. "Mr. Delaney, I'm sorry. That guy—"

"Deacon, did I not make myself clear? Everything you do has an impact on the show. Fighting like that can ruin everything." He's not yelling. He's got that measured voice of a father correcting his son. Not that I have a point of reference.

I almost bring up what the guy said about Soraya, but I don't. The more I think about it, the more it sounds like I'm trying to justify being a pissed-off asshole. "It won't happen again."

Delaney continues as if he hadn't heard me. "We work hard to maintain the image of our dancers. You were supposed to be this year's yokel."

"I'm . . . hang on, what do you mean by that?"

"Oh, you know," he says distractedly. "The country boy. The hillbilly trying to find his way around in the big city. The audience loves that. In season two we had this kid from Mississippi, you'd swear he'd never even worn shoes before. The viewers went nuts. He made it to the finals."

And now they want me to play the country bumpkin. "You didn't mention any of this before."

"Well, we're still trying to work everything out. But after your display last night, we can't very well cast you as the naïve farm boy, can we?"

I'm suddenly very alert. Maybe he's going to kick me off the show! It'd be his decision, not mine. Completely out of my control. And I'd have no choice but to go off to school with Soraya in the fall.

"Although . . ." Delaney pauses. "You know, with your bulk, you might make a good bad boy. You follow?"

I sigh. "Not even remotely."

"You know, the tough guy with the heart of gold. The badass who loves his grandma. Hear me out. Now I'm not saying go get in another fight, but maybe you can show more of your wild side. You don't have a motorcycle, do you?"

"No."

Jean calls to me from in the kitchen. It's time for breakfast.

"Do you have any tattoos or piercings?"

"No."

"Would you be willing to get some? We'd foot the bill."

"No."

Jean calls out again. This time louder.

"Okay. Well, let me think on this for a while. In the meantime, no more brawling, though if you wanted to start smoking, I wouldn't tell you no."

Suddenly, Jean calls out my name, much more urgently than before. And she sounds upset.

I garble a good-bye to Mr. Delaney and rush into the kitchen. The room is filled with smoke. Jean stands next to the stove, staring in horror at a grease fire rising up from the skillet. The smoke alarm starts to blast.

I rush to the fridge and yank out the pitcher of water. Just before I dump it over the flames, I remember something I read. It was from a Donald Duck comic book, but I think it's still true: never pour water on a grease fire.

Then what the hell are you supposed to do? Why don't they teach you this shit in school?

Jean starts coughing, but makes no move to leave the

kitchen, or even move away from the smoke. It's time for action. I throw open the back door. I then gingerly grab the pan by its handle and carry the flaming thing into the backyard, where I drop it onto the end of the gravel driveway. It hisses into the earth.

Jean is still standing by the stove when I return. As I pause to reset the smoke alarm, I notice with horror that she looks upset. Not scared, but like a child who knows they've screwed up and is facing punishment. When she sees me looking at her, she bursts into tears.

I rush over to hold her. "It's okay, Jean. Kind of scary, but no harm done. It's okay."

But she just keeps crying into my chest. And though I keep my sobs inside, a few tears do escape from my eyes.

How is this my life? What's happening?

The thing about Jean is, she does not like to be reminded of her frailties and failures. When she had knee surgery last year, she was up and about far sooner than her doctor allowed. When we were both down with the flu once, she was serving me chicken soup long before she felt better. And now that the fire is safely out, she doesn't want to talk about it.

Not that I blame her for the accident. Not at all. But I did kind of want to know what had happened.

Jean refuses to answer me. Now that her tears are dry, it's like nothing happened. "I didn't know you expected me to be perfect, Deacon. I wasn't aware you never made any mistakes."

"I was just asking . . ."

"Well, instead of interrogating me, why don't you clean up some of this mess? I'm going to lie down for a moment. You know, it's a nice day. I think you should get out of the house for a bit. There's money in my purse if you need some."

Wow. Just . . . wow.

I mean, a fire like that, it could have happened to anyone. And it was probably plenty embarrassing. It's not at all worth getting upset about.

Though as I dump the charred remains of breakfast into the trash, I do worry. I worry a lot, actually.

"And then she just acted like the fire was no big deal. And maybe it's not, I mean, it's not like I'm a master chef. But what if I hadn't been there? What's going to happen when I move out?"

We're sitting in the YMCA cafeteria. Today's not one of Soraya's teaching days, but she's here anyway, helping someone make plans for an ESL class that's starting next month. She sits across the table from me, frowning sympathetically. When I called her and asked to meet, she didn't bring up our argument last night.

"You sound like someone's dad, Deacon. And I mean that in a good way. But stuff happens. She survived over sixty years before you moved in."

I so want to buy into what she's saying. I desperately want everything to be okay. But I should tell the truth.

"The thing is, it's not just the fire. Her driving has gotten a lot worse lately. She's starting to get confused and frustrated. She forgets things. Nothing major, but enough that I'm worried about how she's going to do on her own."

Soraya bites her lower lip and nods. "Have you taken her to the doctor?"

"We have an appointment in a couple of weeks. If I want to see someone earlier, I have to take her to urgent care, and she'll refuse. I'd rather do this gently."

"Maybe it's time she downsized the house. A lot of my students live in retirement villages. No yard care or cooking, people on staff to check in on them. Jean might enjoy a place like that."

I remember broaching the subject with her, and how she was not receptive. "It might come to that. But it's going to be a hard sell. So I was thinking . . . maybe I shouldn't go to Los Angeles."

She takes my hand in hers and begins playing with the hair on my knuckles. "Is that what Jean needs . . . or what Deacon wants?"

I lower my head. "I don't know. I want to be on this show, but I don't want to abandon Jean. Or you."

She smiles. "You're not abandoning anyone. And I think it may be too late to change your mind anyway. Would it make you feel better if I looked in on Jean a couple of times a week while you're gone?"

I can barely stop myself from grabbing her up in a huge hug. "Yes. A lot. You don't know how much."

"Well, I've always liked Jean."

We hold hands and stare into each other's eyes like a couple of twits. Where're the paparazzi now?

"Soraya, I'm really sorry about last night. I know you don't need me to stand up for you." No matter how much that guy deserved an arse beating.

"It's okay. I just hope your TV bosses don't see that clip."

I laugh. "Too late. Now they want to cast me as the badass rebel." I let go of her hand and begin shadow boxing. "What do you think? Can you see me as the new James Dean?"

She shakes her head. "You've got more of a Humphrey Bogart vibe. Or Marlon Brando, before he got fat."

I'm blushing. I can tell. And I don't care. Soraya and

"If this is an attempt at humor, it's not funny."

It's not funny to me either. "I'm going to be half a country away. I just don't like the idea of Jason sniffing around you while I'm gone."

She stands. "*Sniffing* around? What am I, a bitch in heat? How would you like it if I told you to stop hanging around Clara?"

I don't stand up. "Clara's not hot for me."

She whips out her phone. "Well, she's the only one! Have you checked out your page on the *Dance Off* website?"

"I have a page?"

"Listen to this: Deacon, look me up when you get to L.A.! Deacon, if you ever make it to the UCLA campus, my sorority would love to meet you. Deacon, WHO'S THAT UGLY DOG ON YOUR FACEBOOK PAGE?"

She hurls a plastic saltshaker at me. "Every day I worry that I met you too late and that you'll make a life for yourself outside of Arkansas. And then you start beating people up and accusing me of cheating? I don't need this. Not now."

She turns and storms out of the cafeteria. I try to follow, but find my path blocked by a pair of slow-moving seniors who, insult to injury, are holding hands. By the time I get around them, Soraya is gone.

And everyone is staring at me.

Great. Fantastic. On top of everything else, I'm totally blowing it with Soraya.

Jesus, can things get any worse?

Spoiler alert: yes.

TWENTY-EIGHT

SO REMEMBER HOW A COUPLE OF MONTHS AGO, I was a quivering wreck who was too scared to even ask out a girl? I kind of miss that.

Not really, but back then I wasn't worried about Jean. I didn't have to "promote my brand." I wasn't in danger of blowing things with the girl I liked.

Sitting on a park bench, I mentally go over our latest argument. After reviewing the tapes, the refs conclude that it was Deacon who was at fault. Ten-yard penalty, reset the clock two months, to when I was alone.

I take out my phone and text Soraya with a heartfelt and incoherent apology. She doesn't answer.

I look through the social media wasteland. Mr.

Delaney has been busy, sending lists of products I'm to purchase and "casually" use. No more soda pops and retailers; now I'm supposed to be hawking energy drinks, music venues, and body-art establishments. Fine. But no way am I promoting those e-cigarettes. I already feel stupid enough.

Looking through my messages and contacts, I realize that Soraya may have been right. And that's male talk for "Soraya was completely right." Most of my online "friends" are girls, and their messages are all kind of flirty.

I purge all the unread messages. I upload a photo of Soraya and me together at the street fair and post it to my page.

I caption it: *Soraya, a very beautiful, forgiving, intelligent, forgiving, talented, forgiving girl. And a great dancer.*

At least now she'll know I'm sorry.

I buy a can of that energy drink and take a selfie. I delete it. The photo looks more like an ad for chronic depression.

I shouldn't sit here and dwell, but I don't want to go home and start fretting about Jean, either. Hammered by indecision, I do what everyone else does to waste time: play with my phone some more.

There are some neat apps here. This one lets you know where your friends have been. Elijah went to the gaming shop last week. And Soraya went to the Y. And Kelli went to Coffee Lab.

Wait. That was only ten minutes ago.

I never much saw the point of a coffee shop. A restaurant that only serves one kind of drink? But it's nice and cool inside, and not crowded. I spot Kelli working at her laptop, alone at a table.

"Deacon! Wow, I feel so stalked."

I pull up a chair. "How are you?"

"Great. Not 'Reality-TV star' great, but I'm okay."

"How's Hunt?"

"Eh, seven point five for conversation, nine for kissing. But you didn't come here to ask about me. What's wrong?"

I tear open a sugar packet and down the contents. "Soraya . . . we just had a big blowout."

Kelli rolls her eyes. "What did you do?"

I'm kind of offended. "What makes you think I did something wrong?"

She regards me from over the top of her glasses. "Do you really want me to answer that question? Now, out with it, what horrible thing have you done?"

No use denying it. "I got crazy jealous about one of her guy friends. Even though he's a total tool! He's a complete—"

Kelli rolls her eyes. "I can't imagine why Soraya's mad at you. And are you talking about that guy she went to the dance with? Seriously, Deacon? That's who you're freaking out about?"

Her words make me feel a little better. "He plays the guitar."

"Does he have a contract with a major TV studio? He *doesn't*? Tut, tut."

I'm smiling now. "So I'm an idiot."

"Haven't I been saying that these past couple of years? As soon as you men realize that, we'll all be happier."

"Back to my problem . . ."

"Right." She toys with her cup. "Would it help if I went to Soraya and explained what a nice, if sometimes thoughtless, guy you are, and that she should forgive you for your many, many, MANY failings?"

I'm overwhelmed with relief. "Yes! Would you do that?"

"Not a chance." She slurps the dregs from her cup. "This is your rodeo. If I were you, I'd send the most groveling text you can imagine."

"Way ahead of you. Now what?"

"Nothing. You wait. Send her a text a day, saying what a sorry, pathetic wreck of a man you are, how everything is your fault, and if she'd just give you one last chance, you'd be her faithful, obedient slave for life."

I think about this. "I'm not sure—"

"Oh, grow a pair, Deacon. Just tell her you're sorry. If that's not good enough, maybe it wasn't meant to be."

This makes me sad. I'm not ready to give up.

Kelli stands. "My mom's picking me up soon. Walk me out."

We stand on the sidewalk. I'm preoccupied with thoughts of Soraya and how she's probably so pissed she'll never talk to me and how I'm going to end up as a weird middle-aged bachelor who drinks beer at Elijah's house on the weekends.

Kelli nudges me. "It's going to be okay. She'll come around."

"Thanks."

"So when do you start work on that show?"

"July."

She flips her hair. "Well, don't forget about me."

"I won't."

"Liar."

Something in her tone catches my attention. "Kelli?"

She suddenly looks kind of sad. She won't face me.

"Hey, what's wrong?"

"Nothing. I'm just missing you a little, that's all."

"I'm right here." Are all women this confusing, or is it just Kelli, Soraya, Jean, and that girl from the movie?

"You haven't been here for a long time. I've been

texting you all week, but you never responded."

Don't I feel like an ass. "I'm sorry. So many people have been trying to contact me. . . ."

"That I got lost in the shuffle." She looks up. "Two years you followed me around, and I kind of ignored you. And now that you're leaving, I realize I may possibly really miss you."

She smiles, but it's not sincere.

"I'll be back."

"No you won't. And even if you do, I'll be in Little Rock."

I run my hands through my hair, trying to think of a way to phrase this.

"Look. You were my only friend in high school. My only friend ever, at least until a couple of months ago. You think I can forget the girl who told everyone that I wear women's panties?"

She winces. "I shouldn't have done that. Even though the look on your face was kind of priceless."

"Well, I can laugh about that now." Not really. "But I'm going to miss you too. And this isn't the last time you'll see me."

Kelli's looking at the ground. "So you say."

I gently take her face in my hands and point it upward. "This is Deacon Locke you're talking to. I've already screwed things up with Soraya. I'm bound to do the same thing with the TV show." I lean toward her and tap her forehead with my own. "I'll be back."

She stares into my eyes for a few seconds, then smiles and pulls away. "Things are going to be fine with Soraya. She just needs a breather. A little Deacon goes a long way."

She suddenly roughly pushes me in the chest and smiles. "Geez, when did we get so corny?"

"I dunno, but let's not do it again, okay?"

A car honks across the street. Kelli glances at it. "That's my ride. You stay safe in California, okay? If someone offers you a ride, don't get in the car. Even if they have good candy. And cigarettes don't make you look cool. They just make you look dumb."

"I'll miss you too."

She jogs across the street. "Don't tell the cabdrivers you're from out of town. And call me when you get there! I want to sell your embarrassing stories to the bloggers!"

I smile as I watch her go. There are things about this town I'm going to miss. And a couple of things I need to fix before I go.

TWENTY-NINE

STEP ONE: MAKE SURE JEAN IS ABSOLUTELY HEALTHY and safe enough for me to leave town for a while.

Step two: Convince Soraya that I'm not a jerk by . . .

Beats me. Hell, I usually don't even have a step one.

Still, I'm actually doing something. Since I won't be around to help with the house, I'm making sure that it's in good repair for when I'm gone. Jean is at her self-defense class. I take the opportunity to bring in an expert to fix that broken gutter.

Clara dances and prances across the roof, directing the operations. And doing pretty much everything. Elijah sits next to her, gripping the dormers and occasionally holding something in place. I stand on the ground, staying out of their way and sometimes passing a tool to Clara.

"Seriously, guys, anything I can do?"

Clara, who is holding several screws in her mouth, shakes her head. Elijah kind of whimpers.

I take a break from my duties of doing nothing and step back to look at the progress. The repair job is coming along nicely. Clara says they no longer make those big copper gutters, and the replacement section is noticeable. A big stretch of aluminum tubing where a solid metal pipe used to be. Kind of like where you once had a great girlfriend to hang out with, and now all you have is Elijah.

I've texted her two or ten times since our fight the other day, but there's no response. I call, but she doesn't answer. I'm stuck in neutral. I need a change in my game plan.

"Hey, Deacon? When was the last time you had this chimney swept?"

"Probably before I was born."

Elijah, still clinging to the shingles, stares down the driveway. "Heads up, we have company."

Is it Soraya? It's Soraya, right? She's coming here for us to have one more big spat, and then a passionate makeup kiss in the driveway, as Clara looks wistful and Elijah catcalls. I eagerly turn.

Aaaand . . . it's Jason. I recognize his jerkmobile from the time he intruded on astronomy night. What in the holy hell is he doing here? I'll correct his mistake right quickly.

Jason parks and gets out. He walks directly toward me, being careful not to soil his fancy shoes in a mud puddle. He approaches me slowly, almost skittish. It's like I could yell "Boo!" and he'd go running off.

I don't yell "boo."

When he's about four feet away from me, he looks me right up in the eye, but doesn't come any closer. He claps his hands once.

"Deacon . . . is your grandmother here?" He glances around.

"Uh . . . no."

"Good. Because . . . because what I have to say is between you and me." He points a finger at my chest. "I want you to stay away from her."

I'm confused. "But she's my grandmother."

"No, I mean . . ." He looks at the ground, then back up at me. His eyes look angry. "Soraya. Don't call her anymore. Stop bothering her."

Behind me, the construction noises abruptly stop.

"Excuse me, Jason?"

"You heard me." The sentence ends in a squeak.

I'm suddenly aware of how hot it is out here. So very, very hot. I'm sweating. I swallow.

"And you think it's your place to give me orders?" I take a step toward him. He steps back.

"I know her a lot better than you." He keeps glancing toward his car.

I take another step, over the piece of downed gutter. "Jason, back off. I know she's pissed at me, but this is not your business. This is not your fight."

Damn, it's hot out here. I can see rings of sweat forming in the armpits of Jason's crisp, white shirt.

"Soraya will call you when she's ready to talk."

"That's her decision, not yours." I continue to move forward.

He stands his ground. "If you care about her, you need to leave her alone right now."

Clara says something, but I don't catch it. Jason and I are standing eye to eye, with only a vertical foot between us.

"You're a liar. Now get out of my yard."

Jason turns and skutters off. For a couple of feet.

And then he comes back. "Listen to me, Deacon."

I'm done listening. I stick out a finger and thump him in the chest. He staggers backward.

And then his hand shoots out. He pokes me in the

stomach. Right in the stomach.

It hurts.

It's so very, very hot out here. . . .

"Guys!" Elijah's screechy voice cuts through the blurry haze of my mind. I turn to see him scrambling down from the porch roof.

"Guys, hang on! Don't—"

He loses his grip and falls straight backward into the azaleas. Clara shrieks his name before leaping, feetfirst, to the ground.

Jason and I rush toward them.

Elijah staggers to his feet. "I'm all right!" he says, with that goofy smile of his.

"Are you sure?" asks Clara.

He frowns. "Nah, I'm just kidding. I broke my wrist."

He holds up his arm, revealing a twisted and discolored hand. He's still grinning, tears running down his nose.

Clara screams.

Jason and I exchange a panicked look before remembering we're pissed at each other and turn away. The three of us stand there, staring at Elijah, who's clutching his forearm.

"Clara, honey, you wanna drive me to the hospital? You're going to have to fish my keys out."

She sticks her hand into his front pocket and digs around, but Elijah doesn't crack a joke. He must truly be in pain.

I snap out of my helplessness. "Clara, let me drive him!"

Elijah glances at his tiny car, the back of which is filled with Clara's tools. "You stay here. Call my mom, tell her what happened. Don't tell her I've been drinking."

"You haven't been drinking."

"Then you won't have to lie. And Jason . . ." He turns to my nemesis and pointedly nods toward his car. "Amscray. I don't need either of you in the ER with me."

Jason opens his mouth to be irritating but realizes the injured man trumps even his superiority. Instead, he takes out his phone and does something. I feel my phone buzz in response. Without another word, he slinks off to his car and leaves.

I help Clara, who's now crying, stuff Elijah into his car. He smiles painfully at me through the window.

"No dueling while I'm gone. My lawyers will be in touch."

I watch them drive away, leaving me alone.

God, does everything in my life end in catastrophe?

I take out my phone to call Elijah's mother. Jesus, how am I going to say this gently?

Have you ever thought about gravity, Mrs. Haversham?

So there we were, innocently hanging out on the roof . . .

Would you mind if I faxed you over a liability waiver?

And then I notice what it was that Jason sent me. And suddenly, I realize that Elijah is having a better day than me.

Another goddamn video clip. It must have been taken the other day, outside the coffeehouse where I met Kelli. It's just the two of us, talking, when she told me she'd miss me. There I am trying to cheer her up. There I am putting my hands on her cheeks. There I am, leaning toward her. . . .

Oh, shit. What with the angle and the poor quality of the video, it doesn't look like we're talking. It looks like we're kissing.

Who the hell filmed this? What kind of Orwellian nightmare am I living in? I read the name of whoever uploaded this. 2crazy4u had better watch their ass.

With a growing sense of doom, I read the comments.

DEACON LIKES BIG BUTTS AND HE CANNOT LIE.

WASN'T HE DATING SOME ARAB CHICK?

CHRIST, LOOK AT THE ASS ON THAT ONE.

THE DEEPER THE CUSHION . . .

I feel like I'm going to puke. I pray to God Kelli hasn't seen this. She deserves better.

And then the true horror of my situation dawns on me.

Jason doesn't know Kelli. He doesn't care about her feelings.

It's Soraya he likes. And if Jason knows about this, then so does she. He'd make sure of that.

Shit.

THIRTY

ELIJAH'S MOTHER REFUSES TO GET OFF THE PHONE when I call her. It must run in the family. I spend ten minutes assuring her that her son isn't dying of a broken neck somewhere, and another ten getting berated for allowing him to do something dangerous, like be up on my roof. She's driving to the hospital while she talks to me on the phone. Apparently that's not dangerous.

Eventually she lets me go and I rush to Soraya's house. Maybe Jason didn't show her the clip. Maybe she saw it, but she wants to hear my side first. Maybe she doesn't believe everything she sees on the internet.

I'm exhausted by the time I reach her neighborhood. I pause to catch my breath, then rush to her door.

As if things weren't already going great, her father answers. He's not smiling this time.

"Hello, Deacon." He doesn't say "eat shit and die," but it's implied.

"Mr. Shadee, is Soraya here?"

He inhales deeply. "I don't think she wants to talk to you at the moment. And I have to say, I agree."

Oh, goody. He's seen the clip too.

"Mr. Shadee, I—"

"It's okay, Dad. Let me talk to him."

Soraya stands in the kitchen doorway. Her eyes are not bloodshot from tears. She's not dressed in the clothes that she slept in. Her hair is not an unkempt mess.

She's just as beautiful and stylish and together as she always is. Should I be relieved or worried?

Mr. Shadee regards me from under his bushy eyebrows. "Outside, then. Five minutes."

We're alone on the porch. Before Soraya can say anything, I open my mouth.

"I didn't kiss her. I know what it looks like, but I swear, nothing happened."

She looks at me with those brown, brown eyes. "I know. I believe you."

Okay, she believes me. So why does all not seem right?

"Then are we . . . okay?"

She shakes her head. "Deacon . . ."

I feel my heart creak. "Please. Don't."

I use my latent psychic powers to prevent her from talking. I try with all my might to get time to rewind, back before I'd even heard of *Celebrity Dance Off* or had a social media account.

It doesn't work.

"I'm sorry," she says. And I can tell she means it. "I thought I wouldn't mind. I thought famous Deacon could be on the show while I dated real Deacon. But they're the same guy."

"Then I won't do the show!" But even as I say it, I know the words sound forced, insincere. A fake offer that I know she won't take.

"Yes you will. I'd hate myself if you gave this up, and you'd end up resenting me."

"Then how can I make things right? How can I make this work?" If it weren't for my fear of Jason spying on me from his house, I'd get down on my knees.

She turns and stares at the porch lamp. "You shouldn't have to change, not for TV, not for me, not for anyone. And I shouldn't have to worry every time you go to a party or dance with another girl."

I'm starting to lose it. "You have nothing to worry about! I like you! You're perfect, why would I want to be with someone else?"

"Damn it!" she suddenly shouts. "You treat me like

I'm some kind of superwoman! I'm not! I'm insecure! I'm scared to go off to college!"

"So am I!"

"Sometimes I hate who I see in the mirror."

"At least you don't have to squat to see your reflection!"

"I get freaked out when I see you with other girls. I know there's nothing going on with you and Kelli, but it still made me jealous to see you with your hands all over her."

"And I nearly got in a fistfight with Jason today!" That startles her, I can tell. "Soraya, don't you see? You and I, we're totally screwed up. We're meant to be together!"

I reach out a hand to her, smiling desperately. She smiles back. But doesn't take the hand.

"We're both starting new adventures in the fall, Deacon. I think . . ." She rubs her hand across her eyes. "I think maybe we should both start . . . without any attachments."

I physically stagger, just a bit. "I don't want that. I don't think you want that."

She just shakes her head. "You said it yourself, you're supposed to be the bad boy. You're going to be dancing with women, going to parties, meeting famous people. You don't need to be pining away for some girl in Arkansas."

"Listen to yourself! You really think I'm that shallow?"

She twists her hair. "Maybe I'm the shallow one. Everyone thinks you're seeing that Kelli girl behind my back. It's not your fault, but it still kind of hurts. Next semester I need to concentrate on my classes, not be thinking about you, what you're doing and who you're with. And if maybe you'll end up happier in California and I'd just be in your way. You may not believe me, but I think you might like life out there."

"I'm not my father. I'm not going to move to California because it might be fun. I didn't ask for any of this."

She smiles, faintly. "But you have it. And it would make me very happy if you enjoyed it. Be a TV star. Try to make it to the final round. Make me proud. And if you move back to Fayetteville afterward, look me up." She chokes on that last bit.

"I don't understand. I don't understand why we can't do the long-distance thing. I don't understand why me being on TV matters!" I notice Mr. Shadee peek through the living-room curtains.

"Good-bye, Deacon." She touches my hand and kisses my cheek. "I wish I was stronger."

"Well, I wish I was too." Because I'm about to break

down crying. Turning my back to her, I jog toward the street.

"Deacon?"

"Yeah?" I don't turn around. I can't.

"Break a leg, okay?" Her voice comes out as a forced rasp.

"I will."

I make it down the street before the tears start.

It must have taken me a couple of hours to walk home. I don't remember any of it. By the time I arrive at our house, I'm soaked in sweat, my shoes are muddy, and the sun is going down.

She ended it. Just like that. For no good reason. Her boyfriend of a few weeks suddenly plans to move out of state, starts getting in fights, becomes possessive and angry, and shows up in a video with another woman, and all of a sudden she wants me to give her some space.

Damn. I knew I'd do all the wrong things, but this is a spectacular failure, even for me.

My only comfort is I won't be leaving for another couple of months. Maybe if I make a huge effort to be a good boy and not get into any compromising positions, Soraya will miss me and want to see me again.

Meanwhile, Jason is probably already lurking under her bedroom window, playing romantic songs on his guitar. Soraya says that she doesn't have any feelings for him. Well, if she could fall for me, then she could fall for anyone. Especially a guy with money and talent and carefully maintained beard stubble.

The yard is still filled with pieces of gutter and some of Clara's equipment. I need to clean all this up. But not now.

I find Jean sitting in the dining room. Both our places are set, but Jean's already eaten.

"Well, you finally decided to come home." Her voice is uncharacteristically icy.

"I'm sorry, I hope you didn't wait."

"You couldn't pick up a phone and call me?"

Too busy getting my heart crushed. "There was an accident. Elijah fell off our roof."

Her eyes widen. "Is he okay?"

"He's . . ." And it suddenly hits me. With all the craziness with Soraya, I never called and asked how bad Elijah's injuries were. Way to be a friend, Deacon.

"He'll be fine."

"What on earth was he doing up on the roof in the first place?" she snaps.

I'm shocked. I expected her to be concerned, to ask

more probing questions, to insist on baking a casserole to take to his family.

"We were just . . ."

"You may think it's funny to pull stunts like that, but I assure you, I am not laughing. Did it ever occur to you that you're no longer a boy? That maybe instead of jack-assing around with your friends, you could start trying to act like an adult?"

All of a sudden, I'm not thinking about Soraya or Elijah. I'm looking at this woman in front of me, and I'm very scared.

"I . . . all we were doing . . ."

"Deacon, I am a little tired of your excuses, your whining, and your troublemaking."

"I'm sorry." But I have no idea what I'm apologizing for.

"If you're truly sorry, you'll clean up that mess your friends left in the yard. Now, have you eaten?"

"I'm not hungry," I truthfully reply.

"Then I think you'd best go on up to your room. Good night."

"Night."

I wait until I'm alone to start hyperventilating. She's not right. She's not right at all. She was obviously mistaking me for my father back there.

I can't leave. I have to stay here and watch out for Soraya.

I mean Jean. I have to take care of my grandmother.

I pull out my phone and begin to compose a letter.

Dear Mr. Delaney,

It is with great regret that I ask to be released from my contract. . . .

THIRTY-ONE

I GET UP EARLY THE NEXT MORNING TO CLEAN UP the yard before Jean gets up. And by cleaning up, I mean sitting on the porch obsessively waiting for a text from Soraya.

I get an email from Mr. Delaney instead.

> Deacon, I am getting a bit tired of your constant complaining. You were not the only young man we could have selected for this opportunity. We chose you, however, and you signed a contract. If you produce a doctor's note saying that your grandmother is incapable of caring for herself for five months, and that you are the only person available to watch out for her, we will consider

releasing you from your contract. However, we have already spent considerable resources planning for your appearance on *Celebrity Dance Off.* If you do not honor our terms and conditions, we will hold you responsible for lost revenue, to the amount of $25,000, payable at once. Please see article three, section one of your contract for specific details.

I'm terribly sorry that your grandmother is not doing well, but I find it difficult to believe that this happened so suddenly, or that you are the only one who can help her at this time. I think that the money you would earn on our show, as well as additional opportunities this would open for you, would be a greater help to your grandmother in the long run.

As a show of faith, we would be willing to provide you with plane tickets home twice a month for two days, during the course of the filming, subject to future change. We have no wish to cause strife for your family, but we are not prepared to reconfigure the show at this late date. It's time you started doing your part. I notice that a new nightclub has opened in Fayetteville, El Bar Sin Nombre. I think it would be nice if you showed off some of your patented dance moves there this week. Get a friend to take some pictures.

Incidentally, I'm glad you have chosen not to

associate yourself with only one girl. We would like
our female audience members to feel that you're
available. Good choice on your new lady friend, as
many of our viewers can identify with girls of a certain
size.

God, I want to wash my eyes after reading his letter.
So if I try to pull out of the show, he'll utterly destroy
me financially. The only way out is to get a doctor to say
that Jean is nuts. And if a doctor makes that diagnosis—
which would be completely wrong!—wouldn't they have
her committed or something? I'm only eighteen, I don't
think they'd trust me as a guardian.

I also get a note from Kelli.

Forgot I was talking to a celebrity ☹

She's pissed about the video. She never emojis.

I decide to pretend that my problems do not exist
and I concentrate on cleaning up the bits of gutter,
shingles, and other debris in the yard. I've barely started
when Elijah's toy car pulls up the driveway.

He hops out, brandishing his bright-pink cast at me.

"Came by to pick up Clara's drill and nut drivers." He
giggles when he says the last part.

"How's the arm?"

"Terrible. I was nearly forced to amputate it myself
with a pocketknife, but the doctor swears it's just a crack."

"I'm sorry about all this, Elijah." I'd offer to sign his cast, but Clara has already covered 100 percent of the surface with flowers and hearts.

"I'm still alive. Um . . . is Jason? You didn't throw him into the old well, did you?"

"No." But only because we don't have an old well.

He sits down next to me, picks up Clara's cordless drill, and begins revving it in an irritating matter. "What was all that about, anyway? You two were ready to go at it."

I look over at Elijah and realize he's my only friend who's not pissed off at me right now. "Someone shot a video of Kelli and me. We were just hugging, but it kind of looked like we were sucking face."

He looks baffled. "Does Jason have a thing for Kelli?"

"Soraya. He's after her and made sure she saw the clip. She didn't believe him, but she still dumped me. How does that make any sense?"

"Sorry, man."

"Seriously! Is Soraya crazy? Am I crazy?"

He scratches ineffectively at his plaster. "Deacon, you're tall, good-looking, and famous. If you can't hold on to a girl, I'm worried for the rest of us."

I laugh a little. It's nice to talk to someone this week and have it not end in a fight. I almost tell him about

Jean and her problems. But I'm not ready to share that with him yet.

"Elijah, I'm so screwed up. I don't want to be on that stupid show, but I don't see the point of going to college if I don't have Soraya. And is there a way to get her back? What do I do now?"

"Something for yourself," he answers with no hesitation.

"What?"

He faces me. "Do something for yourself. As long as I've known you, you've done nothing but worry about other people. You did whatever Kelli told you, and she never treated you that nice. You took your grandmother to the prom, just to make her happy. You've spent the past month trying to impress Soraya. You agree to do this silly TV show, but your heart's not in it.

"How about you do something for Deacon for a change? I'm serious, man. Tonight. Go crazy. What do you like to do? You name it, I'm in. Let's make a night of it. C'mon."

His enthusiasm is a little contagious. And he's right. Maybe getting out of the house for a while would help clear my head. I could forget about Soraya for the evening. Refresh myself, give me a chance to decide what to do about Jean.

Plus, I really kind of want to say screw everything today. I remember what Mr. Delaney suggested I do.

I smile at my friend.

"You ever been clubbing?"

El Bar Sin Nombre is in the industrial area of Fayetteville, and it blends in. There are no signs, no parking lot, no exterior lighting. I would have taken it for an abandoned warehouse or factory, except for the long line of people waiting to enter.

Elijah, Clara, and I stand across the street, each waiting for someone to make a move forward. I'm dressed in some of my mandatory new clothes. Clara is wearing a surprisingly short miniskirt and sleeveless sweater. Due to his cast, Elijah has to wear a T-shirt.

Clara turns to us. "Are you sure you're up for this? I know things have been rough. It's okay if you'd rather stay home."

I'm touched by her concern for me, but Elijah and Mr. Delaney are right. I need to get out of the house. I'm about to thank Clara when I realize she's not talking to me.

Elijah squeezes her hand. "I'm fine. Can't feel it at all. Now c'mon, are we just going to stand here?"

We just stand there. Eventually, I cross the street.

The bouncer is much shorter than me, but also much wider. He eyeballs the people in line ahead of us. Clara and I pass, but he holds out a hand at Elijah.

"Sorry, kid. Dress up a little next time."

Elijah looks heartbroken. "I couldn't get the cast through the sleeve. . . ."

The doorman is not moved. "Then come back when you get it off. Move aside, please."

Well, so much for dancing tonight. I wonder if there's anything good on at the movies.

Unless . . .

God, do I have it in me? Could I really be that obnoxious?

Clara is looking at me, her eyes wide and sad. I should at least try.

I tap the doorman on the shoulder. He turns and does not smile at me.

"Excuse me, sir. Um, what's your name?"

"Garth." His expression does not invite conversation.

Here goes nothing. "Nice to meet you, Garth. I'm *Deacon Locke*. Maybe you've heard of me?"

No reaction. He just stares. Not only are we not getting in, I just played the "Do you know who I am?" card and got shot down. It's humiliating. I feel six feet tall.

But then his face breaks into a gold-toothed smile.

"That guy from TV! You danced with your grandmother. You're going to be on . . . um . . ."

"*Celebrity Dance Off*," I say in my best radio-announcer voice. "I hope you'll watch. You know, they always ask the contestants where they danced back home, and, well . . ." I pat the side of the building. The people behind us move in closer to listen.

I point to Elijah. "The thing is, it's my friend's birthday, and I said I'd show him a good time. It's not his fault he has to keep the cast out in the open, doctor's orders. I guess that's how it goes on the MMA circuit. So, what do you say? Could you bend the rules for my little buddy tonight?"

Garth beams. "Hey, any friend of Deacon Locke's is welcome here." He slaps Elijah on the shoulder, causing him to wince. "Just try to style it up a little next time, okay?"

We walk through the door, side by side.

"Thanks, Skipper."

"No problem, Gilligan."

The inside of the building is the exact opposite of the outside. Neon tubing, mirrors, strobe lights, and video monitors. All designed to draw attention. The music is loud, but not painful, vibrate-off-your-lungs loud. There are about fifty people in here. Half of them are dancing, the other half are on their phones.

Soraya would have liked it here. She would have already dragged me out onto the dance floor. She would have warned Elijah to dress up a little more. She would have made me not nervous and afraid.

"Deacon?" says Clara. "Would you like to dance?"

It's a sweet offer, but I shake my head. "Later. You two have fun. I'm going to get something to drink."

Within seconds, Elijah and Clara are on the dance floor, moving in time to a beat. They're certainly . . . enthusiastic.

I make my way to the bar. I notice that the older patrons are all wearing over 21 wristbands. Celebrity or not, Deacon Locke is not getting served beer tonight.

The bartender ignores me for five minutes as he takes orders from other people. And when he does finally serve me, he's not impressed when I ask for a Fresa Blaster (#berryblasterific).

I sip the syrupy thing and check my phone one last, last time for a message from Soraya. Nothin'.

"Hey, aren't you Deacon Locke?"

Will this never end? I strap on my smile and turn. Much to my surprise, I actually know the girl who's speaking to me. She's a cute, slender brunette, and I know I went to school with her. Not a clue to her name, though.

She seems to read my thoughts. "Regina Callahan. We had trig together. Had no idea you were a dancer until that craziness on the last day of school. When does that show start?"

"We start filming this summer. Should start airing in September." I think.

She leans against the bar. Unconsciously, I follow suit, and nearly demolish a tray of garnishes. She giggles.

"I'm more graceful on the dance floor," I say, a little defensively.

"Well . . . want to show me?"

Wow, I walked right into that. But she has a nice smile and I can't spend the whole night sitting at the bar, drinking pure high-fructose corn syrup. I take her hand.

Regina isn't as good a dancer as Soraya, but neither am I. As we dance, I find it's kind of nice to not feel outclassed. Since we started in the middle of the song, we dance to the next one too. And the next.

People are watching us. It's clear I've been spotted. Phones are out, and people are shout-whispering to one another over the music. It's just like when I danced with Jean at prom.

Only it's not. Tonight, I'm supposed to have people notice me. I've been told to be in the public eye, so, by

God, I'll do it. I kick it up a notch. I dance faster. I try moves I never attempted with Soraya: dips, twirls, leaps. Regina seems surprised, but as long as I'm leading, she seems willing. People holler and whistle at us. We're the center of attention. And when I move to Los Angeles, it's going to be like this every night.

After what seems like an hour, Regina asks me to stop. "I need a break, Deacon."

I'm soaked with sweat and kind of breathing hard. "Yeah, me too. Do you want something to drink?"

She glances at her nails. "No. Do you, um, want to step outside for a second? It's cooler out there."

That works for me. She leads me out a back door and into a little patio paved with cigarette butts. We sit on a low cinder-block wall.

It's much quieter out here, with just the hum of traffic and the thump of the music from inside. It's also a little chilly. Regina moves closer to me.

"Deacon? Can I ask you a question?"

"Sure," I say, though that's probably a mistake.

"You seemed so sad when you were sitting at the bar earlier. Is anything wrong? Anything I can help with?"

"No, nothing." I'm disgusted that my answer has that whiny "I have a long, sad story to tell, but you'll have to wheedle it out of me" tone.

"Sometimes it helps to talk."

I turn to her and half smile. "My girlfriend. I thought things were great, but she tells me she can't handle the long-distance thing. We just broke up."

Regina looks indignant. "You're kidding me! She really gave you up because you have to go away for a little while?"

Well, I also started getting in fights and attacking her friends and there were some rumors about me and another girl. "It's complicated," I say with a shrug.

"I'm serious, Deacon!" she yelps. "A lot of girls would be happy to go out with you, and be proud to see you on TV. If she's too stupid to see that, then screw her!"

I almost leap to Soraya's defense, before I remember I have no reason to defend her anymore. Not really. "It is what it is."

"Listen to me. You shouldn't waste time on a girl who's not proud of you." She scoots closer to me, close enough that our shoulders are touching. I don't move away. I don't move when she lays her hand on my knee.

"Did you drive your friends here?" she asks after a minute.

"No, they drove me."

"I have my car here. Want to go for a ride?"

I shrug. "To where?"

She kicks the wall with the back of her feet. "Wherever.

We could go out to the country and look at the stars, maybe."

Even I recognize what a total line that is. It's no wonder, I've used it myself. I turn to Regina and smile. "No, thank you."

She smiles, but I can see she looks a little hurt. A girl that pretty, she's probably not used to guys not being interested. At least, guys who aren't totally screwed up in the head.

"Well, maybe some other time. Are you ready to go back inside?"

I shake my head. "Why don't you go on in. I'll come later."

"Oh." She pauses, as if waiting for me to change my mind. When I don't move, she returns to the club.

I'm an idiot. Why didn't I go with her?

Because I'm still hung up on Soraya. And I don't see that changing anytime soon.

That's my problem, isn't it? I can never move on. That's why I'm not excited about doing the dance show, or going to California, or trying to have fun. It's because I don't want things to change.

I want a grandmother who's still at the top of her game. I want a girlfriend who likes street fairs and pigs. I want to go out and not be filmed.

My father abandoned everything, including his own

son, seeking fortune and pleasure. Me, I get it dumped in my lap and I complain about it.

Am I really that different from him?

I see Elijah and Clara leave a couple of hours later. They're laughing and holding on to each other, and I'm almost embarrassed to call out to them.

"Holy crap, Deacon!" says Elijah. "We thought you left. Figured you'd met some girl and . . . well, my mistake."

I nod. "Let's go."

During the ride, Clara alternates between snuggling with Elijah and jabbing him in the ribs as he attempts to drive with one hand.

I wonder if I'll ever have a girl to physically abuse me.

As we pull down the country road that leads to my house, Elijah addresses me over his shoulder.

"Deacon? You wanna come over to my place tomorrow? It's movie night."

I don't feel like socializing. "Maybe some other time."

"You sure? *Missing My Lady* just came out on DVD, and I hear it's really scary."

Yikes. "No thank you."

As we pull into my driveway, Clara turns in her seat. "You know, my cousin Janine is going to be there. She likes to dance."

"I said no." I say this rather forcefully. Clara quickly turns around.

Elijah parks. He's still looking forward, but I can see his eyes reflected in the rearview mirror when I open the door. They don't look happy.

"See ya, Deke. Say hi to the beautiful people for us."

I pause, wondering if I should try to defend myself. "Knock it off, Elijah. I've had a rough week."

"Yeah." He waves to me with his broken arm and pulls off down the driveway.

I slump my way to the house. The lights are all off. I haven't talked to Jean since she yelled at me yesterday. Not that I'm angry or afraid. It's just that I'm . . .

Okay, angry and afraid. I'm scared that the next time I talk to her, she'll be confused again.

Why the hell did I sign that contract?

There's no movement in the house and I sneak upstairs unnoticed. I lie in my empty cell of a room and stare at the ceiling.

Is this what life in Los Angeles is going to be like? A hotel room, night after night, worrying about Jean and wondering about Soraya, while everyone else is having fun?

I need to turn off my brain. I need to not think at all. Too bad I don't have a television in here.

I don't have anything in here to distract me, not even

a radio. I usually only go up here to sleep. I spend most of my time downstairs with Jean.

My phone is dead, and it's only brought me misery recently anyway. I rub my forehead. Is there anything to read up here? I check my desk, but only find that old stack of letters from my grandfather.

Actually, that might do the trick. His puerile descriptions of the food and his socks might help me take my mind off my problems. I take some letters off the bottom of the pile.

Dear Jean,

I'm shipping out tomorrow. I'll be in California for a few days, then Saigon. After that, I'm not sure. I'll let you know as soon as I do.

Jean, I've never been so scared in my life. The guys are talking about how rough things get over there. I don't want to kill anyone. I don't want to die.

I wish I could come home to you. I wish we could go swimming and ride the horses and go cruising. I wish I could hold you.

I'm sorry I can't come home for your dance. All leave has been canceled. I'm sorry, I really would like to see you before I ship out.

I need you to know that there's a very real chance

that I might not come back. I hope that's not the
case. I know we always talked about getting married,
but I need you to know that I was serious. I always
saw you in my future. I've always loved you. I always
will.

If the worst should happen, please look in after my
parents.

I may not be able to write for a while.

All my love,

Howard

Jesus.

I wasn't expecting that. I gently replace the letter. I don't want to read the ones from Vietnam.

The poor bastard. He didn't want to go to war. I mean, I guess none of them really *wanted* to go. Most of them had no choice.

I walk to the window and stare out at the dark night, broken by the lights from the country club down the road.

I do have choices. And it's time I started acting like it.

Jean's doctor's appointment is next week. I'm going to tell her about it tomorrow. And she's going to go, even if I have to carry her. I'm going to let her physician know exactly what's been going on. I'll insist on an honest diagnosis. And if he tells me she's not okay, I'll use his word to get out of Delaney's stupid contract. He can sue me if he'd like, I've got nothing.

If the doctor says Jean will be okay . . . then I'll go to California. And I'll try my damnedest to win. I'll have fun. I'll go home and see Jean when I can. And I'll start college in the winter.

And no matter what happens, I'm going to make things right with Soraya (Elijah and Kelli, too, though they can wait). Maybe it'll happen before I leave. Maybe when I get back and we're in school together.

I don't want her to think of me as a regret.

THIRTY-TWO

I WAKE UP THE NEXT MORNING MUCH LATER THAN I intend to. While it would be nice to go back to bed for another couple of days, I know that it's time to get up and face my problems. First things first, I need to tell Jean about her doctor's appointment.

As I go downstairs, I'm surprised not to smell bacon. I can't recall the last time she didn't cook us a big breakfast on the weekend, though after the fire the other day, we may be having Pop-Tarts.

"Jean?"

No answer. Did she go out? She almost never leaves without telling me. I'm getting an uncomfortable feeling.

And then someone punches me in the back of the head.

It's not a strong punch. I barely feel it. But it's so unexpected that I stagger. Someone just assaulted me in my own home. Someone who is about to have their face busted.

I turn.

It's Jean.

I would love to believe this was just some kind of misunderstanding. Maybe she was trying to get my attention or something and misjudged. But just looking at her, I know this isn't the case.

She's still dressed in her pajamas. She's not wearing makeup. Her hair is disheveled and uncombed. None of this is remotely like Jean. But that's not what scares me.

It's the look in her eyes. Something I've never seen before. I see fear. I see rage. I see anger. And she's directing it at me.

"Jean?"

Her hand snakes out. Her nails rake me across the cheek.

"Get out!" she hisses, in an unworldly voice I've never heard before. This terrifies me more than her violence.

"What are you doing? Stop that!"

Her fist flies, catching me in the chin. There's no pain, but still I fall back.

"Get out of my house! Leave, right now!" She grabs a knickknack from a side table and hurls it at me. She misses by a mile.

What has brought this on? I try to think of what could have made her so mad . . . but I already know. I've known for months. It's nothing that I've done. And nothing I can correct.

Jean—or the thing in front of me that looks like Jean—strikes at me again. She connects to my lip. I taste blood.

She's yelling at me, but I can't understand what she's saying. I'm yelling too. Begging her to stop, to look at me, to come back.

Neither of us understands the other one. Jean begins pummeling me with her tiny fists. It hurts . . . and not just on the outside.

I'm backed against a wall. I don't know what to do. I can't fight her, I can't leave her alone like this, and I can't even restrain her. I might break her.

"Jean, it's me, Deacon! Stop!"

"You're not Deacon! Get out of my house! Get out! Get . . ."

The punches come harder and faster. All I can do is guard my face. I have to get out of here before she ends up hurting herself, attacking me like this. I have to . . .

She's stopped. She's staring at me. Tears fill her eyes. She's breathing rapidly.

"Jean?"

She turns and rushes toward her bedroom. I take a step after her, then stop.

I hear her door slam.

Gingerly, gingerly, I follow. I silently sit down in front of her bedroom.

Jean is sick. And I knew it. I saw how confused and frightened Jean was getting, but I didn't do anything. I wouldn't take her to urgent care. I never forced her to discuss things with me. Because if I didn't say anything, then I wouldn't have to face it, would I?

I was too scared. Scared that she'd have to go away, that I'd lose her.

Deacon, the little boy who was too frightened to do anything himself.

I press my ear to Jean's door. I can hear her softly sobbing.

Not a bad idea. But later.

I call her doctor, but it's the weekend and I only get a recording.

"If you have an emergency, please hang up and dial 911. . . ."

Am I that desperate? If a bunch of EMTs show up at our house, won't that just freak her out even more?

But who else can I call? Not Elijah. And not one of Jean's elderly friends. God, who else do I know? Who else does Jean know?

The answer, of course, is obvious.

With trembling hands, I dial Soraya. She doesn't answer. I leave a message.

"Soraya? It's Deacon. Jean is having some kind of attack. She doesn't recognize me. She hit me. I . . . I don't know what to do. I'm scared. I'm sorry. This isn't your problem, but Jean likes you. Maybe she'd recognize you. I . . . look. If you could come by . . . please. Please."

I hang up.

Soraya calls back in two minutes.

"Stay with her. I'll be right over."

I stand in front of Jean's door the whole time I'm waiting. I knock a few times, but there's no answer. Part of me wants to just bust the door down, while the rest of me wants to collapse, sobbing.

Soraya arrives seven minutes after I talk to her. She rushes into the house without ringing.

"Deacon." She takes my hand and squeezes my wrist as she looks sadly up at me. And just for a moment, I feel a little stronger, a little better.

A little.

She turns to the bedroom door. "Jean?" she calls.

"Jean, it's Soraya Shadee. From dance class at the YMCA. I'd like to talk to you. May I come in?"

There's no answer. What is she doing in there? What if she's hurt? I'm about to knock again when the knob starts to turn. The door opens just a crack. I can't see into the bedroom. Soraya slips in and closes the door behind her.

I wait in the hall for over an hour, my back against the wall and my arms around my knees.

What are they talking about? Why will Jean speak to Soraya and not me?

Maybe because I'm a shitty grandson. I can't believe I even considered being on that stupid TV show. I can't believe I didn't realize how sick Jean was.

Solitude is not my friend. I begin replaying scenes from my life with Jean. I remember a thousand times that I was inconsiderate and rude and just plain mean. Why did I always slam the screen door? How come I didn't help around the house more? Why didn't I encourage her art?

I'm at the point of kicking the door off its hinges when Soraya comes out of the bedroom. She silently motions me to the kitchen.

"How is she?" I ask in a whisper.

She shakes her head. "Not good. I'm sorry, Deacon. I didn't realize things had gotten this bad."

I rap my knuckles against the counter. "I knew it. But I kept telling myself that I was just being overprotective. That Jean would be okay if I didn't think about it."

Soraya goes to the fridge and takes out a jug of lemonade. Jean's lemonade. The special, extra-tart kind. She pours us both a glass.

"You know what has to be done, don't you?"

I can't look her in the eye. "I'm going to talk to her doctor next week."

Soraya stands beside me. "She needs to go to the hospital. Today."

"But . . . what if they . . ." My voice cracks. "What if they keep her?"

She looks grim. "You may have to face that possibility."

"Like hell I do! She can stay here. I can watch out for her."

"Deacon . . ."

"You'll see! She took care of me, now I'll take care of her."

"How did you get those scratches on your face?" she asks evenly.

"Jean was upset. But you know what? I don't care! She can't do anything to me, she weighs like ninety pounds."

"It's not you I'm worried about. You're built like a

wall. If she comes smashing into you, she's the one who's going to be injured."

I remember how I let Jean whale on me, for fear I might accidentally hurt her.

"It won't come to that."

She shakes her head. "What if she needs special equipment? What if she needs someone to help bathe and dress her?"

"Quit trying to turn her into some kind of helpless baby! And if she needs all that, I'll get it! I'll hire someone! I'll get Clara to install equipment we need! You watch, I'll turn this house into a place dedicated to Jean. Somewhere we can take care of her and watch out for her and . . ."

I suddenly shut up, realizing what sort of home I'm describing.

Soraya, I think, realizes she's won the argument but takes no pleasure in it.

My hand shakes hard enough to spill some of my drink. "Maybe if we waited a few days . . ."

"Deacon. The ambulance is on its way."

I take a step away from her. "You had no right!"

She shakes her head. "I didn't call them. Jean did. She was scared and confused and was afraid she might end up hurting you. I think she knew that it was going to come to this sooner or later."

"But why an ambulance? I would have driven her!"

"No. You would have come up with some excuse."

I can't believe what is happening. I call Soraya over here for help, and she lets Jean do something like this. I'm so furious I want to scream. I want to break something. I grab the glass lemonade jug and prepare to smash it to the floor. I stop myself just in time.

"It's okay," says Soraya. "Do it. It'll make you feel better."

It's hard to be violently angry when someone gives you permission. I set the pitcher back on the counter, where it promptly slips out of my hand and dumps its contents everywhere.

I stare at the sticky puddle as it drips onto the linoleum.

"I hate everything."

Soraya grabs some dish towels. "Deacon, Jean made that call ten minutes ago. Why don't you go talk to her?"

Go talk to her while I still have time. Before they come and take my grandmother away.

I want to take Soraya with me. I want her to do the talking. I want someone else to take care of everything.

But those days are over. I go to Jean's bedroom and knock.

"Come in, Deacon."

I expect to find her disheveled and confused, so I'm

happy to see her fully dressed and made up, her hair perfect. Is this what they were doing this whole time while I was going through hell waiting? Playing beauty salon?

Jean sits on her bed, her travel bag next to her.

"Sit with me, honey."

I sit.

"I have to go away for a while."

Nausea sweeps through my body. "We don't know that. Let's wait and—"

"Stop it," she says severely. "You're an adult now. That means facing some unpleasant facts. We both know what's happening, and as much as we'd like to pretend otherwise, there's nothing to be done."

She's giving up. Giving up on herself. And giving up on me.

"Please . . ."

She stands. "Deacon, you know how an actor will dream that he's standing onstage and doesn't know any of his lines? That's been me for the past year or so. You don't know how often I've been talking to someone, nodding my head and agreeing, while I have no idea what they're saying. It didn't bother me much until it started happening when I was with you."

I grab at my hair with both hands. "It's not just you. I don't think I've been making a lot of sense lately."

"That's probably true. But I can't go on like this

anymore. I was hoping to wait until you had moved out, but I think the time has come."

"But . . ."

The doorbell rings. I hear Soraya answer it.

"That's my ride. Walk me out?"

I'm suddenly seized with an icy dread. I give her my arm.

There are two strangers standing in the entryway. One is a young black man in an EMT uniform. The other is an older woman in a business suit. They both smile at Jean when they see her.

"Jean Locke?" asks the man. "Are you ready to go?"

He sounds so sincerely polite that you'd think he was escorting his own mother. I hate him.

Jean takes his arm. Through the open front door I see, not an ambulance, but a sports utility vehicle. The man begins to lead Jean out the door. I rush to her side.

"I'll follow you in the car. I'll be right with you, the whole way. No matter what happens, I'll be right there with you."

But my grandmother only smiles and shakes her head. "No you won't. I don't want you to come."

Soraya, who was standing out of the way in a corner, looks surprised. Not as surprised as I look, I bet. "What?"

"Tonight's going to be rough. I need to do this on my own, without you hovering around. Please try to understand, but I need you not to be there."

She's having an episode again. She thinks she's talking to my father or something.

"Then I'll hang out in the lobby. I'm not going to abandon you. Not now."

"Deacon Locke Junior!" I jump a little at her stern tone. "Listen to me. I know this is hard for you, but it's much harder for me. I need to start the next phase of my life with a little dignity, and a little privacy, and I cannot do that with you hanging over me." She smiles a little. "Please. Let me do this my way. I'll call you when I'm ready to see you."

I'm too stunned to reply. She reaches up and touches my cheek. "Such a good boy. I love you, Deacon. Goodbye."

I don't answer. After a minute, the medic leads her out of our house. And I have the horrible feeling she'll never be back.

Now is the time for me to run down the porch stairs after Jean, embrace her in a huge hug, and tell her everything she means to me. But the strange woman steps between me and the door, blocking my last view of my grandmother.

"Mr. Locke? I'm Namey McName from the Meaningless Acronym Government Department. I'd like to speak with you for a moment."

"Huh?"

"How old are you?"

"Huh?"

Soraya steps to my side. "He's eighteen. He'll be fine."

The woman hands me a business card. "We have your phone number. Please call me at number number number if you have any difficulties whatsoever."

And she joins the others in the SUV. It takes off with a roar. I stand in the doorway and watch it vanish down the road.

Soraya takes my arm. Not in a comforting gesture. She grips me tight, like she's afraid I'm going to go racing down the driveway after them.

But I've lost all energy. I can do nothing. Not even stand up. I drop to my knees.

Soraya gently presses my head to her chest and holds me as I blubber and bawl like a baby.

THIRTY-THREE

SORAYA STAYS WITH ME FOR THE REST OF THE AFTER-noon. I do not leave the couch. She keeps trying to talk to me, to fix me food, to get me to go for a walk.

Yesterday, such attention from her would have caused my head to explode.

Today, all I can do is just sit here.

Jean is gone. My only family. The only one who ever cared for me. My best friend.

And I let her go.

I grip a throw pillow so hard it tears.

"You'll see her tomorrow, Deacon. Things aren't as bleak as they seem right now."

I turn and frown at her.

She drops her eyes. "Or maybe they are. But Jean is a fighter, and she has you. Do you want me to come with you to the hospital tomorrow?"

That would be nice. I'd truly love her support. But what's happening . . . it's between me and Jean. I think I'd rather have privacy.

"Thank you, but I need to go alone. I have a feeling I'll be asking for your help a lot in the days to come."

She gives me a one-armed hug. And she tries to be subtle about it, but I see her glance at the clock on the end table.

"You've been here all day, Soraya. Go on home."

"I'm not going to leave you here alone," she says emphatically.

"I've got to make some calls, try to track down Dad and my aunt. Plus I somehow doubt your parents will let you spend the night."

She smiles. "They don't even know where I am right now."

"What? You need to get out of here. I'll call you when I know what's going on."

She shakes her head. "I'm not leaving. You're not going to sit in this big empty house with your thoughts all night. I know you. You'll go nuts. Come to my house. Have dinner with us."

Yeah. That'd be relaxing. "I'll be fine."

Soraya looks at the clock, then back at me. "Call Elijah."

"Huh?"

"Have him stay over tonight. I'm not leaving until you promise me."

"Soraya . . ."

"Promise me, Deacon."

I give her a weak smile. "I promise. Now get out of here. Your parents are probably pacing the floor."

I walk her to her car. Twice she stops to offer to stay with me. And the offer is tempting, but I know she'll catch hell when she comes home as it is.

She stands in the driveway and looks at me. "About the other day . . ."

"Shh. Don't worry about it."

She hugs me, and I hug her back.

"Anytime you need me, Deacon, just call. For anything. I'll be there."

"I know you will."

And then she's gone.

And I'm alone.

So very alone.

I sit on the porch steps. I lied to her about calling Elijah, of course. The last thing I need right now is his cheery optimism and chatter.

But I cannot go back into this house, where Jean is

not. I cannot wander around those empty rooms. The kitchen, where Jean may never cook dinner again. The living room, with her crocheted lampshades and her three identical paintings of Elvis, James Dean, Marilyn Monroe, and Bogart sitting in a diner. The back patio, where we'd sit and watch the sun set on nice days.

But not anymore.

I have never felt more confused and afraid in my life. And this is coming from a guy who once had to outrun security dogs at a scrapyard when his father needed to "borrow" some parts.

Worst twelfth birthday ever.

But now, it looks like I'm in charge. I'll tell Mr. Delaney that I can't do the show, of course. I'll stay here with Jean. If she can't come home, I'll visit her every day. I guess she'll have to go to a nursing home or something. God, how are we going to afford that?

Well, I could probably get a job at the hardware store with Clara. And . . . I'll figure out something.

I'm going to have to figure out a lot of things, I think. Like how to pay taxes and doctors' bills and who do I talk to about Jean's insurance and can I apply for some sort of assistance?

I don't know anything about that. Maybe that social worker, or whatever she was, can help.

I can do this. I'll work all day, visit Jean in the

afternoons, and maintain the house in the evenings. It has to work. Jean is still in her sixties, she could live another twenty years.

Twenty years.

That reality show pays well, maybe . . .

No! I'm not my father! I'm not going to take the easy way out.

Except tonight. I can't hang around here. I'm leaving. Somewhere. Anywhere.

Yeah, this was a mistake. For starters, I decide to walk, so I'm alone with my thoughts for like an hour. And when I arrive in town, it's filled with people looking for a good time. The bars are crowded, the people are strolling in the warm night, everyone is happy. I want to yell at them, to grab them by their stupid, ignorant fat faces and remind them that my grandmother is very sick and they have no right to be in a good mood.

I'm sweaty and tired and twice as upset as when I left home. Part of me wants to go back, part of me wants to collapse on a bench.

Part of me wants to go screaming off into the night.

I settle for a cup of coffee at that joint where I last talked to Kelli and started all that trouble.

And then, for the first time in a week, my luck is not shitty.

As I walk into the café, someone is walking out. Someone with pretty clothes, luxurious hair, and a beautiful face.

It's Jason. I run into my nemesis on the very night my world falls apart.

For a minute we just look at each other. Not angry looking, but kind of like two dogs who are meeting for the first time.

Neither of us is wagging his tail.

Eventually, Jason claps his hands once and speaks.

"So, are we going to finally do this?"

Any other night, I would have walked away. All those clandestine videos of me, and Soraya being angry with me for fighting . . .

But tonight is different from all other nights.

It's Passover, Jason. Time to taste the bitter herbs of . . .

Sorry, I'm not Jewish, and that was a bad metaphor to begin with. But I really want to kick Jason's ass.

I look down at my puny rival. "Let's do it."

He glances over his shoulder. "C'mon then. The alley out back."

Oh, this is going to be therapeutic.

The alley is the home to the coffee-shop Dumpster. It's cramped and dirty, but well lit. I wait while Jason carefully removes his jacket, watch, and hat.

Except for Skee-Balling that college boy the other night, I've never actually been in a fight before. Unless you count that time in Houston where I had to pull that dude off Dad's back.

But I am a big guy and Jason is fancy.

I won't hurt him too bad. I may even do the manly thing where I help him to his feet after I've knocked him down.

He raises his fists. I raise mine.

This is going to be sweet.

Ten seconds later, he's collapsed against the brick wall of the building, holding his jaw, not bothering to hide his tears.

"You didn't have to hit me so hard," he whimpers. "You could have knocked out one of my teeth."

I'd take great joy in his low state, except I'm collapsed next to him, leaning forward, draining a pool of blood from my nostrils into the street.

Somehow, we both managed to land a haymaker at the same time.

"I think you broke my nose," I mumble.

"Really?" This seems to cheer him up greatly. He passes me a pressed and folded handkerchief. I eject a wad of blood into it, causing me a momentary flash of incredible pain.

Yep, broken.

We sit there and bleed for a while, as june bugs kamikaze into the light fixture.

"Jason?" I'm still looking at the ground to avoid draining blood down my throat. "Is this about Soraya?" I know it is, but I want Jason to admit it. Admit he's been trying to steal her.

"Damn straight," he replies. "You don't deserve someone like that. She's special, and you go and screw around on her."

That stupid video. "I know what it looked like, but nothing happened with that girl. Kelli's just a friend."

"I know."

I don't think I've ever used the word "malicious" before, but that's the only way to describe Jason's smile.

"What are you saying?"

He chuckles, then winces. "You think you're so damn important that people just follow you down the street to take your picture? I know all the baristas here. One of them texted me that you were here with some girl, and I asked him to film you. And you totally looked like you were kissing that girl. At least you did when I finished editing the clip."

It takes a moment to process what he's saying. "You son of a bitch. You set me up."

He shrugs. "So what if I did?"

Is it time for round two? Or am I about to literally kick a man when he's down? "What the hell is your problem, Jason?"

He turns and glares at me, his split lip glistening in the harsh electric light. "I don't know. Maybe it's because I've known Soraya for twelve years and I've been in love with her for eight. Maybe because I've always been the guy she cries all over when she's scared and when assholes are mean to her. And every time I try to show her how much I care, how much she means to me, she says she just wants us to be friends! You know how many girlfriends I've had? None!" He says this like I'm supposed to be shocked. "Because I wasn't willing to give up. Soraya means the world to me.

"And then just when I think she might be beginning to maybe think about starting to feel the same way someday, you fee-fi-fo-fum in and I've been replaced. So maybe I didn't play fair, but you know what? I'm glad. I'm glad I hurt you. I'd do it again."

His wrath kind of frightens me. He's smart, and I wonder just what he's capable of. I almost forget to be violently angry. "Well, your plan worked. She dumped my ass."

"Good. I was sick of you hurting her."

"I never hurt her!" I shout, spraying blood out of my nose and mouth.

He just laughs. "You really are kind of stupid, aren't you? You get famous and then plaster her picture all over your website. You think people didn't figure out who she was? You know she caught hell for dating you, right?"

"What?" This is all too confusing.

He rolls his eyes, then pulls out his phone, a gesture that has proved disastrous for me this past month. "People sent Soraya messages. She always deleted them. Said the comments didn't bother her. But they bothered me."

I look at the device. There is a string of screen caps, pictures he's taken of Soraya's page. As I read the comments, I start to Hulk out again.

MUS-SLIME

TERRORIST IN TRAINING

WHY DOES DEACON WANT TO BE WITH SOME CAMEL LOVER?

UGLY ASS MUZZIE

I hand the phone back before I can read more.

I truly, truly want to hurt someone tonight. Again.

Jason is not done lecturing me. "That's what happens when you decide to parade around a beautiful, intelligent girl like she's one of your reality-star sluts. That's how people treated her. And her family. It really upset Mr. Shadee. And you didn't even realize it was happening. Too damn clueless."

I remember how Soraya's father requested I leave her out of my quest for glory. I remember some odd comments Soraya made about the internet. I remember how Mr. Oinky came into her life.

And still, I had no idea this was going on.

Jason continues to rant. "Maybe I don't have your build and your brooding-loner thing, but at least I care about her! At least I . . . I . . . um . . . oh, Jesus, Deacon, don't cry."

I wipe my hand across my eyes, smearing blood everywhere. "I'm not crying."

"Yes you are." Just a touch of glee under the false concern.

"It's not about this. It's about . . . Jean."

"Your grandma?"

"She's in the hospital. She . . . her mind is failing. I don't know if she's ever going to come home again. I don't know what the hell to do. And I never meant to hurt Soraya. I care about her too much. And when you showed her those video clips . . . do you think that made her feel good? Were you thinking of her, or thinking of yourself? Who really hurt her, Jason?"

He doesn't answer. We sit there in the grit and grime, pissed off as hell at each other and our own shitty luck.

In an attempt to move on, I try to give Jason back his handkerchief, but he just shakes his head and stands up.

"Let's go."

"Where?" I climb, unsteadily, to my feet.

"The emergency room. You have to get that nose fixed before it heals like that and you get even uglier."

"I don't need your help."

"C'mon. You're twice my size. It'll give me great pleasure to say I put you in the hospital."

I'm too tired, too confused, and in too much pain to argue. I follow Jason back around the building.

"Deacon?" he says, just before we reach his car. "I'm sorry about your grandmother. I would have backed off if I'd known. But listen. Things look bad now, but I think you've kind of hit rock bottom. You can't sink any lower."

"So that means things are bound to get better, right?"

"No. Not at all. But I hope your grandmother comes through okay." He smiles, just slightly. "Now get in the car. I don't have all night."

THIRTY-FOUR

AT EXACTLY SEVEN IN THE MORNING, JEAN CALLS me on my cell phone.

"Deacon, if you'd like to come see me at the hospital, I'll be ready at eight o'clock."

"I'll be there, Jean."

Actually, I'm already there. Jason dropped me off at the emergency room, even bringing his car to a complete stop to let me out. After a surprisingly long delay in a surprisingly empty waiting room, a doctor bandaged up my nose. I'm not sure he believed that I fell in the shower, but I think all ER staff are used to evasive answers, halftruths, and outright lies.

It was nearly midnight by then. I sat in the cafeteria

until morning, making plans for the financial future.

I can probably earn ten dollars an hour at the hardware store or wherever. That's about $1,600 a month, before taxes.

Jean owns her house outright, so there's no mortgage payment. Now let's say for food and gas, $500 a month. Utilities and taxes, another $500. Insurance and things that haven't occurred to me, maybe another $500, but I have a feeling I'm underestimating.

So far, so good. But if Jean has to go into a nursing home, I have to take that into account. How much would that run?

I do a quick Google search. When I see the cost for a private room in a decent-looking facility, I'm sure I'm looking at the yearly rate, not the monthly.

It's about five times what I could earn in a month. I desperately search for grants and assistance for this sort of thing, but I don't understand any of the websites I find. They all seem to imply that help with this thing is hard to come by, and the waiting period is long.

Also, it's illegal to sell your kidney, at least in this country.

Soon my table is covered with empty coffee cups and napkins with scribbles all over them. People begin to join me in the cafeteria, elderly people and nurses about to start their shift. No one notices me.

The numbers. The damn numbers. I cannot afford to take care of Jean.

Even if I became a TV star, it wouldn't be enough. Though it would certainly help. . . .

Maybe I'll be able to track down Dad and he can do something. Or my aunt Karen. I think she'll be headed for Sturgis this time of year. . . .

The alarm on my phone buzzes. It's seven forty-five. Time to face Jean. I plaster on a smile. I cannot let her know the desperate nature of our money situation.

I stand in the corridor, hovering outside her room. Suddenly, I'm scared. I'm scared that when I go into that room, the person there won't be my grandmother. She won't recognize me again. That maybe I'm already too late.

I hesitate, then knock.

"Come in!" sings Jean. I peek through the door.

I'd expected to find Jean lying in her bed, but she sits at a tiny desk, dressed, primped, and powdered. Her face splits into a smile when she sees me. Then she frowns, staring. For a second, I'm afraid she doesn't remember who I am. Then I realize she's startled by the bandage across my nose. She smiles again.

"Eight on the dot. I knew you wouldn't make me wait."

We embrace.

"I'm sorry, Jean. I'm . . . sorry for everything."

She pushes me away to arm's length. "Sorry for what? I'm the one who should be apologizing. I haven't been honest with you. Sit down, we need to talk."

I sit on the bed. Jean used to take such pride in the living room, the parlor, the dining room, and now her guests have to sit on the bed.

"Deacon, several years ago, I was diagnosed with early-onset dementia."

I wince. A real diagnosis from a doctor. The words don't mean much to me, but obviously, they're not good.

"It was right before you moved in," she continues. "My doctor advised me not to take on the responsibility of raising a child, but I wasn't about to let your father turn you into a junior gangster. I thought you were worth taking care of, and I was right."

I will not get choked up. I will be strong for Jean. "You probably saved my life."

She smiles. "I think you would have survived, somehow. But things are starting to slip. I'm losing my marbles, honey."

"No!" I shout. "It's just age. You're just a little confused sometimes."

"That's because I'm such a good BSer. Most of the time, I'm fine. But more and more often . . . it's hard to talk about. Like with the fire the other day. Or—was it yesterday?—when I didn't recognize you. I'm slipping, and I don't need to be living out in the country by myself."

I stiffen my spine. "You won't be. Not now, not ever. I—"

She cuts me off. "I spoke to my lawyer yesterday. It's all been arranged."

The room seems very cold all of a sudden. "What's been arranged?"

"I'm moving into an assisted-care facility. A place where someone can watch out for me. You said it yourself, that house is too big."

"Jean, I meant like a condo or something!" I sputter. "And it was a dumb suggestion. You already have a place to live. *We* have a place to live! Just come home. We'll work all this out."

She pauses before answering. "I've sold the house, Deacon. The golf course has been after that land for years. They'll take possession in the fall."

I jump up. "What? How did all this happen? Where are we going to live? You can't decide something like this after one bad night! Who's your lawyer, I want to talk to him!"

"Sit down! Right now. Calm yourself. This wasn't a rash decision, I planned for this over a year ago."

I fall back to the bed, stunned. She seemed so adamant about not moving when I brought it up. "And when were you going to tell me?"

She glances to the window, then back to me. "When you were away at college. Or in Los Angeles, whatever you decided."

My utter shock must show on my face. "Don't worry," Jean continues. "Peggy's son is in real estate, he'll help you find a nice apartment when you start college. And your things will be put in storage in the meantime."

"My things!" My fingers grip the plastic mattress beneath me. "What about me? Why didn't we discuss this? Why didn't you talk to me?"

She frowns. "You would have argued. You would have fought me on it. I didn't want you to find out until everything was settled. But my little episode last night . . . it's time for me to move out. You won't believe how much the country club is offering, apparently they want to add another nine holes or something. I'm going to send some of the money to your aunt. . . ."

"Jean . . ."

"And use some to pay for your schooling."

"No. Please."

"And the rest will go for my living expenses. I'm going to be moving into the nicest little—"

"Stop it! Stop it!" I know I sound like a little boy

throwing a tantrum, but I can't take this. I can't take Jean giving up on herself. "You don't need to move to some kind of home! You have a home! With me. I'll take care of you." I kneel down in front of her, but I'm still looking her in the eye. "Forget selling the house. Forget moving away. I'll watch over you. All the time. For the rest of your life."

She slaps me.

Not hard. Not at all. But I still stagger backward slightly.

"Deacon Locke, get ahold of yourself! You are a wonderful young man, but you are still very much a child. You're acting like I'm going to get better. I'm not. It's going to get worse and worse, and I'm sorry, but you just are not capable of dealing with things that are happening. There may come a point where I won't be able to do much of anything for myself. I can't even remember how you hurt your nose. Do you realize how bad that scares me?"

I'm tearing and snotting. "That actually happened last night. But Jean, don't you understand, I'm not Dad. I want to do this! I want to help you."

"If you really want to make me happy, then get your ass to California and be on that show. That would really make me excited and proud."

I nearly slap myself. "You honestly think I'm going to

leave the state now? You think I'm that shallow?"

"No. I think you've been given a wonderful opportunity that I'm not about to let you squander."

I'm starting to get angry. "Well, this isn't your decision. If you want to sell the house, I can't stop you. But this is my life, and I'm going to spend it watching out for you."

I expect more arguments, but she gets a sad, faraway look in her eyes. "Deacon, you know your grandfather Howard was wounded in the war, right?"

"Of course." Did she honestly think I didn't know that? Or does she not remember that I know that?

"The thing is, something happened to him over there. Long before he lost his leg. I'm not sure what. He never talked about it. But he wasn't the same man when he returned. He was angry and bitter and scared. He couldn't sleep, and when he did, he'd wake up screaming. He'd get sullen and not talk to me for days. He'd sometimes punch out the wall or pick a fight with your father. We didn't understand the psychological side of things, back in those days.

"And I stood by him. I learned to deal with his moods and his anger. I taught myself not to make loud noises or to sneak up on him. And when he passed away, there I was, nearly sixty, with no education and kids I barely talk to. I did it because I loved Howard. And I'd do it all over again. But I'm not about to make you go through all that. Honey, I know what it's like to take care of someone who has a lot of problems upstairs. It's not fun."

I never knew this about my grandfather, but it changes nothing. "So you expect me to just abandon you?"

"Posh. I expect you to visit me at least twice a week, once you start college. But I also expect you to be on that TV show and have the time of your life. I'm still going to be here when you get back."

Everything is happening too fast. "I don't have to decide right now."

"Yes, you do. And I'm still your grandmother, and I'm still in charge until you leave home. So I'm telling you, go be a TV star. It would make me very happy."

And part of me, a selfish part of me, knows she's right. Knows that I cannot take care of her, and that selling the house is the prudent thing to do, and that I shouldn't pass on the dancing show, for the money, if no other reason.

But it doesn't stop me from hugging Jean and crying. I can't sit in her lap, of course, but I kind of squat on the floor and let her hug me as I sob.

She sobs too.

After a while, we both lose momentum. She passes

me a box of Kleenex, but it hurts too much to blow my nose. Jean notices.

"What *did* you do to your face?" she asks.

I smile, sheepishly, as I dab the mucus away. "I kind of lost it when they took you away. I went to town and picked a fight."

"Deacon Locke! Did your father teach you nothing? I mean, I know he taught you nothing, but still . . ."

"It's not like that. It was about Soraya."

She raises an eyebrow. "I doubt she needs you to fight on her behalf. But please tell her thank you for helping me yesterday. She's such a sweet girl. I'm so glad she's in your life."

I wince. "We're kind of . . . just friends for now."

This seems to genuinely surprise Jean. "Why? What happened?"

I shrug. "It's complicated. Probably all my fault."

Jean's eyes twinkle. "I'm an old woman, and I've seen a lot. And what I'm about to say comes from forty years of marriage."

"Yes, Jean?"

"It probably was your fault. Even if you didn't do anything, it's still your fault. Go apologize to the girl."

Losing her marbles, my ass.

THIRTY-FIVE

IT'S A BEAUTIFUL DAY. THE SUN IS SHINING, THE BIRDS are singing, and I'm about to pass out from exhaustion. I want to go home and sleep in my bed, while I still have a home and a bed.

I have a lot of decisions to make, a lot of planning to do. But first things first.

It was an arduous trek to Soraya's neighborhood. I should have gone home to get the car but what I have to say can't wait. I'm going to be very busy in the next few months, with Jean, with moving out, and . . . appearing on that show. While I still deny that it's going to happen, Jean seems to have made up her mind.

And maybe that's not such a bad thing.

But I have to tell Soraya how much she means to me, and how much I appreciate her. And how I'm sorry I caused problems for her and her family.

True to my recent run of bad luck, Jason is in his front yard, weeding a flower garden. He stands up when he sees me pass by. I notice a huge, purplish bruise developing on his face, and I'm not as pleased as I would have expected.

He grins at me, raises his fists, and throws a fake jab. I join him in his yard.

"How's your grandmother?" he asks.

I shake my head. "Not good. She's going to have to move into a . . . place."

He sighs. "Sorry, man."

I shrug. "Well, at least she'll be here in town where I can keep visiting her."

"Yeah."

There's nothing left to say, but it would be awkward if I just walked away or punched him in the stomach. "How about you, Jason? What're you doing in the fall?"

He flicks a speck of dirt off his immaculate gardening clothes. "I'm going to UALR. Good music program there. It's time I got out of Fayetteville." He looks over at Soraya's house. "There's nothing keeping me here anymore."

I don't feel guilty. Soraya makes her own decisions

about who she dates. It's not Jason. And it's not me.

I extend a hand. "Enemies?" I ask.

He shakes it. "Always."

I walk to Soraya's house. One of their cars is gone. Hopefully that means her parents aren't home. She answers my knock.

"Hey! How's . . ." She stops, noticing my face. "What happened?"

"Um, I slipped in the shower."

She tilts her head, her brown eyes boring into my lying brain. "Really. Because I talked to Jason earlier. He looks like someone cracked him in the jaw, but he says he fell off a ladder."

"Yeah. Small world." My foot jiggles and I rub the back of my neck.

Fortunately, Soraya lets it drop. "How's Jean?"

Damn. I'd managed to stop worrying about her for five minutes. "Not good. She wants to go into a home. And sell our house."

She shuts the front door behind her and gestures to a couple of chairs on the front porch. We sit.

"I'm so sorry, Deacon. How's she taking all this?"

I shrug. "Better than me. She knew this was coming. Me, I was too dumb to realize it."

"You weren't dumb. You just love her and don't want to see her suffer."

I nod. We sit.

"Soraya? She thinks I should still do the show. But with her health problems, they'd almost have to let me out of my contract if I asked."

"So what are you going to do?"

I knead my eyes with my knuckles. I'm so tired I'm almost seeing spots. "The thing is, I kind of want to. Maybe it's for the money, or the fame, or so I don't have to watch the house get torn down. But these last couple of months have been weird. I think I'd like to go to California, and I think that makes me a terribly selfish person."

To my surprise, she grips my hand. "No it doesn't. Jean isn't dying. She's going to be around for a long time. But this opportunity won't last. Jean told me herself. It makes her very happy to see you do amazing things like this. To start earning a little cash. To save up for school. Um . . . you are still planning on enrolling next semester, right?"

"Yeah."

"It's not my decision, but I think you should go. And I don't care what my father says, I want you to tell the world what a great dance instructor I was."

I kind of wince. "Soraya, I'm sorry. Jason showed me what people were messaging you."

She snatches her hand away. "It'll be a cold day in

Arkansas when I give a shit about what some yahoo with an internet connection thinks about me. I'm not some kind of damn Disney princess who needs a man to come and save her. I've been handling assholes all my life. Yes, it bothers me. Yes, sometimes it scares me. And yes, it really helps to have friends like you and Jason to lean on. But when it comes down to it, I can live my own life. Jason and my father never really understood that, and neither do you."

I lean back in the metal deck chair, which creaks in protest. "I'm trying to understand."

"Well, you're not totally hopeless." She smiles at me. I hope she'll take my hand again, but she doesn't.

"Listen," I say after a moment. "Do you think you'd still be willing to look in on Jean while I'm gone?"

"Of course I will. I promise."

"Good. That makes me feel a lot better." I drum my fingers on the armrests. "And maybe, when I come back at Christmas, you and I could—"

"Deacon," she interrupts. "Let's worry about that when the time comes. Okay?"

"Okay." Not really the answer I was hoping for, but it's something.

"Right now, we need to get you home before you pass out in Mom's begonias. C'mon, I'll give you a ride."

"In a second." I scoot my chair closer to hers. We don't

374

hold hands, but just kind of sit there for a bit, watching the unimpressive view of houses across the street.

My life is in chaos. I have no idea where I'm going or what I'm going to do when I get there. But for the first time in my life, I have a few good friends. A little self-confidence. Some fleeting popularity.

The future is just a little less scary than it once was.

EPILOGUE

REMEMBER THAT MOVIE ABOUT THE GUY WHO'S ready to kill himself on Christmas Eve, but instead ends up having a huge party with all his friends and family?

I never liked that movie.

It's late December, and I'm engaging in my two least favorite activities: moving and entertaining. My father did both of those a lot.

Elijah is in my new mini kitchen, helping Clara prepare the party snacks. "Hey, Deacon, do you have a colander?"

"In the cabinet, I think." I'm not really sure what exactly I have here, other than my bed, a couch, and a TV. Most of the rest of my stuff is still in storage, along with all of Jean's possessions. It's going to take me months to go through everything.

Our house is gone. They're already landscaping for the new fairways. It seemed surreal when our home was no longer there, but when I saw the bulldozers leveling astronomy hill . . . I won't be back.

It's just as well. Adam helped me track down this little apartment near campus. When school starts, it'll be a quick walk to classes. And a quick drive to visit Jean.

I sit down next to my grandmother on the couch.

"I'm so excited for tonight," she says. "How many people did you say are coming?"

"Nine or ten. Just a few friends." I told her that twenty minutes ago, but I don't mind repeating myself. I'm just glad she's feeling well enough to come to my party. Some days, she gets confused and it's not quite safe for her to leave the facility.

"It's so good to see you." She smiles up at me, her makeup perfectly in place. There's a salon at the nursing home and I made sure she has plenty of credit there.

"It's great to see you, Jean. I'm sorry I haven't been around for a while."

"Posh, you've been busy. We'll see each other at Christmas. Um, won't we?"

"Of course we will. We're going to have a nice little dinner here at my place."

She squeezes my hand. "How wonderful. Will . . . will your father and your aunt be there?"

I hate explaining this part again. "I'm afraid they can't make it. But they promised to visit soon."

Extending the Christmas invitation had been the first time I talked to my aunt since the summer. She was sorry to hear about Jean's illness, thankful for the money, and didn't come out to help me with Jean. As for my father, who knows? He's dropped off the face of the earth.

There's a knock at the door and guests start to trickle in. Kelli, Hunt, Adam, along with some friends of friends.

I find myself rushing to greet guests, serve drinks (mostly leftover Fresa Berry Blasters), and dart back to the couch to make sure Jean is okay. Fortunately, Elijah relieves me of some of this duty. I'm not sure Jean understands anything he says, but she's hardly alone in that regard.

After half an hour, people start gravitating toward the television. This is, after all, the reason they're here. As I make sure everyone has a place to sit, there's a final knock.

I take a deep breath, plaster a smile on my face, and open the door.

"Hello, Soraya. Hello, Jason."

Soraya, of course, looks fantastic. College agrees

with her. She's more adult, more mature. And—I never would have thought this possible—more beautiful. God, that face.

Jason looks exactly the same. I'd like to say he's one of those guys who peaked in high school and now has trouble finding his place in the world, but he's just as confident and well dressed as ever.

We all exchange greetings. I almost close the door behind them when I realize there's someone else with them.

"Deacon," says Jason, "I'd like you to meet my girl-friend, Rosemary."

I guess you'd call Rosemary attractive, if you're into the whole blond, slender, classic-beauty type of thing. We shake hands. While I'm glad Jason is no longer pursuing Soraya, it amuses me that he's gone for someone based on her looks. This girl probably has a double-digit IQ.

"I've been following you online," she says. "I'm a bit of a fan."

"Oh, you like *Celebrity Dance Off*?"

"What? No, I meant the blog you do with Adam Fernandez. I'm a physics major myself. Later, I'd like to talk to you about your views on the future of the space program."

As I go to put away everyone's coat, I catch a glimpse of Soraya sitting on the couch and talking to Jean. Soraya has been wonderful. She visited Jean while I was away, and sends her letters and little gifts. Even on Jean's off days, she asks about Soraya.

Unfortunately, I don't always have a lot to tell her. I spent most of June and July settling Jean's affairs, then flew off to California to do the show. Soraya started college, and while I managed to fly back twice to see Jean, there was no time to do anything else. Soraya and I kept in touch via social media, but that kind of slacked off after a while. When I moved back to Fayetteville last month, I got busy finding an apartment and registering for college. I haven't seen Soraya in person since early July.

"Hey!" calls Elijah. "Everyone get in here! The show's about to start."

My guests all move toward the TV. Soraya scoots over so I can sit between her and Jean. And it's such a small couch.

I'm so distracted, I almost don't notice the familiar theme music to *Celebrity Dance Off.* The show has aired every week for the past month and a half, but this is the episode where contestants start doing their huge production numbers and risk being eliminated. I wasn't excited about watching this one, but Elijah and Clara had insisted on seeing it with me. And since everyone was out of school for break, I decided to make a party of it.

Funny, a year ago the thought of inviting even a couple of people over would have caused me to play sick. Now, I'm sorry the apartment isn't bigger.

Everyone is silent while the host of *Dance Off* announces the contestants.

"And from Fayetteville, Arkansas, teen internet star Deacon Locke!"

My guests cheer. Jean claps. Soraya shifts in her seat. I feel her hand brush mine, though that might have been an accident.

We watch the clips of each contestant practicing with their professional dance partner. Elijah whistles when he sees me with Tatiana, the Russian dancer I'm paired with.

"She's lovely, Deacon," says Soraya.

I'm a little embarrassed when they show that clip of the two of us having kind of a tickle fight. It had been a difficult rehearsal, and the director decided Tatiana needed to "spontaneously" go after my ribs. They shot five takes of her running her fingers all over me, as I pretended to not enjoy it.

Next come the contestant interviews. I wince when I see how wooden and nervous I look. The host plays that original clip of Jean and me at prom, and I explain, for the thousandth time, why we ended up going together. The producers had originally wanted to fly Jean in for an interview as well, and I was forced to explain why that couldn't happen. They simply told the audience she was "ill" and left it at that.

I do mention Soraya, my great dance teacher back home. But I don't say how, for a few glorious weeks, she was so much more than that.

Finally, the actual dance competition. True, we'd all danced in the previous episodes, but that was just to build up interest in the various teams. This is where the real contest starts.

Tatiana had decided we should dance the Charleston. She looked great dressed as a flapper. I didn't care for my vintage 1920s suit, but the wardrobe people insisted it was fine.

"Looking sharp, Deacon," says Kelli. I'm glad the hubbub over that stupid video of us died down quickly, and that Hunt took her at her word that it wasn't what it looked like. They're still dating. And I've officially become the platonic male friend she calls to bitch about her boyfriend. I'm comfortable with that role.

My apartment is silent as everyone watches our routine. It's not bad, a hell of a lot better than I could have done without Soraya's lessons. Or, for that matter, a month of intense training from Tatiana and a crew of professional choreographers. But they don't show that part on TV.

The fact is, though, Tatiana is the one with the talent. I'm just kind of following along. And when it's time for a team to be eliminated (the result of the judges' decision, along with a complicated system of the studio audience's votes), we're the first to go. My friends boo.

"Stupid democracy," says Elijah.

I shrug. "Hey, it was fun."

And it was. Though I was initially worried about leaving Jean for three months, she did great. Every time I called her she insisted she was fine and I should go out and have a good time. We pseudo-celebs and our partners all became quick friends. Los Angeles isn't that great of a city, but we all enjoyed ourselves in the down time, sightseeing and eating out. I got really drunk for the first time with a couple of other dancers. And I remember the night I left, when Tatiana kissed me and told me to come visit her someday. . . .

"Deacon?" asks one of Clara's friends. "Are you going to do any more TV shows?"

I laugh. "I think that was my last chance. Well, I did get an offer to be on *Celebrity Cage Fight*, but I said no thank you."

Everyone laughs. Soraya squeezes my hand for real.

"Deacon!" says Jean. "Don't be so modest. Tell them what you're doing this summer."

I was hoping she wouldn't remember that tonight. It's not a done deal, and I doubt anyone here is interested.

"It's nothing. My friend Adam is visiting the Guiana Space Centre next June. He invited me to come along."

Everyone murmurs appreciatively.

"Wow!" says Elijah. "Goin' to Africa."

Clara whispers something in his ear.

"South America, I mean."

I'm glad the brawl at Adam's place last semester didn't piss him off too much. Actually, he's been a big help planning my coursework and degree program. The U of A is a solid science school. And now that I've given up on dancing professionally, I can go back to watching those little white dots in the sky. Astronomy, my first love.

Soraya laughs at something Jean says, and I take a sidelong glance at my ex-girlfriend.

Astronomy, my second love.

My guests hang around for a couple of hours, but soon people begin to trickle out. Elijah, Clara, and I solidify our new year's plans. Jason and I shake hands and smile insincerely at each other.

Finally, it's just Soraya and me, with Jean dozing

lightly on the couch. We stand awkwardly in the kitchen, not sure how to pick up a conversation from five months ago.

"Jean looks well," says Soraya, busily stacking dirty dishes in the sink.

"Thanks. She has good days. They treat her nice, and I see her as much as possible, now that I'm back."

"She's lucky to have you in her life."

I duck my head. "So how are you liking college?"

She smiles. "It's wonderful. Not so scary, once you get your feet wet. I guess I'll see you there next semester."

"I'm looking forward to it."

Silence falls as we pick up the party debris.

There's so much I want to tell her. How I thought of her all the time in L.A. How I've had a few dates, but nothing serious. How my feelings for her haven't changed, but I'm too afraid to mention it, because I don't want to drive her away. How I wonder if maybe I'm being obsessive. And that maybe she's moved on.

"I probably should go, Deacon."

"Um . . . okay." Stupid unseasonably warm weather. What I wouldn't give for an ice storm about now.

"Deacon?"

"Yes?"

She looks at me, an unreadable expression on her

face. "I guess I'll see you in January. Give me a call. We'll get together."

"Yeah. Let's do that."

She reaches, uncertainly, for her coat.

And suddenly, music fills my small apartment.

We both look toward the living room. Unnoticed by either of us, Jean has gotten up and turned on the stereo. It's a slow-dance song. One I remember from our lessons at the Y, all those months ago.

Jean looks at me intently, then nods at Soraya. I turn.

"Soraya? Would you . . . would you like to dance?"

She smiles. "I thought you'd never ask."

She puts her arms around my neck. I place my hands on her hips. And we slowly move back and forth across my kitchenette.

ACKNOWLEDGMENTS

THIS BOOK WOULD NEVER HAVE HAPPENED WITH-out help from a lot of people. First and foremost, my editor, Claudia Gabel, who always pushes me to do my very best. You've made my dreams come true ten times over. I'd also like to thank my beta readers, Kate Basi, Ida Fogle, Antony John, Connie Schertel, Kelsey Simon, Heidi Stallman, and Amy Whitley. Thanks for catching all my boneheaded mistakes. Finally, a huge debt of gratitude goes to my wife, Sandra, and my daughter, Sophie. Thank you for putting up with my distraction, self-doubt, and hours at my desk. You never stopped believing in me.

BRIAN KATCHER is the author of the Stonewall Book Award–winning novel *Almost Perfect*, along with *The Improbable Theory of Ana and Zak*, *Playing with Matches*, and *Everyone Dies in the End*. He lives in central Missouri with his wife and daughter. When he's not writing he works as a school librarian and contributes to the Forever Young Adult book blog. He once drove 150 miles to attend junior prom at his date's school, and it was worth it.

The author with his wonderful grandmothers,
Katie (left) and Belle (right)

Also by
BRIAN KATCHER

The cover shows the title *The Improbable theory of ANA & ZAK by Brian Katcher*

"With perfect comic timing and outrageous twists, *The Improbable Theory of Ana and Zak* will have you cheering for the underdog."

—Robin Constantine, author of *The Promise of Amazing*

KATHERINE TEGEN BOOKS
An Imprint of HarperCollins Publishers

www.epicreads.com